Pooches and Pubs
A Doc and Daisy Mystery for Dog Lovers

Dr. Stacey Bonner, DVM

Contents

Chapter 1

Cat Tails Pub

My name is Daisy MacVety. I am a fluffy dog with a fluffy head and long, curled-up tail. My heart belongs to Sue. My mind belongs to crime—crime solving, that is. I am Sue's sleuthing partner. I have the nose for it, and she has the knack for solving our southern town's impromptu murders and mayhem.

My two-legged companion is Sue Mac Vety. Since retiring from her veterinary clinic, Sue has solved mysteries in our quaint, increasingly famous riverside town. Visitors descend every summer for sunshine, and calm water floats on the sparkling spring-fed river. One jump in the refreshing cold river is a game-changer on a one-hundred-degree day. Sue says the effects of one chilly immersion last about an hour.

The transition is so transformative that some say the river has healing powers. It's like a hot bath on a bone-cold day, except the healing is from a cold dip on a scorching day. Sue says swimming in the cold water holes or walking in the creek numbs her sciatica. I like how the water cools my belly after a long walk on the trails.

We live in Sweetwater Springs, which you may have heard of. There, people save cats from alligators and fall in love, young and old. People say that seniors fall in love like teenagers. However, there is the occasional murder to deter the idyllic nature of our peaceful abode.

Many locals did not want the mayhem of popularity, but what do you do when everyone loves your town? We have the best tubing, kayaking, snorkeling, diving, and pub grub on the river, and walks on the riverside trails. Did I mention the spectacular beauty of the clear, cool water gurgling through lime rock in the underground aquifer?

I didn't know what an aquifer was until we moved to Sweetwater Springs. Now I know it's an underground river where many Floridians get their drinking water—some of the cleanest and purest water in the world—until recently. But how the river got dirty is a story that weaves through the mysteries of Sweetwater Springs.

The crystal-clear river has the best bird-watching, turtle-watching, and alligator-watching almost anywhere. My favorite is watching turtles climb up the bank of our cove to lay eggs. I'm not a fan of alligator watching, but they are easy to find and hard to spot because they are camouflaged. You can see gators at the river's edge from the walking trails or on the river. You'll find them floating amongst the duckweed or sunbathing in the lilies when you float—yes when you float downriver. Sue won't let me walk past the nests during alligator mating season. She says alligators like to eat dogs better than people.

We live on the river, but I'm not allowed to soak my belly in the cove behind my house because of the alligators. A small, a medium, and a large alligator live in the small cove. Sue watches them swim for food in the early mornings and evenings. The biggest alligator disappeared, and someone said the gator trapper had taken it to the rock up the river. Sue thinks he more likely took it to Heaven, but around here, folks don't talk about stuff like that—even if it's legal.

Today, Sue is taking me to Cat Tails Pub for lunch. Sue will eat a salad, and I'll get ice cubes floating in a bowl of water—and a French fry left over from the last customer if I'm lucky. Sue only eats French fries on Sunday, but usually misses a fry somebody left behind. I scarf it up before she sees it.

Cat Tails is owned by Sue's friends, Tori and Dave Pedri. They moved to Sweetwater several years ago, and her parents bought the pub for them as a wedding gift. They knew nothing about cooking or business, but got a great chef and manager—who lives near Sue. As it turned out, Tori loved the pub and small-town life more than Dave did.

Tori was especially fond of the river life. Most people docked their watercraft by the bar to enjoy the pub. I like to ride to the pub on Sue's kayak. Tori would meet her friends at the dock and help them tie off to the cleats before they frolicked at the bar. Tori knew everything about Sweetwater Springs: its beauty, the gossip, the latest watercraft, and the local tension over the river. No matter what anyone thought, Sweetwater Springs was growing, and Cat Tails Pub was booming.

Tori adored the laughter of children jumping in the cold water and the tales of the small-town drinkers at the bar. This was a pub where everyone knew your name, your partner, and whether you had your eye on a new boat, car, or motorcycle. Everybody came to Cat Tails Pub—rich or poor, beautiful or not, farmer or city girl. Yes, there was room for everyone at Tori's bar; most were regulars.

Tori was a natural as a bartender, absorbing the stories of people, places, and things. Dave hated such trivia and longed for a life back in Miami, where boats were yachts instead of kayaks, girls wore strappy dresses instead of tank tops and cut-offs, and his wife wasn't having much fun at a life he hated.

I was especially fond of being called Daisy instead of "Cute Dog" when Sue took me to Cat Tails Pub on the kayak. I was not fond of owners who didn't pay attention when their dogs growled at me. Yes, this happened a time or two—and Tori hired a dog bouncer to remove them. Dave said the pub shouldn't allow dogs, but he was outnumbered by customers who brought more dogs than ever. Most of them were friendly. If not, the dog bouncers escorted the biting dog and owner to the parking lot.

Sue says I'm a connector dog. That means I connect with people because they like to pet me. First, they call me a cute dog, then they say hello and pet me, most often my fluffy head. I like how they say "Cute Dog" because they sound excited. Their tone of voice means more than words when people talk to me. I liked how Tori spoke to me sweetly, but Dave usually ignored me.

My favorite thing about Tori was that she always remembered to bring me ice cubes for my water bowl. I say this in the past tense because Tori is now missing. Nobody knows what happened to her, but Sue wants to investigate her friend's disappearance, now a cold case.

Tori has been missing for almost six months. Without a trace, she disappeared into the wilds and wetlands of Mia's Run—a sparkling creek on Baldwin's Ranch four miles upriver— during a kayaking trip with Dave.

Her disappearance was followed by the most extensive search and rescue Sweetwater has ever seen. They brought hounds and shepherds, even a Sheepadoodle. Have you ever heard of them? Me, I'm an Aussie Doodle. I'm soft—Aussie. I love water—Poodle. No matter how many generations, I'll have instincts from my breeds.

By the way, I don't care what anyone tells you. You can't deny a dog's instincts, though you can modify them by combining them with other breeds. I like swimming from my Poodle roots, sleeping as a dog, and running from my Poodle and Australian Shepherd roots. From walking around Sweetwater with Sue, I have long legs and a lean body.

We have been walking around Sweetwater Springs to see if anyone has clues about what happened to Tori. Sue insists we will learn the truth.

According to Dave, he dropped Tori off when they were kayaking at Mia's Run to talk to a friend, went home for snacks and a drink refill, and when he came back, she was gone. He insists an alligator took her—but he's a Miami boy—and the search for her clothes, body, or body parts proved nothing.

I hope Miami Dave knows more about sharks than alligators because nobody in Sweetwater Springs believes an alligator took Tori. Locals know an alligator wouldn't have devoured a grown woman and her clothes. Even the largest alligators—like the one that used to live behind my house—hide some for later with larger meals.

The enormous search and rescue for Tori lasted two days, with helicopters, night vision, and locals trudging through swamps in tall waders. Kayakers brought their boats to scour the narrow creeks for the woman who had become dear to them for her love of the river. Mostly, dogs weren't allowed in the swamps where snakes and reptiles lurk, but Sue and I scoured the river banks in her kayak without success. Tori was gone, and the locals would miss her.

Today, Sue is meeting Phil Coleman at Cat Tails Pub. Phil is a land buyer for Thomas Baldwin, who owns Baldwin Ranch. I don't know much about Phil, but I can sniff him out for his intentions. Dogs can smell emotions and report to their owners.

It is a scorching day in August that makes me want to soak my belly in the river. On days like this, I can feel the sun on my backside and my nose, where the fur doesn't grow. I love to walk early in the morning to avoid the most intense heat. Since we're meeting Phil for lunch, it's too late for a shady walk to the pub.

Sue opened the garage door for the short drive to the pub. My short nails skidded on the living room tile as I skedaddled to the car. "Load up, Daisy!" she said, opening the car door.

I was happy to comply because I loved to go anywhere with Sue. I was fond of the pub she had mentioned as our destination, but I missed Tori's smile and the ice.

"Hi, Dave," Sue said when we passed him at the outdoor bar near the river.

"Hi, Sue," he replied, ignoring me as always.

"Any news about Tori?" she asked, although she would have been among the first to be notified if there was something new.

"I wish there were," Dave said. "I'm tired of running this pub alone."

Whenever we talked to Dave, it was always about the work. I wondered if he missed Tori, but Sue wouldn't ask. Instead, she took a deep breath and sighed so only I could hear her.

"It keeps you busy," Sue said. "Work was the only thing that kept me going after my husband passed away."

"Busy at work, I don't want to do," Dave replied. "It's hard to keep help at the pub. I'm always picking up the loose ends after somebody. People don't stay at their jobs anymore. We train them, and they leave."

"Can I get a cup of ice for Daisy?" Sue asked, changing the subject. He passed her a cupful.

"There's a man over there waiting for you," Dave said, pointing to Phil, and he waved, exposing a bulge beneath his shirt.

"Be careful," Dave said. "He thinks he lives in the Wild West."

Phil carries a silver-engraved handgun in a concealed leather holster with a silver concho. I think that's weird, but what do I know about guns—I'm a dog. Oh, by the way, Sweetwater Springs has a concealed weapons carry law. The locals have gotten a peek at the weapon despite its concealed nature. Word spread quickly about the silver engraving and the concho.

"He works for Thomas Baldwin," Sue replied. "Baldwin wants to build a luxury hotel on the river and a Wild West Theme Park."

"Tell me about it," Dave said as if he hadn't heard about it thousands of times. "The whole town knows he carries that gun."

"He doesn't keep it a secret," Sue agreed.

"The Dude is delusional," said a random man at the bar. "I wouldn't buy a used car from him."

"I wonder if Baldwin knows he totes that gun," Sue said.

"Everyone knows he carries it," Dave replied. The question is, does Baldwin know how he flashes it?"

Thomas Baldwin was Sweetwater Spring's first and only billionaire. Most billionaires lived at the beach, but Thomas Baldwin had the good sense to build his mansion on a spring-fed, cool, and comfortable river year-round. Phil Coleman bought land in Sweetwater Springs and all around the county for him. Baldwin wanted everything he could get.

"Are you going to Baldwin's housewarming party this weekend?" Sue asked.

"I'm planning on it," Dave replied, and the random man said he wasn't invited.

The housewarming party was the first of its kind in Sweetwater Springs. Mia Baldwin planned the grand event, which gave Sweetwater Springs' business owners and special friends a tour of the magnificent property where she and her husband, Thomas, lived. Two hundred invitations had been signed, sealed, and delivered for the party. I wasn't invited.

"Daisy wasn't invited either," Sue said, rubbing behind my ear. "She goes almost everywhere with me."

"Do you own a business?" he asked.

"Not in Sweetwater Springs, but I have a veterinary hospital nearby, in Haywood. "My daughter is the chief veterinarian now that I retired."

The man rattled off three questions about ticks and fleas before he continued: "I don't want Baldwin to build that hotel, let alone that Wild West theme park. The river is polluted enough without five hundred more random people to swim in it all summer long."

Tori would have enjoyed solving the dilemma plaguing Sweetwater Springs residents. Tori believed the river pollution could be solved with the proper diagnostics and treatments. Dave preferred to stay out of it. "I hear you," he said.

"What if the river was cleaned up?" Sue asked.

"It ain't going to be cleaned up," he said, walking toward the river. "It keeps getting dirtier and dirtier. It used to be crystal clear to the bottom. The only difference is a whole bunch of people are using the river when it used to be just us locals."

"What if it could be cleaned up?" Sue asked again.

"Are you going to bring in a vacuum cleaner?" he asked, and Sue frowned. "I know people with good ideas," she replied. "It takes legitimate expert science, money, and politics to get things done."

"Well, ain't that interesting?" he said. "The expert folks say cow dung polluted the river."

"I've heard that."

"It ain't the cows done it," he said. "Them cows upriver been here my whole life. The only thing that's changed is the number of people."

These were the topics Tori listened to and loved, but Dave hated. "I want to go back to Miami," Dave said as a young woman in baggy jeans and a black T-shirt walked past.

"Nobody's stopping you," the man said, but Dave did not reply.

Phil Coleman waved again while we were talking. "That wild west cowboy wants to talk to you real bad," the man said, and Dave agreed that Phil didn't like to be kept waiting.

Sue took the cupful of ice and picked up a dog bowl with water on the way to the table where Phil was seated. I found two French fries on the ground—practically a record—before Sue caught me and picked up the rest.

"I'm Phil Coleman," the man said, exposing the bulge near his hip.

"Nice to meet you. I'm Sue Mac Vety. This is Daisy."

"I've heard of Daisy before," Phil said, rubbing my head and mentioning nothing about Sue. "She likes to kayak."

"Yes, she does. She's the captain."

"Have you been to Mia's Run?" he asked of the creek that led to Baldwin's mansion.

"Many times. It's one of our favorite places on the river."

Phil wore his button-up camp shirt with a T-shirt underneath to cover the bulge. I sniffed the bulge, but it was firmly attached.

"Your dog seems interested in my handgun," he said. "Do you want to see it?"

"No, thank you. I'm not a gun person."

"Suit yourself," Phil replied. "It's a beautiful handgun. A masterpiece."

"What do you need with a six-gun masterpiece?" Sue asked.

"It's my signature," Phil replied. I like it. Toting it brings joy."

"What are you planning to shoot with it?"

"Nothing. Anything that chases me. It makes me feel safe to have it. What do you have for protection if something chases you?"

"My voice. I can be loud when I yell."

When I finished sniffing the bulge, I lay down beside the table. Phil was odd, and I didn't trust him, but for now, he seemed harmless.

"What do you want to talk to me about?" Sue asked.

"I'll get straight to the point, Sue," Phil said. "Thomas Baldwin wants your clinic. He wants me to buy it."

Sue's eyes popped, and her mouth gaped. She frowned. "What could Thomas Baldwin possibly want with my clinic?" she asked.

"I don't know, ma'am," Phil said. "I'm just the buyer."

"The clinic has been in my family for thirty years," Sue said. "My daughter is the head veterinarian since I'm retired, and I have no interest in selling it."

"Mr Baldwin is willing to swap the clinic and land for a far nicer, bigger piece of property," Phil said. "You should think about it," he added. "He's a mighty man. You'd be better off having him as a friend than an enemy."

When he was leaving, Phil added, "I like your Fedora."

"Thanks, it's my signature," Sue replied, tipping her hat and scowling at the bulge that made him smile.

Sue sat at the table for thirty minutes while I lay in the shade before we departed for home. I had never seen her so distracted. I suspected she thought she might have felt threatened. Something was amiss. In time, all would become clear.

Chapter 2

Loretta's House

L oretta MacVety is Sue's daughter. Now that Sue has retired, Loretta is the chief veterinarian at Haywood Veterinary Clinic. I love Loretta, but I have mixed feelings about what she does to me at the hospital.

Sometimes, she jabs me; some call them shots, while others call them vaccines. They come in a plastic tube with a needle. Sue says vaccines keep me healthy since I walk with her in Sweetwater Springs, where we meet many people and other dogs.

The needles are so sharp I barely feel them. Dr. Loretta is good at giving me shots. Her assistant pets me so that I don't notice the shots. Afterward, she gave me a dog cookie, which wasn't as good as a stolen French fry, but I appreciated the effort.

Sometimes, Loretta prescribes itch pills if I have a terrible itch after a haircut. The itch pills keep me from licking a raw sore. Sue hides them in a dog food ball, so I eat the pill. She thinks I don't know this, but I do. It's the only time she gives me a ball of dog food. It doesn't take a genius to see the ball of food makes me quit itching.

Loretta also prescribes yummy-flavored pills every month to keep me healthy. It makes me suspicious when Sue calls me to the bathroom for a yummy pill that prevents fleas, ticks, or heartworms, but she has a good reason. She doesn't want the cat to eat any of the yummy pills. I eat them in the bathroom because my pills could make Toby sick.

Toby was an alley cat, but now he lives with us. Sue says alley cats and alligators put Sweetwater Springs on the map. Toby likes to ambush me; we have pretend fights, but don't play rough. We make Sue laugh, and she says we love to show off.

Today, we are going to Loretta's farmhouse. I'm excited to go anywhere with Sue, but I'm delighted because I get to see my three dog cousins.

"Load up, Daisy," Sue said, opening the car door. I knew what day it was because she didn't take my leash when we went to Loretta's house. Today, I will run to my heart's content in Loretta's big fenced yard—about three minutes—and take a long nap in Loretta's living room with my dog cousins.

I love to run in Loretta's yard—I am a tall, spirited, long-legged dog. My cousins love to run, too, but not as much as me. All three of us are Doodles or, technically, Mutts. We are half-Poodles and half Something Else—Golden Retriever, Bernese Mountain Dog, or Australian Shepherd.

Now, don't get me wrong. I like to meander with Sue in Sweetwater Springs, but running at Loretta's farm is the Best thing ever. When we arrive at Loretta's house, I race to her front door, hips in full flexion and extension for the short course from the car to the house. It's my favorite time to play with other dogs. Getting ambushed by a cat is fine and dandy, but a dog needs time with her tribe.

My cousins wait for me behind the door—a massive threesome of black and white fur with curled and fluffy tails. My best friend, Luna, aka Luna Tic, is all black. My sister, Leela, aka Lee, is red and white, like me, except I'm spotted— aka Red Merle. Lee has a red saddle and a white body, aka parti-color. My cousin, Stevie, aka Steve, is black and white. Steve was a COVID-19 baby. She was born shortly before COVID and didn't get to socialize with other dogs as a puppy because of the quarantine.

Luna is mischievous, Leela is serious, and Stevie is needy, but Sue prefers to call her affectionate. Some might say I'm needy, too. Sue says I'm an affectionate dog. Loretta says I have Only Dog Syndrome.

"Hello???" Sue says, opening the door to her daughter's house.

I race past my cousins, nails tapping on tile, for three minutes of running glory in the backyard. My cousins can run around the backyard anytime, but this is my moment—Freedom to run circles in the sunshine, chase friends in the grass, and bark at Sue and Loretta's horses. They prance by the fence to be part of the best thing ever.

"Hi, Mom," Loretta replies, approaching the moments of joy in the backyard. "Are they having fun?"

"It took courage to open the door!" Sue replied, not wanting them to slam the door against the house, as three hundred pounds of fluff can do.

Sue and Loretta watched us running circles and smiled. "Have you been busy at the clinic?" Sue asked.

"Always!" Loretta replied. "I love it."

Loretta had the energy of her father and the soul of her mother. For Loretta, good was the greater good of humanity and women. She had the nerve to speak her mind and stand her ground. At 31, she was beautiful, dedicated, adventurous, and caring with her patients, family, and friends.

Stevie was first to return after the romp, and Lee joined her shortly after that. Sue had to call Luna and me back to the house because we had been enjoying ourselves in the bushes, where Lee had dug a hole. Luna and I got blamed for the dig, like always. Lee never got blamed for anything, although she was sometimes guilty. Stevie was likelier to put her head on somebody's lap than be part of the mischief.

Luna was every dog's best friend who came to play at Loretta's farm. Loretta's friends would bring big dogs and little dogs to her dinner parties. Luna likes to teach everyone a bad habit or two. Her favorite misguided activity was to teach the big dogs counter-surfing.

When Luna thought no one was looking, she would stand on her hind legs, shift her head sideways, lay it on the counter, and stick out her long tongue to grab a morsel of food. Loretta called it counter-surfing.

Although I didn't enjoy food as much as Luna, who was getting chunky from her kitchen adventures, I liked to counter surf.

I had never thought of counter-surfing before Luna taught me. Later, I tried it at home. Toby often left tasty morsels of cat food on the counter where Sue fed him. Cats are much more sloppy with food than dogs, so I decided to clean up after him as Luna had done with Loretta's crumbs. Since cat food tastes better than dog food, salvaging the leftovers was worth trying, but Sue disagreed with the sport.

"Luna taught Daisy how to counter-surf," Sue announced. Loretta agreed that it was more likely for the naughty one to teach the nice one than vice versa. Lee got attention for being good, and Stevie got attention for being needy. Luna was the mischievous one, and her doggie guests loved her for it.

"The naughty ones have the most fun," Loretta said, and Sue smiled.

Sue gathered salad fixings from the refrigerator—baby spinach, black beans, blue cheese, and leftover grilled chicken—while Loretta made spicy herbal loose-leaf tea in the teapot. They agreed on balsamic dressing to complement the salty toppings and served lunch at the kitchen table.

I lay under the table with my cousins, who barely moved throughout the meal. Lee, who never counter-surfed, would be first to scarf up a crumb on the floor. Still, she maintained her girly figure better than Luna. I had the best figure—not to brag—but I worked at it with exercise, a healthy diet, and the occasional tidbit.

Sue believes eating a healthy diet is the best way to lose weight. Not to be mean, but Luna looks like a fat black sheep when she gets a haircut. Now, it's not all about looks but about health. Luna is my young and healthy best friend, but I want her to be my old and healthy best friend when the time comes.

Loretta added honey to her tea and passed Sue the teapot and strainer.

"I'm glad your new teapot doesn't drip," Sue said. "I hate making a mess on your tablecloth,"

Loretta explained. "A slow pour helps, but the shape of the pot matters, too."

"Are you going to Baldwins' housewarming party this Saturday?" Sue asked after she had poured the tea.

"I wouldn't miss it," Loretta replied. "How many chances do we get to explore a billionaire's property in Sweetwater Springs?"

"Baldwin is the only billionaire in Sweetwater Springs," Sue reminded her.

"The rich usually live on the coast," Loretta replied. "The beach is hot in summer, but the springs stay cool. It's a relief to enjoy the river's cool water."

Sue stabbed a forkful of spinach and toppings. "We don't get as much damage from storms in Sweetwater Springs," Sue said. "It's safer for houses, too."

Loretta agreed it was strange that more wealthy people didn't choose river life in the countryside. "Maybe it's a blessing," she said. "Sweetwater Springs is bulging at the seams already from growth."

Sue mentioned the owner of Cat Tails Pub. "According to Tori, the locals keep arguing about the increasing population and its effect on the river."

"Is there any more news about Tori since her disappearance?" Loretta asked.

"Same story from Dave—an alligator took her."

"That's unlikely considering the massive search," Loretta said, and Sue agreed that the alligator would have left something behind.

"Are Tori's parents going to the Baldwins' housewarming party?" Loretta asked.

"They've been spending more time with the Baldwins since their daughter's disappearance," Sue said. "I would expect to see them at the housewarming."

Tori's parents had connections in Miami that brought watercraft, high-tech surveillance, and dogs to the swamps. Her father had many friends from all walks of life, some of whom owed him favors. After Tori disappeared, they rented a house in Sweetwater Springs to pursue the search and honor her memory as their only daughter.

"The locals don't want Baldwin to build the hotel," Loretta said.

There were two sides: one wanted development and more jobs, and the other wanted the river to be used by a smaller population. Both sides wanted to clean up the river's pollution, but needed the best plan.

If the experts found a way to clean up the river, Tori would support the hotel. Her father, Gio, planned to work towards cleaning it up in her honor after her disappearance. Gio had the connections, and Baldwin had the money to make a difference.

First, they had to determine how it got polluted—nobody believed anybody. Gio said the experts who proposed the pollution factors were as corrupt as the politicians. Everyone believed sewage had contaminated the river and caused algae growth, but Gio did not believe cattle had contributed much to the sewage contamination. No cattle grazed beside the river but were blamed for much pollution.

The cattlemen agreed with Gio, who had many connections in farms and businesses. Whatever people thought of him, Gio knew people who got the job done.

Have you met the man with the silver-engraved handgun?" Loretta asked after she sipped her tea.

Sue said, "Phil Coleman. He buys land for Baldwin. I met him yesterday."

"He's creepy," Loretta said. "He wants to buy the clinic. He was pushy about it, too. Like a car salesman who latches on and won't let go."

"Daisy didn't like him," Sue said, and I raised my head when hearing my name.

"What does he want with the clinic?" Loretta asked.

"He didn't say," Sue replied. "Thomas Baldwin told him to see if we'd sell it."

"I don't want to sell the clinic," Loretta said. "Why would I want to do that?"

"Who knows what he's up to?" Sue said when she finished her salad. "I'll snoop around and see what I can learn about him."

"He dared to flash his silver-plated gun at me!" Loretta growled, rising to carry her plate to the sink. "Who does he think he is?"

"Some people say he thinks he's back in the Wild West."

"He's bizarre," Loretta said. "I don't like being pressured by anyone. Especially somebody flashing a gun."

Loretta was cute and petite but more formidable than she looked. I suspected Phil Coleman should reconsider before he flashed his gun again. "I don't know what's going on around here," Loretta said, "but it's time we found out."

"Would you like to kayak Mia's Run with Daisy and me tomorrow?" Sue asked, and Loretta agreed because she had the day off.

Mia was Thomas Baldwin's wife. He named everything in her honor, including the proposed Wild West Theme Park, to be built following the hotel.

"Didn't Tori disappear on Mia's Run?" Loretta asked.

"Yes, on the Baldwin property," Sue said. "Almost six months ago."

I was excited to hear Sue was taking me to Mia's Run. I loved kayaking the river and looked forward to the trip. Tomorrow, I could sit on the boat, get called a Cute Dog, and enjoy the ride with the wind in my face.

Chapter 3

Peter and Stanley's House

When we arrived home from Loretta's house, Toby awaited us inside the front door. He sat sweetly, looking at us with big green eyes on his round, striped face. My first impression was that he had spent time sleeping on the bed while we were away. Still, he took time away from his favorite, sneaking into the bedroom to greet us at the door.

Sue did not let Toby sleep in the bed at night because he was a pouncer. Toby didn't jump on anything; he launched in full spring from the floor to whatever. Since Sue was not fond of being pounced on while sleeping, Toby got left out of the nightly sleeping arrangements in the bedroom. He made up for it by sleeping on the bed whenever he could while Sue was away.

"Hi, Toby," Sue said, stroking him under the chin. "You're a good little man."

Toby launched onto the counter, where Sue kept his food bowl out of my reach. My food was on the floor, where he could sample a nibble of leftovers, but he rarely did because—-as everyone knows— cat food tasted better. It was one of life's strange injustices, but sleeping on the bed was a better alternative for me than cat food on the countertop.

Toby was a stray cat from the neighborhood. The local Trap-Neuter-Release clinic veterinarians spayed, neutered, and vaccinated stray cats from two nearby colonies. Still, some were too wild to be adopted and returned to the colonies. The residents of Sweetwater held fundraisers for the cat rescues. Some strays, like Toby, were community cats who needed a home. They were sweet and made good housepets.

Peter Gardner, who lived on our street, managed the nearby feral cat colony with funds from a local philanthropist. He previously worked at the cat rescue, but when it ran short of funds for spays and neuters, he returned to his first love—cooking. Now, he works as the head chef at Cat Tails Pub.

"Let's talk to Peter," Sue said, grabbing my leash off the chair. "Maybe he can tell us more about Phil Coleman."

I was excited to go to Peter and Stanley's house, which is only a few houses down from Sue's on the river. Peter is the best cook in the neighborhood, and we have potluck dinner parties there. He used to own a restaurant in Miami, but he sold it when he and Stanley moved to Sweetwater Springs. Before Tori disappeared, Peter accepted a job as head chef and manager at Cat Tails Pub.

His partner, Stanley, is an attorney who commutes to Miami when he can't work from home. Attorneys are working increasingly from home, and Stanley prefers the slower-paced life of Sweetwater Springs. We heard the roar of his sports car earlier. Stanley purchased the car as a gift to himself to make the Miami commute more enjoyable—to the disdain of our neighbor who despised the high-pitched twang—but loved the goodies and treats he brought as consolations.

Sue called Peter and announced her intentions, and he welcomed us at the front door upon our arrival.

"Come in, Doc," Peter said, patting me on the head. We followed him to the living room, where Stanley sat on the couch with a large orange tabby cat on his lap.

I stood at a distance, not sniffing the cat, who looked like he didn't want to be bothered by a dog's friendship. Stanley had adopted the growing cat after Peter had to give up on a feral cat from Miami who had proven too wild to tame as a housecat.

"It's good to see you, Sue Ellen," Stanley said, "Pardon me if I don't get up, but O.C. is just too comfortable."

Sue studied the cat, which bulged with contentment from the big man's lap. Stanley was fond of luxuries that he bestowed upon himself and his friends, two-legged and four-legged.

"You are feeding him too much," Sue said, and Stanley agreed he should do better. "He loves it so much."

"He's not going to love to move when he's older," Sue replied.

Until now, chastising Stanley about eating and feeding habits had been in vain. Stanley loved to eat and believed everyone else loved it as much as he did. It was odd how some liked to eat while others seemed to live for it. I liked the food as much as the next dog, but I was also the fastest dog at Loretta's because of my trim figure, while Luna moved like a black sheep, except when counter-surfing.

"What brings you to Paradise Point?" Stanley asked. Their house was at the end of River Drive, facing the confluence of two rivers. The view of the wetlands across the crystal-clear spring-fed river was spectacular from the grand windows.

"A lot is happening in Sweetwater Springs," Sue replied. I wanted to catch up and clarify a few things."

"I'm at your service," Peter replied, sitting beside Stanley. What can we do for you?"

"Do you know Phil Coleman?" Sue asked Peter. "I saw him at Cat Tails yesterday morning. He had a strange, unexpected request—almost more of a demand."

"Yes, of course," Peter said. "He carries a silver-plated gun and sits on the corner table. When he flashes it at people, it makes them feel like his requests are a demand."

"He flashed it at Loretta," Sue replied. "I saw the bulge but declined to look at it when he tried to show it to me."

"He's not supposed to flash it at anybody," Stanley said with a deep sigh. "It's called a concealed weapon for a reason."

"What on earth does he want with you?" Peter asked.

"He wants to buy the clinic," Sue said, and Peter gasped. "You and Loretta don't want to sell it."

"Of course not," Sue replied. "He's a buyer for Thomas Baldwin and claims not to know what he wants it for."

"That's outrageous!" Peter said. "I knew he was a buyer for Baldwin—but what would he want with your veterinary clinic?"

"Who knows?"

"Some mega-wealthy entrepreneurs want a piece of everything," Stanley said. "Baldwin has been buying up property for a long time."

"He owns most of the property across the river from Cat Tails Pub," Peter added. "Almost two hundred acres of prime land for a hotel and Wild West Theme Park."

Thomas Baldwin bought the property from Luke Wilson, who had also considered building a hotel and water park on the parcel. Eventually, Luke decided he didn't want to develop Sweetwater Springs if he wanted to live here. As the second-wealthiest man in Sweetwater Springs, Luke Wilson became a philanthropist instead of a developer. He was the financier of the cat food and veterinary treatments for the cat colonies on Cypress Street, up the hill from River Drive, and funded other local fundraisers.

The locals were less impressed with the hotel plans than Baldwin. Although some saw it as enterprising and a source of good jobs, others saw it as a threat to the river. Tori monitored the local opinions before she disappeared, but Dave couldn't have cared less. He had been listening to the development disputes in Miami for a long time and preferred other pursuits.

"Did you know Dave and Tori when you lived in Miami?" Sue asked as I padded into the kitchen for a drink of water, and Peter followed with an ice cube for the dog bowl.

"I went to high school with both of them," Stanley said. "They seemed like the perfect couple back then."

"What made you think so?"

Stanley said, "Tori wanted a fresh start. She lived in the shadow of her parents. Dave wasn't afraid of her. He gave her friendship and doted on her with little gifts and attention."

"Some people thought her father had mafia ties—high in the hierarchy—maybe a boss," Peter added after he popped two more ice cubes into the bowl and returned to the living room.

"Speculation," Stanley said. "If he had mafia ties, they would have been sworn to secrecy."

"Kids were afraid of Tori, and they looked down their noses at Dave."

"Dave was from the other side of the tracks," Stanley explained.

"Tori's family was wealthy compared to Dave's family," Peter continued. "As everyone knows, her parents bought them the pub as a wedding gift."

"To marry Tori was Dave's quickest route to a successful business," Stanley said.

"Tori would have been better off without him," Peter added. "They argued in front of the staff. It wasn't good for morale. He dragged the staff down; he dragged the pub down."

"Tori loved the pub, the locals, and Sweetwater Springs," Stanley said, and Peter added, "I don't think Dave expected to hate it so much."

"What will Dave do now?" Sue asked.

"I guess the same thing as he's been doing. Run the pub without her."

"Can Dave sell it?"

"I'm sure there is a clause that the pub goes back to her parents if she dies," Stanley said, and Peter countered, "Speculation."

"You're right; I haven't seen the prenup."

"Dave couldn't do it without your cooking," Sue told Peter. "You're the best thing that ever happened to the pub."

"Neither of them are good cooks," Peter said, and Stanley countered, "You're not a cook, you're a chef—and an excellent chef at that."

Sue took a deep breath and sighed. Tori's disappearance was getting more complicated, but every tip helped. She loved solving mysteries as much as she loved diagnosing cases before she retired. It was the same critical thinking—just a different outlet for it.

"Are you going to the Baldwins' housewarming party this weekend?" Sue asked.

"We'll be there with bells on," Peter said.

"Cowbells, that is," Stanley added, but Sue understood, and he didn't explain.

Sue stared out the magnificent window at the sparkling river for a long time before she rose to leave. The ripples toward the west implied the direction of flow toward the sea. I was tired of looking at the orange cat who didn't want to see me. The water was good, and the ice had been fun, but I was ready to go home to play with Toby, who liked me.

The ice reminded me of Tori, who remembered how much I loved to bob for the cubes in a bowl of ice water. Now Tori was gone, and I missed her. A land speculator with a silver gun wanted to buy the clinic for Thomas Baldwin, provided no reason, and it made no sense to anyone. Loretta was unclear about his motives, irritated by his pushy manner, and angry about his flashing a gun.

Tomorrow, Sue and I will kayak to Mia's Run with Loretta. I can't wait to go home, eat dinner, and sleep. Sometimes, when I sleep with a problem, I wake up with a brainstorm. With any luck, this was one of those crazy old nights.

Chapter 4

Jessica and Chris' House

The following morning, Sue awakened early and put on her bathing suit for the kayak trip to Mia's Run with Loretta. I could smell the suntan lotion she applied for the trip and wondered if it was as bad for the river as for the coral reefs, where Sue had read it caused bleaching. I don't know much about suntan lotion, but Sue sometimes puts it on my nose where the fur doesn't grow. I wouldn't say I like it, but Sue says she doesn't want me sunburned.

Frankly, I think there must be a better way to avoid sunburn. Sue wears sun shirts and hats and puts lotion on her legs and face. I've seen dogs with sunglasses and hats, but I have a very long nose, and Sue doesn't think a dog hat would shade my nose. Sometimes, we see people attach umbrellas or sunshades to their kayaks. Sue says that's an excellent idea, but we're working on it.

When Sue dresses, Toby extends little striped feet and arms under the door. The morning ritual makes Sue smile. She bends to pet his feet before letting him in the bedroom. He races across the tile floor and launches on the bed to greet me.

Sometimes, Toby chases the flowers on the bedspread. Mostly, he wants to rub against my body before we leave the bedroom. I am used to the love ritual and rarely leave the bed before he greets me. Toby and I snuggle for a moment before we begin the day.

I am eager to potty in my tiny dog yard, have breakfast, and get on the river today. Mia's Run is my favorite creek on the river. Still, I know Sue will do some things before we leave. She drinks coffee, and the smell reminds me of breakfast because she fills our bowls with dog kibble on the floor and cat kibble on the counter when she brews it. Everyone knows Toby's food tastes better, but I'm happy to sleep on the bed.

I lay by the mat while Sue practiced yoga, which she has done daily since she adopted me as a puppy. Sue says she couldn't get out of the kayak without it. Sometimes, she poses on all fours and arches her back like a cat. Sometimes, she poses on all fours with her body in an inverted V and her arms in front of her like a puppy.

I think yoga looks like the stretches I do when I stand up after a nap. Toby watches her, too, but he is more likely to stand on the mat and get in the way of the poses. I've seen Toby do some of the same stretches as Sue when she practices yoga. Somebody must have copied the animals when they invented yoga long ago.

Sue and Loretta both practice yoga. Loretta is thirty-something—I can never remember— and practices yoga daily, too. She says it relieves stress from her body and shoulders. Her five-year-old daughter, Lucy, and her husband practice yoga with Loretta. Sue says she loves to see it pass from generation to generation.

We usually walk around the neighborhood after Sue practices yoga. Today, we skip the walk for the river trip. I am excited to see Luna, who loves the river as much as I do. Sue loads the kayak, and I hop in the truck for the ride.

We will launch the kayak upriver behind Jessie and Chris's house. Mia's Run is only a short paddle from Jessie's house— they can see the entrance across the river. Chris bought the home to surprise Jessie after they fell in love. I loved it because I could jump off the concrete seawall into the river and dog-paddle back up the stairs to the backyard.

Jessie and Chris kiss a lot and hold hands almost everywhere they go. At first, Chris told her he loved her once a day, then twice, three, and sometimes ten times a day. Jessie says it's the most romantic relationship she's ever been in. I think they're made for each other.

Jessie and her nine-year-old daughter, Beth, used to live with us when Jessie was getting divorced from her hot-tempered doctor husband back in Haywood. If Chris has a temper, I've never seen it. Jessie says he's the most patient man she's ever met.

Jessie is a nurse. Her sidekick is healthy cooking with bold flavors. Since Sue got to know her, she's been writing a cookbook and sharing recipes with families at the elementary school. She wants Peter to add some of them to the menu at Cat Tails Pub, where they dine weekly.

Jessie and Chris are the only people who saw Dave and Tori paddle into Mia's Run the night she vanished. Chris thinks Dave should have been more upset when he left without her. They've been discussing it for almost six months without a resolution. Jessie is convinced that Tori is dead.

Loretta drove to the riverfront home with both kayaks in the truck bed. She opened the front door, and Luna rocketed out of the truck for a race on the fenced property. Of course, I would lead, but she didn't care. She chased me in circles three times around the yard—one of the biggest on the river.

Jessie and Chris walked to the truck to help Sue and Loretta unload the kayaks and take them to the river while we chased each other. When we were finished running, we lay on our bellies by the Adirondack chairs close to the river, where the foursome would chat before the trip.

"It's good to see you," Jessie said as she hugged Sue. "I miss our breakfasts on the back porch, but not those three alligators in the cove."

"Me too," Sue said. "Our breakfasts got me outdoors, but now I'm more likely to eat indoors unless I have company."

"Will you see gators here?" Loretta asked as she surveyed the crystal clear water where it would have been easy to spot them.

"A few," Chris replied, and Jessie added, "Never right behind the house, like the ones that lived in your cove."

Jessie had always been afraid of alligators, but Sue insisted she worried more about me than herself because alligators are likelier to prey on dogs than people. Therefore, I could not jump into the cove with all four feet—then or now.

"I'd like to buy a place near yours for Daisy," Sue said. "I could sit by the river, and she could swim whenever she wants to."

"You're welcome at our place whenever you like," Chris said, and Jessie continued, "Our home is your home."

"It's sweet of you to offer," Sue replied, smiling at her friends.

Loretta watched the sparkling river flow by the house. Upriver, near the headwaters, the river was clear. Downriver by Sue's home, it was more tea-colored because it mixed with the waters from the Tannahoochee River.

"It's beautiful here," Loretta said. "If I lived here, I'd never leave the backyard."

"Your backyard is nice too, with horses entertaining you in the pasture," Jessie said, and Loretta agreed that it was fun to have animals.

"What brings you to the river today?" Chris asked.

Loretta replied, "It's a beautiful day to refresh on the water, but I wish that were all there is to it."

"What do you mean?" Jessie asked.

"A man has been pushing me to sell the clinic," Loretta said. "He says he's buying for Thomas Baldwin, and I was hoping to shed some light on his motives."

"I've never seen Thomas at Mia's Run," Chris said. "But sometimes we see Mia."

"You're right to paddle early in the morning," Jessie said, looking towards the creek's entrance. "None of the Baldwins come to the creek when it's busy."

"Are you going to their housewarming party this weekend?" Sue asked.

"We're looking forward to it," Jessie said. "We're new to Sweetwater Springs, and we don't own a business here, but we live close to the Run, so Mia invited us."

"Mia brings her dogs to the clinic," Loretta said as she rubbed Luna's chest. "We were invited because we own the clinic, and I'm her veterinarian."

"What's with Baldwin wanting to buy your veterinary clinic?" Chris asked, frowning.

"Darned if I know," Loretta replied. "But the man who made the offer carried a gun."

"We've seen him at Cat Tails," Jessie said. "It's weird."

"He does business in the corner, like a loan shark in a pub," Chris said.

"Or a bookie," Jessie added.

"Or anyone else doing unscrupulous business with a gun," Loretta said.

"I've heard Tori's father is with the mafia in Miami," Jessie said. "His name is Gio."

"I've heard Gio is getting tight with the Baldwins since Tori disappeared," Chris added.

"Why do you think Phil Coleman carries that silver-plated gun?" Loretta asked.

"It sounds like the Old West," Jessie replied. "Thomas Baldwin wants to build a Wild West theme park on the property he bought from Luke Wilson. Maybe he's trying to fit the part—or perhaps he's delusional."

"It sounds like the mob—sell me your business, or I'll kill you," Chris countered. "Maybe Phil Coleman works for the mob—and says he worked for Thomas Baldwin."

"Maybe he works for both," Jessie said.

"What would the mafia want with my business?" Loretta asked.

"To launder money," Chris said, and Loretta was enraged.

"I've been an honest, hardworking veterinarian my whole life!" Loretta said. "I'd never sell my clinic to launder money."

"We will get to the bottom of this," Sue said.

Loretta replied, "I would never launder money for the mob."

Just listening to Loretta's screech made me nervous. I had never heard her sound so upset. She was, for the most part, an even-keeled person. I licked her hand to make her feel better, but she pulled it away.

Luna put her head under Loretta's other hand, and she softened. "I'm ready to paddle the kayaks," Loretta said. "I need a moment to pull myself together."

"Remind us what happened the night Tori disappeared," Sue said.

"We saw Dave paddle into the creek with Tori at 6:00 PM. It was before the time change, and the days were shorter. Dave paddled out at 6:30 without her."

"He tells people he dropped Tori off to talk to a friend she saw in Mia's Run," Sue said. "Dave says he paddled home for snacks, but when he returned, she was gone."

"We stayed here until after dark that night," Jessie replied. "It was a beautiful, clear evening, and we roasted marshmallows by the fire."

"That is when the alligators are most active, and it was the beginning of the mating season," Chris added.

"Dave never came back," Jessie said.

The conversation was over, but the search for truth was beginning. Sue and Loretta were on a quest to unravel the evolving details of Tori's disappearance and Phil Coleman's strange and aggressive behaviors. One thing was sure. Loretta was brilliant, but she wasn't as patient as Chris. Nothing—not even a gun-toting mob thug—could make her sell the clinic.

Chapter 5

Mia's Run

S ue and Loretta boarded the kayaks and held onto the seawall while they waited for Luna and me. I jumped off Jessie's seawall and landed on the kayak with four feet. It was an easy launch for me—about two feet from the seawall to the kayak. I landed securely, but Luna had less experience with the maneuver and nearly fell off the boat.

Sue and I kayak almost weekly, year-round. Sometimes, we miss a river trip for a holiday or an event, but we rarely miss more than a week or two for other activities or weather. Sue says I might kayak more than any dog in Sweetwater Springs, but it's not like anybody takes polls on kayaking dogs. Sue says she wants to buy a trolling motor for upstream trips, but is still in the thinking stages.

Sue has thinking, planning, and doing stages where she brings her plans to fruition. She is not one to rush into things but to consider them thoroughly. I suspect we might see the trolling motor shortly after she solves the mysteries of Tori's disappearance and the man's motive with the silver-plated gun.

It's 7:30 AM on a Thursday, and we are the first people we see on the river. Weekends can be busy in August, but weekdays are slower. Renters from the B and Bs stay for days, weeks, or months, but most people kayak on a day trip from the nearby cities on weekends.

The early morning sun is warm but not blazing like it will be later. High, puffy clouds dot the sky, bringing moments of shade to the sunshine. Tall trees flank the sparkling river, the only shade without clouds. I'm glad it's early for many reasons, but mostly the good weather.

It is a short paddle across the river to Mia's Run. "How are you doing, Loretta?" Sue asks as we paddle slightly upstream.

"Excellent!" she replies. "The current isn't strong to paddle against."

"Is Luna alright?" Sue asks, twisting backward to look at my dog friend seated in front of Loretta on the kayak.

"She's found the perfect place to sit and stay dry," Loretta replied.

"That won't last long," Sue said. We will tether the boats just past the creek's entrance and walk upstream shortly. Luna can swim or walk, or sometimes I carry Daisy under my arm if she's tired."

Mia's Run was a special place, about a quarter of a mile long and narrow. It was one of the few places we could walk in the river for a distance. Tall trees and cypress knees bordered the crystal-clear creek, fed by small springs and the biggest one near Thomas Baldwin's mansion. There were trails through the wetlands, but none led to the Baldwin mansion, where the housewarming party would be on Saturday night.

The housewarming party was a rare opportunity for those fortunate to be invited—I wasn't one of the lucky few because I'm a dog. Most locals had seen Thomas Baldwin about town or would recognize him from photos, but few had met the billionaire with a vision to change Sweetwater Springs into the home of a Wild West Theme Park. Some might have predicted the luxury hotel, but nobody expected the Wild West theme park he dreamed of.

The public was invited to explore the hauntingly beautiful Mia's Run, but not the fenced-off estate. The Run was shallow and walkable in the crystal-clear Spring water. I loved cooling off during a dog paddle on scorching summer afternoons. This morning was mild, and the springs felt good, but I wasn't hot while Sue paddled to Mia's Run.

Thomas Baldwin named nothing after himself but everything after his wife, Mia, who would be the legacy of Sweetwater Springs with hotels, springs, theme parks, and pubs. Sue thought it was sweet of him, but I thought nothing of it. I wouldn't care if they built a dog park in Sweetwater Springs and named it Daisy's Dog Park. I'm more interested in the moment than a legacy park.

I wish I had been invited to Baldwin's Housewarming Party. I know it's a big, fancy event, but Sue and Loretta are veterinarians, and bringing a dog wouldn't be so unusual. I have a good sense of smell and can be the icebreaker with chilly people. Sue would be much more popular with me around. Luna is a different story.

Sue lodged her kayak into the wetlands at the creek's border, followed by Loretta, who docked next to her. Luna popped off Loretta's kayak before I did and swam to the other side of the creek.

"Should I put a leash on her?" Loretta asked.

"I put a leash on Daisy," Sue replied. We usually see people and other dogs here, but no one is in sight today."

"I'll take it with me," Loretta said. "Luna is enjoying the water her way."

Luna splashed, hopped, and doggy paddled in the creek while Sue and Loretta hiked waist-deep down the middle of the creek.

"She loves it," Loretta said, and Sue recalled my first run in Mia's Run when I swam alone for the first time.

There were parts of the creek where I could dog-paddle with my front legs and touch the bottom with my rear legs, which I favored for a downstream walk. Upstream, Sue usually let me walk closer to the side, which was shallower. Sometimes, I dog-paddled criss-crossed from one side to the other.

"This is beautiful," Loretta said, observing the great canopy of trees that crossed the river. "The water is so clear."

"It's not far to the main spring," Sue replied. "And there are little springs along the way."

"It must be one of the purest creeks in the world," Loretta said. "There's no one on this side of the river for miles except Thomas Baldwin and Luke Wilson."

"Do you think they are in cahoots to keep it private?" Loretta continued.

"I think it's a swamp that needs to be private," Sue replied. "Luke sold the swamp and surrounding land to Thomas Baldwin to avoid projects in Sweetwater Springs."

Loretta put Luna on a leash, and we tiptoed through the shallow creek toward the main spring. Sue carried me under her arm as we walked upstream to enjoy the scenery. We approached the fence surrounding the mansion, and we saw three women in the high, dry woods.

"Is that you, Tori?" Sue gasped, shocked by her appearance after vanishing months ago.

Tori was thin and ghostly yet alive and well. Despite the warm weather, she wore a black cape from head to toe. I recognized her immediately as the woman who fed me ice at Cat Tails Pub.

"Yes, it's me," she said, looking at Sue with hollow eyes.

"Why are you wearing that cape?"

"I'm hiding from Dave," she replied. "I don't want anyone to recognize me."

"Do you want to talk about it?" Sue asked.

"You can't tell anyone you saw me," Tori said. "No one. Do you promise?"

Sue looked at Loretta, then back at Tori. "I promise not to tell anyone," she said, and Loretta agreed.

"Dave said you were talking to a friend when he left you here on the kayaking trip that night."

"I talked to Dave before he left," Tori said. "My friends found me the next day."

"Dave is no friend," the older woman said, extending her hand in greeting. "I'm Mia Baldwin."

The younger woman said, "I'm Sarah."

"It's nice to meet you," Sue said, "although this is a most unusual circumstance."

"I'm your veterinarian," Loretta added. "I look different in a white coat than in a bathing suit and sunhat."

"I thought I recognized you," Mia said.

"Many locals think you're dead," Sue told Tori. "They miss you at Cat Tails."

"I miss them too," Tori replied. "I loved the pub. Dave didn't. We fought about it all the time."

Sarah looked at me and said, "You have a Cute Dog."

I was so accustomed to being called "Cute Dog" it seemed like my nickname. I walked toward Sarah and nudged her hand with my long, furless nose.

"She likes me," Sarah said.

Tori added, "Is that Daisy?"

Sue smiled at her excellent memory. I loved Tori, but she saw many dogs at Cat Tails Pub. I was impressed that she remembered me.

"You have a good memory," Sue said. "Yes, this is Daisy."

"Daisy was one of my favorite customers," Tori said. "Of course, I remember her."

I was honored; I had no idea I was one of Tori Pedri's favorite dog customers. As I walked toward her, she reached down to pet me.

"Daisy got attacked at the pub by a dog twice her size," Tori said. "The dog bouncer had to escort him to leave. We changed the dog seating rules after that. I'll never forget Daisy."

"Do you have many dog fights at the pub?" Loretta asked.

"No, that was the first and only. Dave wanted to shut down the dog-friendly seating, but I insisted we keep it."

"I hope Daisy's attacker didn't instigate your breakup," Sue said, and Tori replied, "If so, it was inspired."

Mia said, "I have three dogs, but two are protection dogs for the property, and the third is a homebody. I'd love a dog to come to the housewarming party as the furry guest of honor."

I couldn't have been more thrilled to hear the unexpected request that I attend Baldwin's housewarming party. I was so excited that I felt frozen and nearly forgot to breathe. It was an honor to be the only dog at a party.

"Can Daisy come to the party?" Mia asked, and Sue accepted instantly. "She'd love to!"

"Since Daisy is the honored guest, I'll seat you and Loretta at the table with Thomas and me. Luke Wilson will join us with Val and Gio Pedri."

Loretta frowned when she heard Gio Pedri's name, but she couldn't say much about him since he was Tori's father. Instead, she asked, "Do you know why Phil Coleman would want to buy our veterinary hospital?"

"I didn't know he wanted to buy your veterinary hospital, and for that matter, I don't know why Phil Coleman works for Baldwin Enterprises," Mia said. "He is an irresponsible con man."

"You can say that again," Sarah agreed. "He'll play two sides against the middle and join the winner."

Loretta groaned at their answers, which didn't alleviate her fears about a mafia buy-in. Phil Coleman could be up to almost anything, and nobody liked him. Still, it had been a fruitful trip. Luna and I got to kayak and swim in the creek.

Best of all, Tori was alive, and she remembered me. I had been invited to Baldwin's housewarming as the doggie guest of honor. I could sniff out danger for Sue. There was much to learn at a billionaire's party—and for now, I thought Mia was a perfect match for Thomas.

Chapter 6

Jessica and Chris

I stood with all four feet on the kayak while Sue paddled back to Jessie and Chris' house. I am a tall dog, so people notice me when I'm standing before Sue. Most people say I look happy on board, but I'm primarily interested in everything on the river.

I love to see the trees, birds, and dogs that stand in their backyards and bark at me. One day, a dog jumped out of his backyard into the water and swam toward the kayak. He had a fearsome bark rather than a friendly one. I was glad he turned around and swam home because his owner was nowhere in sight.

Sue wants a house on the river where I can jump in, too. One day, she may buy one. Coming outside daily would be fun, and I'd jump in the river whenever possible, but I'm happy to live on the cove. I'm not allowed to swim, but we have friends there. I love the catwalk around the neighborhood, where we found Toby.

Sue says Jessie's house was the best buy on the river before she knew they could build a second house on the property, making it even better. Chris is building the second house himself, closer to the river. He knows a lot about buildings and is sometimes asked to help with the fixer-uppers in town.

Loretta paddled her kayak back to Jessie and Chris's house behind Sue. Looking back, I could see Luna lying down, tired. Luna is not as conditioned as I am for swimming in the cold water. Still, she was excited and had fun on Mia's Run.

Chris meandered to the river to help Sue and Loretta pull the kayaks out. "Jessie is making coffee," he said as Luna and I bolted toward the house. "Please join us."

Everyone else walked up the slight slope to their original house. Inside the house was a definite fixer-upper. The walls were covered in great oak panels that would have been spectacular in a riverside cabin fifty years ago. Today was different, but it was a lovely chore for Chris, who enjoyed construction and renovating.

Jessie looked up from her coffee pot. "You two look like you saw a ghost," she said, and Sue swallowed hard. Sue and Loretta were sworn to secrecy, but seeing Tori alive had been a jolt.

"No, just Mia," Sue said, biting her tongue.

"She seems like a nice lady," Jessie replied. "She comes out every morning before the crowds to swim the creek."

"Mia didn't recognize me at first," Loretta said.

"Your white veterinary coat is a bit more professional than a bathing suit," Jessie replied.

"Did you see anyone else?" Chris asked as Jessie poured coffee for every-one

"No, Mia is the only person we saw," Loretta said, and her voice squeaked as it did on the rare occasions she distorted the truth.

"Why do I think you may be leaving something out?" Jessie asked, but she didn't push for more information. Her friends were processing or distorting information, but the truth would come later.

Jessie poured coffee for everyone and set a loaf of homemade bread with no processed ingredients and a bowl of fresh fruit on the table. She also gave

Luna and me dog biscuits from a box. We didn't mind. The biscuits were delicious and crunched perfectly into tiny tidbits we ate from the floor.

"Mia invited Daisy to the housewarming party," Sue said.

"That's fabulous," Jessie said. "How nice for you and Daisy."

"Daisy is the doggie guest of honor," Loretta added. "Luna wasn't invited."

"Daisy is practically famous in Sweetwater Springs," Jessie said, rubbing Luna's head for consolation. "Everyone knows her from kayak trips, restaurants, and walks."

If you were friendly, helpful, or furry and four-footed, you could be famous in Sweetwater Springs. It didn't take celebrity or politics to be appreciated in our small town. I was most honored that Tori remembered me, but Sue didn't mention Tori because she wasn't supposed to reveal her secret. Luna chewed the biscuit, oblivious to anything that was said. She got extra morsels because she was distracted.

"Did Luna like the kayak trip?" Chris asked.

"She loved it," Loretta replied. "The creek was awesome. She had so much fun dog-paddling in the stream."

"Sometimes we see a woman in a black cape by the creek," Jessie said, and Sue cringed. "It's odd because it's too hot to wear it."

"Do you think it's Mia?" Sue asked, trying to sound authentic.

"We've seen a woman in a black cape with Mia," Chris said.

"Maybe she has a skin disease," Loretta suggested, trying to avoid the topic of Tori hiding from Dave in a black cape so no one would recognize her. "Some people can't get any sun but love being outdoors."

"I hadn't thought of that," Chris replied. Some people cover up head to toe to avoid the sun."

"They usually wear white in summer," Jessie said, and Loretta agreed it was an unusual color.

Chris passed two more dog biscuits to Luna and me, who scarfed them off the floor before I could eat mine. "You need to share," Loretta scolded Luna, giving me a biscuit just as Jessie's older Doberman, who used to live at Sue's house before Jessie moved in with Chris, joined us. The Doberman was so stiff from arthritis that she could barely walk on the floor, but she was a trooper to participate, and Jessie gave her a biscuit.

"I'll get you some medicine to help with her arthritis," Loretta said. "I'll bring it to Baldwin's housewarming party."

"That's kind of you," Jessie said. "The big dog bed she sleeps on keeps her from jumping up and down on the couch," she added. "I don't mind if she sleeps on the couch, but I don't want her to hurt herself. Chris made her a slope to get on and off the bed."

"I love old dogs," Sue said. "She's forever young in spirit, no matter how old she is."

"The yoga mats help her with traction," Loretta added, and Jessie said they had made a big difference."

Chris gently rubbed the old Doberman behind the ears, and she groaned with pleasure.

"Mia Baldwin has two Dobermans," Loretta said. They are good dogs and well-trained, but aren't social for parties."

"Some dogs protect while other dogs connect," Sue said. "Daisy is a connector; Mia's dogs are protectors, but they all have love to return when their families love them."

"Did you ask Mia why Phil Coleman wants to buy your clinic?" Chris asked when he had finished sharing the dog biscuits.

Loretta groaned as she recalled the conversation, which revealed nothing about his motives or allegiances. "Yes, sir, I did. I can only tell you that Mia Baldwin does not like Phil Coleman, and she speaks her mind."

"She says he's an irresponsible con man," Sue added.

"I wonder why Thomas Baldwin keeps him as a land speculator," Jessie said.

"Men don't always see these things in people—or they can overlook them for their strengths," Loretta said.

"He has purchased a lot of land for Baldwin Enterprises," Chris said. "He gets the job done."

"How many people does a land speculator work for?" Jessie asked, and Chris replied, "An independent land speculator can work for whomever he wants. He can buy with other investors if he wants to."

"Like Gio," Loretta said.

"Our veterinary hospital is not land speculation," Sue said. "It's a building, land, and a business from a lifetime of our family's work."

"Phil Coleman has an angle," Chris said, and Loretta agreed that we didn't know what it was.

"For some reason, Thomas Baldwin likes him, and Mia Baldwin doesn't like him," Sue said.

"Why do you think Thomas Baldwin is getting tight with Gio Pedri?" Jessie asked, and Chris suggested that enterprising men liked to have partners they could count on.

"Mia Baldwin called Phil Coleman irresponsible," Sue said.

"Yes, she did," Loretta replied. "She called him an irresponsible con man."

"What's with that?" Jessie asked, and Sue said she'd follow up on it.

I could feel the tension mounting from under the table where two sleeping dogs lay beside me. For now, there were more questions than answers, but Sue liked to solve problems. She was not one to let sleeping dogs lie but more likely to leave no stone unturned.

Jessie's daughter, ten-year-old Beth, meandered into the dining room with her cat, Boomer. Beth lived at Sue's house before Jessie and Chris fell in love. I could smell Boomer from a distance, which brought fond memories. Boomer was my playmate before Sue adopted Toby. Our adventures filled a book, but here's a synopsis.

During a rainstorm, Boomer arrived on Sue's driveway, scraggly, thin, and drenched, to join our family of indoor pets. Near death, he was a young kitten when Sue found him and revived him. Beth fell in love with the kitten and named him Boomer. He became her constant companion during Jessie's lengthy divorce from her hot-tempered father. Everyone loved Boomer, but Beth needed him most.

Now, Boomer was a full-sized cat with a round head and round eyes, like many of the cats of Sweetwater Springs. It didn't take a wholesome romance novelist to see that Boomer and Beth loved each other more than ever. He was her first friend in Sweetwater Springs, but now she had other two-legged friends who might help solve a mystery.

"Hi, Sweetie," Jessie said as she entered the dining room. Look who's here!"

"Aunt Sue and Aunt Loretta!" she exclaimed, racing for hugs. Although they weren't related, Beth called all of her mother's besties, Aunts, or Uncles.

"Oh my Gosh, how you've grown," Sue said, and Loretta agreed that she must be an inch taller.

"You just saw me a week ago," Jessie said, and Loretta suggested it might be a growth spurt.

"How's Daisy?" Beth asked as I came out from under that table to greet her.

"She's good. She's delighted to see you."

"Boomer misses Daisy," Beth said, hanging her head. "He doesn't have anyone to play with now that he doesn't live with Daisy. Mom's Doberman is too old to play—and he never liked to play anyway."

"Daisy misses Boomer, too, Honey," Sue said.

Beth joined us for homemade bread, jams, and fresh fruit while Boomer sat at the door looking outside. Ignoring three dogs, including Luna, who could be a pest, didn't make them not there, but he seemed content. Today wouldn't be a playdate for Boomer and me, but I'm sure he was happy to see me.

When Beth finished eating, she asked, "Mom, can I go to Missy Bryan's house today?"

"Of course, Honey," she said. "I'll drive you there."

"Is Missy Hank Bryan's daughter?" Sue asked.

"Yes, as a matter of fact, she is," Jessie said of the daughter of the mayor of Sweetwater Springs.

"Where does your friend live?" I asked. "I'd like to talk to Hank Bryan."

"On the Green Cove," Beth said, since the cove had turned green from past years of sparkling turquoise.

"Do you want to kayak to her house with Loretta and me?"

"No thanks, Aunt Sue, it's too far. Maybe another time."

Beth had let Sue down sweetly, as Beth would do. "Can you pick me up and return to my house for dinner tonight?"

"We should ask your mother about that," Sue said, and Jessie agreed she'd love to have Sue—and me— for dinner.

"What can I bring?" Sue asked.

"Anything you like," Jessie said, "Just be sure it's healthy."

After Jessie left with Beth, we boarded the kayaks, and Sue and Loretta paddled towards home. Luna was a quick learner and boarded with ease the second time around. I thought we would have time ahead of us, but that was good with me. Sue's friends were my friends—two-legged or four-legged—and there was much to learn.

Chapter 7

Rita's House

When we got home from the kayaking trip, I sprawled out on the floor in a configuration Sue called Long Dog because I was stretched out from head to toe. Toby stared out the window as he often did. Cats are so much alike. Boomer did the same thing to avoid eye contact with Luna at Jessie's house. Cats think you can't see them if they can't see you.

It's not true, of course, but we are talking about cats. Their brains are tiny and much more limited than a dog's brain, which is much bigger and more diverse. Cats know what they know—which is ingenious in its own right. That said, Toby is much less discerning about people than I am.

I can sniff out good or evil, happiness or sadness, tenseness or calm, and report my findings to Sue. If Toby sniffs anything terrible, he becomes increasingly annoying. This mostly happens because he thinks someone doesn't like him. I wonder what he'd do if the land speculator came over, but one thing is sure: that will never happen.

When they finished bringing the kayaks to Sue's house, Loretta asked, "What do you want to do about Phil Coleman, Mom?"

"I'll find out what I can about him," Sue said. "I'll stop by Rita's house after I take you back to pick up your truck at Jessie's."

Rita had been a school teacher in Sweetwater Springs for almost forty years. She knew nearly everyone who grew up here, and if she didn't have them in her class, she heard about the best or the worst kids from other teachers—sometimes throughout their lives. She taught third grade but had friends who taught middle and high school. Sometimes, Sue took me to Rita's class to join the kids at reading time.

"Coleman worries me," Loretta said. "I wonder if he's spent time in jail or —-worse."

"We might have to dig elsewhere to find out about his criminal record," Sue said. "But Rita can tell me about his demeanor in school."

"I'll bet he spent time in detention," Loretta replied. "He's cockeye and pushy at the same time. Conceited with nothing to be conceited about."

"Except his silver gun," Sue reminded her.

"There is that," Loretta said, frowning and clenching her jaw. "I wonder why Mia called him irresponsible."

"Maybe she was being nice," Sue said, and Loretta laughed. "I'm sure she could have called him worse."

"I'll find out what I can about Mia from Rita while there," Sue said.

"Mia seemed friendly," Loretta continued. "Down to earth."

"She's a nature lover," Sue said, and Loretta agreed. "Like us."

Currently, Toby was staring out the window, enjoying nature, like Sue and Loretta—or, more likely, capturing the lizard of his imagination that lives on the back porch. He often captured lizards, but Sue took them away from him. Most of them were small, but he was attracted to their quick movement—and size didn't matter to Toby. A small lizard was just as fun to catch as a giant lizard. I'm sure Toby dreamed of catching lizards when he took his frequent naps.

"You have a nice cat," Loretta said. "I'm glad you found Toby after Beth left with Boomer."

"I miss Boomer," Sue said, and Loretta praised her for letting the child take him.

"I wouldn't have it any other way," Sue replied. "They were made for each other."

"True Love is a pleasure to see," Loretta said, stroking Luna under the chin. "Especially between a child and a pet."

"I'm glad Beth is making friends," Sue added, watching Toby jump at the sliding glass door. "And Chris is good for both of them."

"He's a good man," Loretta said. "Jessie was lucky to find him."

Toby jumped airborne in front of the sliding glass door before returning to the couch for a nap, while I sprawled on the floor to keep my belly cool. Dreams could be better than life, especially for a cat who rarely lived his dreams. I slept with one eye open while Sue and Loretta recalled the day's events.

"I knew Tori and Dave were having problems, but I didn't know it was bad enough for Tori to go into hiding," Sue said.

"It's going to be hard to keep it a secret," Loretta replied. "She's been missing for months, and people are worried about her."

"She owes everyone an explanation," Sue agreed. "Where has she been hiding, and who has taken care of her?"

"It sounds like Mia takes care of her," Loretta said. But who was Sarah? How often does Tori get outside in that black cape?"

"Good questions," Sue said. "The answers will come in time."

"Tori has a big heart," Loretta said. "She means a lot to the community."

"Much more than Dave," Sue replied. "He's distant and chilly, like he doesn't want to be here."

"If Dave wants to return to Miami, why doesn't he just leave?" Loretta asked.

"Maybe he can't," Sue said. "Tori's parents gave them the pub as a wedding gift. It can be hard to walk away from men like Gio."

After Sue returned home from taking Loretta to retrieve her truck, she called Rita, who lived across the street, and welcomed us for a visit. Sue grabbed my leash, and I raced to meet her at the door. Every walk was a treat, no matter how short, and I enjoyed seeing Rita and Fred. Better yet, Sue enjoyed my enthusiasm.

Rita greeted us at the front door and escorted us to the family room, where her husband, Fred, observed an upriver view of the bridge. She brought a tray with tea and biscuits for everyone else while she offered me a jerky treat.

"What's up?" Rita asked after she poured tea.

"I saw Mia today," Sue replied. "It was the first time I met her, but Loretta is her veterinarian. You might know her since she grew up in Sweetwater Springs."

"I've been thinking about Mia lately. Rita replied. "She was in my third-grade class. Mia was sweet and caring as a child—loved the guinea pig I kept for a pet in my classroom. We're looking forward to the house-warming party this weekend."

Fred was not so enamored. "Baldwin just wants to suck up to potential investors for his hotel and enterprises," Fred snarled, as he often did. Fred could be as grumpy as Rita was lovely. The two were opposites, but it worked.

"Maybe so," Sue said. "I don't know him, but he has a land speculator named Phil Coleman who wants to buy the clinic."

"For what?" Rita exclaimed.

"Darned if I know, but he has been a horrible upset for Loretta. He flashed a silver handgun like he was threatening her to sell. I met him at Cat Tails Pub the day before he went to see Loretta. He offered to show me the gun—called it a masterpiece— but I wouldn't let him."

"That's crazy," Rita said.

"I've seen him at Cat Tails Pub," Fred added. "He sits in the corner and meets with people—shady looking and otherwise."

"How strange," Rita said. "I wonder what he's up to?"

"Did you have Phil in school?" Sue asked, and Rita said to give her a moment to place him. "Yes, I remember him."

"Phil didn't have many friends in elementary school," Rita recalled. "He picked a few fights and was known to kick and run. Later, he found his calling to excel as a football wide receiver in high school— he was good-looking and popular and got the girls."

"That's quite a transition," Sue said. "From elementary school bully to popular football superhero."

"He was still very self-centered," Rita said. "He loved his name in lights. As I recall, Phil and the mayor were rivals in high school."

"Hank Bryan?" Sue was surprised. "Over what?"

"Hank wanted the girls, but he wasn't as athletic or good-looking as Phil. Hank was competitive at golf rather than football, which the girls admired back then. He liked to hunt and had a room full of trophy heads."

Sue sipped her tea and said, "I'm going to see the mayor when I pick up Jessie later."

Rita sipped her tea and continued, "As I recall, Phil dated Mia Baldwin in high school—years before she was a Baldwin."

"Are you kidding me?" Sue said, "Phil dated Mia in high school?"

"Mia was beautiful. One of the most beautiful girls in Sweetwater Springs. She could have chosen any boy she wanted."

"Beautiful and nice," Sue replied. It must have been hard for her to befriend jealous girls."

"Mia always had friends," Rita replied. "She tried to help people wherever she could—then and now. She grew into her own very nicely."

Sue wanted to say Mia was helping Tori, but couldn't reveal it. "I wonder if Thomas knows Mia dated his land speculator in high school."

"Who knows?" Rita replied. "Thomas adores her for naming everything after Mia, as he does."

"How long have they been married?" Sue asked.

Rita replied fifteen years. It was the most sensational wedding in Sweetwater Springs. It was on the property where they live now, but we weren't invited.

"How nice for them," Sue said. "They're living a dream."

"Mia had some rocky spots," Rita replied. For her, it was not all cake and ice cream."

"What do you mean?" Sue asked.

"She disappeared for a year in high school. When she came back, she was different—melancholy. She never returned to her full, vibrant self—she was still sweet but more serious."

"Strange," Sue replied. "Something must have happened to her."

"How did she meet Thomas Baldwin?"

"She opened a card and gift shop in town. According to Mia, Thomas made every excuse to buy a card so he could see her. They fell in love, and the rest is history."

"His first wife was a piece of work," Fred added. "She had everything, but she was never satisfied."

"That's unfortunate," Sue said. "For both of them."

Rita added, "He learned a lesson and did better with Mia. I'm happy for them."

Sparkles meandered into the living room while they talked and rubbed my head. Everyone we knew on River Drive had a stray cat as a house pet, and Sparkles was the first to be adopted. Like Toby, he was a community cat. He had a story like every cat, but it was time to go.

"I'll see you at the housewarming," Sue said as she rose to leave. "Oh, by the way, Mia invited Daisy. She is the doggie guest of honor."

"That's wonderful," Sue said. "It sounds like being a billionaire's wife hasn't changed Mia a bit."

Chapter 8

The Mayor's House

W hen we got home from Rita's house, Sue was stewing about something. I lay on the kitchen floor, snuggled in a ball with my fluffy tail tucked between my legs, while she sifted through the refrigerator. Jessie's invitation to dinner was unexpected, but Sue would not go empty-handed. She decided to make jalapeno poppers with the fresh jalapenos Loretta gave her from her garden—baked, not fried—because they were just as tasty—and Jessie would appreciate the healthy angle.

Sue gathered the ingredients—cheese, jalapenos, and bread crumbs. It was an easy appetizer with loads of flavor. Loretta had first introduced her mother to jalapeno poppers at a murder mystery dinner party, and they became one of their favorites. Frankly, Luna and I wouldn't bother to counter-surf for jalapeno poppers unless morsels of cheese fell on our heads.

Luna tried a jalapeno once, and that was more than enough. Not me. I'll take her word for it and forego the flaming mouth that sounded miserable and unrelenting. One day, Luna will learn to have more discretion, but for now, she gobbles before she samples the goods.

I lay motionless near the cabinets while Sue assembled the poppers. Toby jumped on the counter to investigate, continuously sticking his nose in everything except Sue's cooking. He sniffed the cheese from a distance and avoided the hot peppers altogether. Some people say dogs are more intelligent than cats, and others say cats are smarter than dogs. From my observations, Toby is more intelligent than Luna.

Sue used to be more hesitant about letting Toby on the counter, but she allowed distance observations. She let him watch the preparations as long as he stayed away from the food. He quickly became bored with the cooking ingredients. Toby preferred cat food, and Sue served him only the best. He ate a tidbit of cat food and left as quickly as he arrived.

I was drowsy from our busy day of kayaking with Luna and visiting Sue's friends. After her prolonged absence, I was happy to see Tori and excited to be the honored guest—and only dog—at Baldwin's house-warming party. I almost fell asleep, but Sue would nearly step on me and wake me up.

Sue stewed about the day while scattering cheese on the jalapenos. Sometimes, she talked to herself while working. "Mia dated Phil Coleman?" she muttered. "What does he want with the clinic? He claims he wants it for Thomas Baldwin, but is that true? Why on earth is Tori Pedri hiding at the Baldwin estate?"

Sue had more questions than answers. "I can't believe Phil Coleman and the mayor were rivals in high school. Phil and Hank were opposites, then and now—from a school jock and a golf star to a con and a public servant. "What did Mia see in both of them, and why did she pick Phil?" Sue grumbled. "Why did Thomas Baldwin keep Phil if the man was such a disgrace?"

Sue pondered the questions when she pulled the poppers out of the oven. She set the roasting pan on the counter to cool while she showered and dressed to pick up Beth at the mayor's house before dinner. It had been a long day, but time passed quickly.

"It's time to go, Daisy," Sue said, attaching my leash to my collar, and I jumped up with renewed enthusiasm after my brief nap. "Let's get Beth."

Sue drove up the hill on River Drive, past Cypress Street, where Sparkles and Toby came from. Nobody knew where Boomer came from, but everyone knew he had enough adventures to write the first love story in Sweetwater Springs. She crossed over Main Street and turned into the more elegant subdivision—the finest in town— where the mayor lived.

The mayor lived on Green Cove, formerly known as Turquoise Cove, before the increasingly abundant algae destroyed the sparkling water. The residents of Green Cove had the most precise view of the river's health from observation. It was not a happy sight for locals who loved the river, especially lifelong locals like Hank Bryan, who watched its demise. For some, like Hank, the cove was love. It was a massive loss of money for others whose property values plunged into the abyss.

For a few, like Phil Coleman, purchasing a house in Green Cove when the market hit bottom was a lucky break and a bargain. He was the first buyer when the cove turned green with algae and home prices dipped.

Unlike the river, the cove was not spring-fed by hundreds of tiny springs that renewed its crystal-clear beauty. Here, in the cove, what flowed in from the river stayed because there was no moving water to push it out. After hundreds of years of turquoise splendor, it turned green with algae.

The experts proposed several reasons, mostly sewage and primarily agricultural from cow manure. But the locals knew the cows had been there for over a hundred years when the river stayed sparkling, clear, turquoise blue. Now, with thousands more visitors, the cove was green. Common sense prevailed amongst locals that Green Cove was a problem of increasing population.

Hence, there was a massive debate between cattlemen and meat eaters who didn't believe cows were the problem. The experts declared otherwise, and the non-beef eaters loved them for it. The developers mostly didn't care about the river—-except for a few like Thomas Baldwin, who wanted to live in Sweetwater Springs for a lifetime.

Sue pulled her car into the mayor's driveway to pick up Beth. I jumped out of the car to escort her to the front door. Glancing at the Green Cove behind the house, I knew one thing: I wouldn't drink that water if you paid me!

Hank answered the door with his wife, Rene, at his side. "It's good to see you, Sue," he said. "It's been a long time."

Sue avoided Green Cove on the kayaking trips for years. Considering how spectacular it had been before the algae took over, it was just too hard to look at. Most of her friends lived in town or on the main river, which was compensated for by the sparkling clarity of the springs.

"It's sad, isn't it?" Hank said, pointing at the green cove and sensing Sue's despondence.

"It's hard to believe it happened," Sue said, veering her observations indoors. "You have a beautiful home."

"With no view," Rene added. "Sometimes, I keep the curtains shut so we don't have to look at the cove."

"Do you think it will clear up?" Sue asked. "Many polluted rivers have been salvaged and renewed."

"It will take a think tank to figure it out and find a solution," Hank said. "The experts are presenting a dismal projection for the future."

"We may be dead by the time they clean it up," Rene said, and Sue scoffed, "I hope not."

"Is this Daisy?" Rene asked, reaching down to pet me, and Sue affirmed. "I've heard about Daisy," Rene said. "You're practically famous."

"Daisy is more well-known than I am," Sue replied. "Thankfully, she doesn't let it go to her head."

"Are you going to the Baldwins' housewarming Party?" Rene asked.

"I'm looking forward to it. I just met Mia Baldwin today."

Hank stiffened at Mia's name, and his wife said, "Hank wanted to date Mia in high school, but she had no time for him."

"That's fortunate for you both," Sue replied as if she didn't know about the rivalry.

"Phillip Coleman is scum," Hank said. "Always has been, always will be."

"He lives in the house two doors down from us," Rene added. "He bought the house at rock bottom because of the algae, and it's already worth more than he paid for it."

"He must think the algae will clear up," Sue said.

"He must know something I don't," Hank said. "The research doesn't look good."

"Not all research is good research," Rene said. "You and I both know that, but not everyone will admit it."

"In this case, I hope you're right," Sue said, and Rene added, "There must be something we can do to improve the conditions of the cove."

I lay on my belly, stretched in a long dog on the carpet. It was itchy, and it smelled like feet. I wasn't sure why people liked carpets, but Hank and Rene were pleasant.

Someone yelled at another person from down the street while Sue and the Bryans were talking. It was a man's voice, not followed by anyone else's; it was just his. "That's Phil Coleman," Rene said. He always yells at his wife, and she never yells back."

"How unpleasant," Sue replied. "She must feel trapped."

"Maybe she thinks he'll hit her if she talks back," Rene said. "He's very controlling."

"Why does she stay with him?" Sue asked, and neither of them had an answer. "We aren't friends with them," Hank said, and Sue wasn't surprised.

"What's his wife like?" Sue asked.

"Pretty and reserved," Rene said. "I could be friends with her if it weren't for Phillip. Now, I would have to pretend not to know about everything I know."

"Can you hear what he yells at her about?" Sue asked, and Rene said no. "They have a daughter about our daughter's age. I would prefer it if she came to our house, but sometimes she and her friends go to her house. They went today."

"Beth went to Phil Coleman's house?" Sue asked, and Rene confirmed it. "Yes, for about an hour before they came home."

"Our daughter thinks Phil is creepy," Rene said, and Sue mentioned that she had heard someone call him that before.

"He's a snake in the grass," Hank said, "The whole town would be better off without him."

These were infamous last words that we often heard in one version or another. Hank Bryan didn't like Phil Coleman, and neither did anyone else.

"He flashed his gun at Loretta," Sue said. "He wants to buy the clinic."

"Was that supposed to impress her?" Rene asked.

"It made her nervous at first, then angry," Sue said. "Phil Coleman has no right to twist her arm—or anyone else's with that flashy silver gun."

"He's delusional," Hank said, and Sue mentioned he wasn't the only one who thought so.

I sat up when Beth joined us in the living room while Sue talked. "Are you ready to go home, Sweetie?" Sue asked, and Beth confirmed.

"Daisy is the guest of honor," Sue proudly revealed before she left.

"How fun!" Rene said. "We'll look forward to seeing you both there."

There wasn't a soul in Sweetwater Springs who wouldn't have "Killed to go to the Baldwins' housewarming party." He was the town's only billionaire. Everyone, no matter how rich, poor, hardworking, lazy, conniving, or ethical, wanted to see how the man who might change the face of Sweetwater Springs forever lived at his mansion on the springs.

Chapter 9

Sue's House

S ue and Beth hopped into the car to drive back home. I sat in the back seat, where I often did. I was comfortable there, and Sue said it was safer for a dog to ride in the back seat than the front seat. She had tried the doggy seatbelt for my front-seat rides, but neither of us was impressed. It was hard to lie down with the seat belt on, and if I could lie down, it was nearly impossible to change positions.

"I made some jalapeno poppers to take to your mom's house," Sue said.

"I've never had them," Beth said. "Are they hot?"

"Baking them takes away some of the heat," Sue replied, but some are hotter. Loretta says there's usually at least one ultra-hot popper in every batch—and there's no way to know which one it is until you taste it."

"Did Aunt Loretta grow them in her garden?" Beth asked, and Sue affirmed.

"I wish I could grow a garden," Beth said. Mom spends a lot of money on fresh vegetables and worries they're sprayed with pesticides."

"She's right to feel that way," Sue replied. "If you want to know the fertilizers and pesticides used on your vegetables, you must grow them yourself."

"Mom doesn't want to grow a garden because she doesn't want to use fertilizer so close to the river," Beth said.

"You can grow your vegetables in a container," Sue said. "The fertilizer won't seep into the river if it's in a container."

"I've heard of container gardens," Beth said. "Our teacher told us about them."

"You have a smart teacher," Sue replied. She's teaching you to take care of the planet. Loretta uses a container to control the soil better. She uses a bit of natural fertilizer, but it doesn't leach into the aquifer."

"What's natural fertilizer?" Beth asked, and Sue explained. "She makes compost from her leftover food scraps and horse manure."

Fertilizers and sewage were dirty words in Sweetwater Springs. I had probably heard more about fertilizers and sewage than any dog in America. The experts believed fertilizers made the algae grow in the river— like the grass on the land. Most of the locals thought this was true because it made sense. Still, it was hard to convince the old locals who grew up with fertilizer to grow planet-friendly grass that used less or required none.

The more significant argument was about the cows since only a few long-term locals believed cow manure was to blame for the algae. I wondered if any farmers would be attending Baldwins' housewarming party. Almost everyone believed human sewage was a problem with the increasing number of people. But there wasn't a single cow on the river. Not one.

I like cows. They stand on all fours in the pastures and look peaceful. We see cows when Sue drives through the countryside to visit Loretta. They should make cow manure into compost and enforce container gardens. Hank Bryan could be the first to make the law.

"The Green Cove looks bad," Beth said. "Mr. Bryan said he'd like to move but doesn't want to give up on it."

"There are a lot of folks working towards improving it," Sue said. "It will happen in time."

"Do you believe that, Aunt Sue?"

"Absolutely!"

Once, Sue drove to a chain of lakes that had become perfectly clean of algae after years of turning green. She took me on a long leashed walk around the lake bordered by a cow pasture. After the cows were relocated, the algae cleared. This made sense because cows lived on the lake, contaminating it with manure, which acted as fertilizer to grow algae. Not so in Sweetwater Springs, where the closest cows lived miles from the river.

I sat up and looked out the window as we approached our home. As everyone knows, dogs have a homing instinct. I learned more about cows, fertilizer, and manure than a dog should know, but I understood it could be significant to the future. I am ready to stop at Home Sweet Home before we leave for Jessie's house.

"Can you help me assemble the poppers on a serving platter?" Sue asked Beth, and she agreed.

"They're delicious!" Beth said, popping a cheese-filled pepper into her mouth.

"Do you like them?" Sue asked.

"I love them."

"Not too hot?"

"No, they're just right."

Toby joined us in the kitchen, rubbing against my fuzzy neck as I lay on the floor. His fur was softer and shorter than mine because mine had grown since my last grooming. "They love each other, don't they, Aunt Sue?" Beth asked before Toby jumped on the counter.

"Very much," Sue said.

"It must have been lonely for you when I took Boomer," Beth said. "I'm glad you found Toby."

"I missed both of you," Sue replied. "And I missed your mother and Chris coming over, too."

"Do you love Toby as much as Boomer?" Beth asked as he approached her platter to greet her, and Sue said, "I do love Toby as much as Boomer. Toby and Boomer are two of my favorite cats of a lifetime."

Sue reminded Beth to wash her hands after she petted him."My mom won't let Boomer on the counter," Beth said. "I'd rather wash my hands."

"You must listen to your mother, Sweetie," Sue said. "But we do things a little differently here."

"Different Strokes," Beth said, to quote her mother. "We certainly do things differently at my house, too."

"How do you mean?"

"Missy's mom fed us hot dogs on store-bought bread, potato chips, and cookies for lunch. Later, we had a bowl of ice cream for a snack."

Sue heard processed food and sugar—two big no-nos in Jessie's world. We were stepping out of a dog's comfort zone to talk about those things, but I had heard much about them.

Sue asked, "Did you like it? Beth answered, "Yes, it was delicious. All of my friends eat hot dogs," she added.

"It's good to step out now and then," Sue said. "Are you going to tell your mother about it?"

"No, I'll eat healthy food at home and skip what other people do."

Sue smiled, and I knew she wondered how it would turn out. Jessie had good ideas, but she was a fanatic about healthy eating. She had no idea how Beth would eat as an adult, but she expected some balance. Jessie insisted that living on fresh fruits, vegetables, and lean meats was much healthier, but it could be expensive. She was working on a cookbook with more economical recipes.

"Did you have fun with Missy?" Sue asked as they assembled the jalapeno platters.

"It was SO much fun!" Beth replied. "We also went to her friend Anita Coleman's house. "

"Is she Phil Coleman's daughter?"

"How did you know?"

"His name is coming up a lot lately. He made a bad impression on your Aunt Loretta. He wants us to sell the clinic to the Baldwins."

"You can't sell the clinic!" Beth said. "Boomer goes there!"

"We don't want to sell the clinic, Honey," replied Sue. "Phil wants to buy it. He got pushy with Aunt Loretta, and she got mad at him."

"I don't like him," Beth said. "He's mean to his wife. He yelled at her."

Sue was pensive, and I knew she felt uncomfortable. Phil Coleman was a rotten egg, and nobody liked him. The list of people who disliked him was growing, and Hank, Loretta, Nella, Beth, and Mia were already on it.

"Do you remember what he yelled at her about, Honey?" Sue asked.

"He said her party dress was ugly, and she had better shape up if she expected him to take her to Baldwin's housewarming party. Then, he yelled at her to make his lunch and said if she didn't make it soon, he'd find someone who would."

"What did she say?"

"Nothing," Beth replied. "She went to the kitchen to make his lunch."

Sue worried most about the women who didn't stand up for themselves. Sometimes, it meant they were submissive; other times, it meant they were in a dangerous situation and couldn't speak up for fear of repercussions.

"Did you like Anita's mother?" Sue asked.

"Yes, she's adorable. She played a game with us and offered to have a tea party for us. She's beautiful, too, but he gives her no compliments—just insults."

"How long did you stay?"

"Not too long," Beth said. "Anita wanted to play at Missy's house. I think her father embarrassed her."

When Sue and Beth finished assembling the poppers, we climbed into the car and drove to Jessie's house. Now, I had less room in the backseat with a box full of poppers joining me for the ride. Sue had a small car and had no intention of buying a bigger one, but I could make do with whatever room she left. Sue says I can go from a long to a small dog in a blink.

"Am I allowed to go to the Baldwins' housewarming?" Beth asked as we drove to her house.

"No, Honey, I'm sorry, it's for adults only," Sue replied.

"Adults and Daisy," Beth reminded Sue.

Beth carried the poppers into the dining room and set them on the table as appetizers.

"Those look delicious!" Jessie said, and Chris agreed as they ate them at the table. "Can I have the recipe for my cookbook?"

Jessie's "CHEWS for Fitness" cookbook was her pastime and hobby. The recipes in it were Cheap, Healthy, Easy, Wholesome, and Spicy. Sue's contribution was the Easy recipes, but each recipe was most, if not all, of the above.

Beth talked about her day while we ate smoked, grilled chicken on a bed of spinach with a balsamic vinaigrette for dinner. She omitted the part about eating the hot dogs, but described Phil's demeanor with his wife. "He's not a nice man," she said, and we agreed he lacked integrity and polish.

Sue described Phil's opportunism in buying the house on Green Cove dirt cheap when the housing market dropped.

"I haven't been to the cove in ages," Jessie said. "We are spoiled with the crystal-clear river behind our house."

"If somebody asked me where I wanted to go next, I'd say home," Chris agreed. "This is a paradise."

"If you don't revisit it, it's easy to forget how polluted Green Cove is," Sue said.

Redman, the Doberman, joined us in the dining room with stiff legs and a happy spirit. He stood beside Chris because he was too stiff to sit. "He never complains and never gives up," Jessie said as Chris rubbed his back, which he loved.

Sue talked about the housewarming party, and everyone wondered who had been invited. "What will I do while you go to the party?" Beth asked.

"Maybe you can stay at Luke Wilson's place," Sue said. Everyone agreed it was a good plan since his 94-year-old mother, Sophie, wasn't attending the party. "I'll call him tonight to confirm, and he'll probably offer to pick us up at my house."

"That would be terrific," Beth said. "I love his dog, and I adore his nephew."

Chapter 10

Luke's Mansion

L uke Wilson was the second-wealthiest man in Sweetwater Springs
and a well-known hotelier in Florida, but he didn't want to develop
the small town where he lived part-time, like Thomas Baldwin. He had
considered building a luxury hotel in the paradise he called home, but
called it off when he realized how much the river and small-town life meant
to the locals. There was bound to be happiness and discontent with
development, and Luke had brought jobs and hotels to the bigger cities.
He decided to sell off some of his local properties and leave Sweetwater
Springs for his favorite philanthropic project—saving cats.

Mr. Wilson—I call him that with all due respect—was the financier of
the cat food, testing, and prescription flea products for the local colonies
on Cypress Street. He and Peter Gardner shared the work that brought
cats scampering for their attention. Sometimes, they worked together with
Sue on the treatments. Peter took the cats to the local TNR veterinarians
for spaying and neutering, where he used to work before he took the job at
Cat Tails Pub. I had nothing to do with the transportation of cats, but I
enjoyed seeing the felines when Sue took me on neighborhood dog walks
with her friends.

The cats brought Sue and Luke together—although I think I had something to do with it since Sue was walking me around the neighborhood
when she first met him. He showed up to meet her, accidentally on pur-

pose, when he knew she was walking me. That's how I met his hound dog, Artemis, who was friendly and playful. Since there's no unleashed-dog park in Sweetwater Springs, I love to visit my dog friends who have big yards and love to run and play.

Sue says she and Luke are just friends, but I could live in that big yard with Artemis if she changes her mind. As you know, I have a tiny yard, just big enough for a potty break, and the rare race in a circle with myself. I have a wonderful life and am grateful, loyal, and kind to my family and friends, so I'm not complaining. But a dog likes to stretch her legs and run sometimes.

Luke spent weekdays in the cities where he built hotels and came home to Sweetwater Springs on weekends. His mother, 94-year-old Sophie, lived in his mansion with his sister, nephew, and dog, Artemis, year-round, so the home was never empty. His vast yard was a wonderful place for me to romp and play with Artemis—which I did every chance I got.

Beth was especially fond of Luke because of Boomer. She was the first to notice how much Boomer loved Luke, and she suspected he already knew the kitten when Luke came to her birthday party. It was the loudest anyone heard him purr when he made bread on Luke's neck. As everyone knows, you could write a book about Boomer's adventures—and you can sometimes find one in the Little Free Library, which we pass on our morning walks.

It was finally Saturday—the day we had been looking forward to—for the Baldwins' housewarming party. Luke's mother and sister had happily agreed to watch Beth while we went to the party. Beth was excited to see Luke's nephew, whom everyone believed she had a crush on. I would have loved to visit with Artemis, but being invited to the housewarming party was even better.

Sue wore a sleeveless black dress with a single strand of pearls and beige platform sandals. For the occasion, she painted her nails red. I could not see red, but she mentioned the color, and I believed her. I had never seen her dressed so elegantly, as she usually wears shorts, tanks, and oversized shirts around the house.

I got a shower and a hair dry, followed by a combing of my fluffy head and tail. I loved the shower, but I wouldn't say I liked having my tail combed. It was better than going to the groomer, who made me itch.

Loretta was the first to arrive at our house. "You look beautiful in that pink and green suit!" Sue said of her daughter's floral ensemble with the oversized jacket.

"Thanks, Mom. You look marvelous—very classy and elegant."

"I don't get many chances to dress up," Sue said. This is a special treat."

"I can take the jacket off if it's too hot, and I brought a raincoat in case it drizzles during the tour."

"I'll bring my summer trench coat," Sue replied. "It's seen a lot of miles and served me well."

"It hasn't rained in a week," Loretta said. "But it looks like it's coming tonight."

"I'm sure they'll have a big tent set up for cover," Sue replied, "but it does put a damper on a walk through the estate."

"I want to take photos," Loretta replied. "Sometimes, a misty rain can be nice for that."

"You can't take a bad photo on Mia's Run," Sue replied. "It's spectacular in any weather."

"I'm excited about tonight," Loretta said. "It was special of Mia to offer to let us sit at her table."

Sue reminded her, "With Gio and Val," and Loretta recalled what Chris had said about buying the clinic to launder money.

"I don't think we should say anything to them tonight," Sue said. "Let's just let it play out."

Loretta agreed since they barely knew Tori's parents. "It's going to be hard not to tell them Tori is alive," she said, and Sue agreed that despite the skimpy details of their daughter's disappearance, they should honor her request.

"Phil Coleman could hide a package under a trench coat," Sue said.

"He had better keep it covered tonight!" Loretta spewed. "I never want to see that crazy gun again."

Luke Wilson arrived next, driving his oversized black SUV that would hold the entourage. He greeted me enthusiastically and gave me a doggie treat from the stash he kept in his glove box.

"Hi, Luke," Sue said while I devoured the treat, and Loretta added, "It's good to see you."

"You ladies look spectacular," Luke said, hugging Sue and Loretta. "I've missed you."

"There's been a lot happening here," Loretta said. "Mom's kept you informed while you've been gone."

"Yes, she told me about Phil Coleman wanting to buy the clinic for Thomas Baldwin—or someone else."

"Have you met Phil?" Loretta asked.

"You can't be a land investor without knowing Phil Coleman," Luke said, and Loretta responded, "What do you think of him?"

"He's slick, but many are," Luke replied. "You have to read the signs."

"Do many of them carry a handgun?" Loretta asked.

"If you mean concealed carry, I've never seen one."

"How well do you know Gio and Val?" Sue asked.

"I've heard a few things, just like everyone else. But no one knows anything. They are sworn to secrecy."

"Do you think they could be mafia?" Loretta asked.

"There are a lot of them down south," Luke replied without elaboration.

"You're not making me feel better," Loretta said, and Luke apologized. "I'm sorry, but I don't know more than anyone else."

Luke was part Irish, but his mother, Sophie, was Italian from Sicily. She was as fiery as Luke was calm, and at 94, she didn't falter. Sophie had an opinion about everything and always spoke her mind. I liked Sophie but kept a distance from loud people, whom I found unpredictable. Sophie remembered her roots as dogs do.

Jessie, Beth, and Chris arrived next, and Beth burst through the door to greet us. "Uncle Luke," she said, throwing her arms around him. "I'm excited to stay at your house tonight. Thank you for letting me come over."

"My nephew is excited to see you," Luke said. He's been talking about you all day."

"No, he hasn't," Beth blushed, and Luke assured her it was true.

"We'll drive separately if you don't mind," Jessie said, "In case somebody wants to leave early."

"No problem," Luke said. "We'll see you at the party."

Chris stroked me on the back by the tail before they left, and I groaned because I had an itch there. "See you later, Doggie Guest of Honor," he said. "You'll be the hit of the party."

I lunged out of the big SUV, landing front feet first when we arrived at Luke's mansion halfway downriver from the Baldwin estate. We didn't have much time there, and I wanted to run around the big lawn with Artemis, who was waiting. I don't get the difference between a mansion and a house—both have four walls and a cool floor somewhere to rest my belly on. But I love, love, love a big yard.

Beth climbed out after me and quickly found Luke's nephew, who was also waiting. The two were about the same age and enjoyed the same activities—swinging on tree swings and jumping off rocks into the cool river. They wouldn't swim tonight because nobody swam after dark in Sweetwater Spring because of the alligators. They'd probably play video games and watch a movie.

After the run, I lay by the Adirondack chairs with Artemis while Sophie joined her son and the two ladies he would accompany to the housewarming party.

"I wish you would come with us," Luke told his mom. Sophie replied that she didn't care for parties much anymore, much less the Baldwins, who didn't act as if they lived on the same road as her. "They never wave," she said, and Luke suggested she might need new glasses. "They're very friendly, Mom," he said.

"Have you met Mia?" Sue asked, and Sophie said she had seen her briefly. "We are seated at the table with her and Thomas."

"Well, we aren't financing her husband's hotel," Sophie said. "It's time for Luke to come home to relax."

"I have too much energy to relax, Mom," Luke replied. "You know I like to keep busy."

"Your lady friend could keep you busy," Sophie said. "I'm sure she could make you a fine Honey-Do list."

"I do like those lists," Luke said, and Sue smiled.

"Gio and Val Pedri are seated with us, too," Loretta said when her mother was done beaming.

"Mafia types," Sophie said. "I can spot them when I see them. You know my family is from Sicily."

It was much more than Luke had said, but Sophie lacked her son's filters. As a nonagenarian, she believed she had earned the right to speak her mind.

"Phil Coleman is trying to buy our veterinary clinic," Loretta said.

"Who's Phil Coleman?"

"He's a land speculator, Mom. You saw him at Cat Tails Pub. He sits in the corner."

"One of those!" Sophie said. "I've known them all my life. They'll sit in the corner of a restaurant and make deals—with anybody who has the money."

"He carries a gun," Loretta said.

"Of course he does," Sophie said, "Sell me your business, or I'll kill you."

It wasn't the words Loretta wanted to hear, but they were close to what Chris had said. Phil could be dangerous and needed to stop engaging in aggressive crusades. Whatever he wanted the clinic for, she needed to find out. Tonight could change her plans.

I jumped in the SUV, and we bid farewell to Sophie. "I almost forgot to tell you, Daisy is the Dog of Honor," Sue said, and Sophie agreed I deserved it. "I'll see you after the party. I can't wait to hear about it."

Chapter 11

The Housewarming

S ue had never taken me on the kayak past the fence that bordered Mia's Run, so we were unfamiliar with the vastness of the Baldwin estate. Tonight was the first time we would encounter and explore the massive plot of land that Thomas and Mia Baldwin called home. It was a dog's paradise with short, shorn lawns that tickled my belly with blades of grass. The lawns were so wonderful I could have stayed there all night, but Sue wouldn't let me.

After all, I was the doggie guest of honor at the first-ever Baldwin housewarming party. Indeed, it was an honor for anyone to receive an invitation. Most people got an invitation in the mail, but in my case, it came directly from Mia Baldwin by word of mouth. I am a strong proponent of humility in all things, but does it get any better than that?

Loretta says Ms. Mia invited me as an afterthought. Still, I think she's jealous that Little Miss Perfect Leela, Naughty Luna, or Sweet, Shy Stevie didn't get invited to the most famous housewarming in the history of Sweetwater Springs. I love my dog cousins, but if Loretta wants them to be invited to parties, she needs to take them to places more often. If you wanted an invitation, you must be seen rather than invisible.

"Would you have taken Luna to the party if Mia had invited her?" Luke asked Loretta as I sat tall and proudly next to him in the front seat of the

SUV. In the most proper of my seated positions, I was almost as tall as Luke, watching everything as we approached the gate's pillars.

"Luna is not ready to be a party girl," Loretta replied, chuckling at the possibility of Luna at a smorgasbord of the best dining in Sweetwater Springs. "I fear she'd embarrass me."

Luke laughed at the counter surfing she might inspire, and Loretta suggested Mia might look elsewhere for a new veterinarian if she knew the truth about Luna.

I had rarely counter-surfed without Luna, but joining her standing two-legged by the lunch feasts at Loretta's house was fun. She had taught me to be stealthy and quick in conquering the leftovers. Tonight, I had to be proper and polite in the presence of filet mignon and fried chicken. There was the chance something would fall to the ground, under the table, as it did at Cat Tails Pub. Sue might be so distracted by talking to the guests that she wouldn't notice when I scarfed it up.

"Luna is still young," Sue said hopefully, but no one was convinced my curly-haired cousin would outgrow her first love.

Frankly, I don't know why anyone was concerned about the limits of my good behavior. I would be leashed all night, sniffing out good and evil as always in Sweetwater Springs. Most people never suspected my detective skills, as I was meant for undercover work.

"There's Phil Coleman's car," Sue said, and Loretta tensed because she didn't trust him.

"I hope Phil leaves his gun at home," Loretta said, and Sue replied that he wouldn't be the same man without his nasty crutch, as she had taken to naming the silver-plated masterpiece.

"He's a strange one," Luke said, and everyone agreed he was an oddball at best in a town that was more like Mayberry than Dodge City.

Sue said, "Strange is safer than dangerous."

Loretta agreed that Phil could seem unstable in Mayberry, but his personality wasn't unusual in Dodge City, where chaos and lawlessness prevailed.

Luke mentioned that all booms and golden years were subject to cons and scammers. "Surely, you aren't the only person he has offended with his tactics," he said.

Sue added. "We can look into that theory tonight. I wish he'd explain why he wants to buy our livelihood."

I could smell the tension in the SUV when Loretta demanded, "Phil must stop treating people like they have no choice but to give him his way."

A light rain drizzled on the windshield, and Luke turned on the wipers as we passed through the parking lot of well-maintained cars and trucks owned by Sweetwater Springs' predominant officials, farmers, and business owners. I twitched my nose and sniffed the moist dirt through the mist when he cracked the windows. It had a pleasant smell and reminded me of a life experience, like truffles. Sometimes, I confused real life with dreams and wondered about the truffles since Sue wasn't fond of buying them after she nearly stank the mailman out of his truck when a bottle broke before delivery.

I wanted to ask Sue about the truffles, but she didn't speak my language. I enjoyed the real or imagined memory and returned to listen to the conversation.

"This is quite the parking lot of old socialites, woke newbies, farmers, and down-to-earth business people," Luke said, observing the hash of luxury late model, mid-line, and newer gas and electric vintage vehicles. The oldest was a diesel truck from the '70s, and Luke mentioned that some older model cars got better gas mileage than new ones. "Improved emissions reduced the gas mileage," he said.

"For every action, there is an equal and opposite reaction," Loretta reminded him.

"Baldwin must want a partner for his countryside adventures." Sue said, perusing the car-studded field of dreams, "At least that's what some people think."

"Business is more fun with partners," Luke agreed. "There is more arguing with a partner, but some people like that. Risk is the spice of life."

Sue reminded him, "Sophie doesn't want to enter the Baldwin prospects."

Luke said his mother had nothing to worry about. "When I retire, I want to build a front porch and rock with you."

Sue smiled. Although they had never dated, growing old with Luke seemed enchanting.

"There's Hank Bryan's car," Sue pointed at the late-model sedan. "Phil and Hank had a crush on Mia in high school, and Phil won," she announced.

"Surely everyone in high school had a crush on Mia," Luke said, "I would have if I grew up in Sweetwater Springs."

Loretta suggested he should avoid talking about other women if he wanted to rock on the porch with her mother.

"You're kind of old-fashioned for a thirty-something, right?" Luke asked, and Loretta said she always stood up for her mother.

"I understand his first wife was a gold digger," Sue said, "and Mia is his soul mate. His first wife was never satisfied, but Mia has his back."

"That's why Mia will have a town named after her," Luke said, and Sue agreed that the best partnership came when people had partners who protected them from the backstabbers.

I felt like we were driving through the fog as we passed the melange of vehicles, and the windshield flooded with condensation from the more fantastic rain after a hot day. I recalled, with fondness, that Boomer had arrived on such a day after a summer thunderstorm. Sometimes, the rain was the only relief from the scorching heat that embroiled Sweetwater Springs in Summer.

Frankly, I loved the rain. Sue usually took an umbrella when we walked in the rain, but I didn't want her to share it with me. I liked feeling the drizzle through my furry coat, which protected me from the water like duck feathers. If I were a bird, I would have liked to have been a duck.

Rain was good for ducks and trench coats. I trusted rain and ducks, but I didn't trust trench coats. It was too easy to hide the unexpected and the unpredictable under a trench coat.

"Is that Gio Pedri's truck?" Luke asked, observing the older model truck, which was perfectly maintained and had a newer paint job.

"Yes, I believe it is," Sue replied as she had seen the vehicle at Cat Tails Pub.

"Has anyone heard anything more about his daughter?" Luke asked of Tori Pedri, whom almost everyone had missed.

I could feel Sue and Loretta cringe at the question and smell their disgust. Both women were too honest to lie, but Tori had made them promise not to disclose her whereabouts. She was alive, and half the town thought she was dead. Sue, Loretta, and a woman named Sarah were Tori's liaisons to maintain the story, and many details had yet to be explained.

"Can't Gio afford a better truck?" Loretta asked about the classic model.

"The mob doesn't like to draw attention to their money," Luke said. "They want to forego the audits and spend cash on experiences they enjoy."

"Do you mean like fine dining and events?" Loretta asked, and Luke suggested it was true. "They buy houses and cars with laundered money to explain where it came from."

"You mean they buy legitimate businesses to filter the extra cash from illegal businesses and convert it to traceable and taxed money for houses and cars?" Loretta asked, and Luke agreed; it was true.

"They like to purchase businesses that can funnel cash, like restaurants, pubs, and other small businesses. Sometimes they buy failing businesses so they don't have to put much staff into running the business, but they can funnel the cash through it."

"And what about veterinary hospitals?" Loretta asked, feeling a fume coming on so strong that I could smell it. "I have a successful practice with clients who trust me, and it isn't a cash business," she said. "People pay with credit or debit cards, but rarely with cash."

"It wouldn't be hard to increase the cash business without drawing attention to your cash flow and books," Luke suggested. "Many businesses are an easy target for laundering dirty money."

"Well, my clinic is not one of them!" Loretta tooted as we passed Gio Pedri's truck. "I can promise you that!"

"Why would Thomas Baldwin want my clinic?" Loretta asked, and everyone agreed we didn't know. "I won't ask him at his wife's housewarming party," Luke said.

We passed a truck belonging to a cattle farmer accused of polluting the river with cow dung from far upstream. "I wonder if Phil Coleman also tried to buy his property?" Loretta asked, observing the luxury truck that could pull a loaded cow trailer.

"Maybe he wants to turn it into a theme park," Sue replied, and Luke agreed he had heard of the Wild West theme park of Thomas Baldwin's dreams.

"How do we ever know the truth?" Loretta asked. Luke replied that it could be challenging to decipher the motives from the ulterior motives.

Everyone agreed we had a lot to learn. People were interesting—infinitely interesting when you listened to their stories. Luke parked the SUV near the tent that covered the townsfolk from the rain. I hopped out of the SUV from the back seat to explore the estate with my two-legged friends and inspire the truths that lingered within the confines of the big top.

Chapter 12

Baldwin's Mansion

T he Baldwin estate was crawling with people. I couldn't imagine how
long Sue would take to filter through the guests and discuss things a
dog didn't need to hear. My two-legged friends talk about all things that
make no difference to dogs. Words are weird to me. They are great for
narration and explanations, but the conversation is another matter that I
leave to Sue.

I'm a listener, not a speaker. I listen to everything: tone, inflection,
mood, friendliness, irritability, or anger. I may lie on the grass and pretend
not to be listening, but I am. That way, I've learned a lot about Sue, as well.

Sue pretends not to know as much as she does. She knows more than
she says. She is forever collecting information, but sometimes she has to
make something called small talk to get there. I can tell by how she smells
that small talk is not her favorite topic. I never smell excitement when Sue
talks small, but sometimes it leads to interesting information.

I can tell when Sue is happy to see someone or if she'd rather move on.
For example, when we dropped off Beth at Luke's mansion, she was happy
to see Luke and his mother, Sophie. The feelings were mutual, as it was
with people who were true friends.

Loretta departed to socialize on her own. "I'll catch up with you later,"
she said, closing her umbrella and waving to Peter and Stanley, standing
with a man wearing a cowboy hat she had never met.

Mia was the first to approach Sue and Luke after we found shelter from the drizzle under the big tent where dinner would be served. "It's good to see you," she said. "Thank you for coming to our housewarming party."

Sue was excited to see Mia, and I knew she wanted to get to know her better. "Thank you for inviting us," she replied, and Luke shook hands. "It's good to see you again, Neighbor," he said.

Luke lived closest to the Baldwins of anyone in Sweetwater Springs, but they had no neighbors on their riverfront property, the biggest on the river. The frontage, which was wetlands, occupied almost half the river's length. The Inland was high and ordinarily dry, but the land was moist tonight. My four feet were black from the rich dirt of the lawns.

"I love your decorations," Sue said, "Your flower arrangements are spectacular!"

"The flower shop owner is a friend of mine," Mia replied. "I've known her since grade school."

The dainty florals ran the length of the oblong tables where guests would be seated. They were interspersed with candles in bell jars, ceramic water birds, and cowboy boots. "That's quite a combination of themes," Sue said.

"The ceramics are hand-painted," Mia replied.

"By a local artist?" Sue asked, noting the perfection.

"By friends," Mia said as a young woman greeted us. "Do you remember Sarah?"

"Of course, from our kayak trip on Mia's run, it's good to see you, Sarah," Sue said, explaining their prior meeting to Luke before she glanced toward Jessie and Chris, whom she had told no one else was there but Mia.

"Sarah and her friend painted them," Mia said without providing a name or mentioning if she'd be at the party. "Thomas loves the river and horses. I'm sure you've heard about the riverside hotel and the Western theme park he wants to build."

"Yes, of course," Luke said, "The whole town knows about his projects."

"Thomas loves the river as much as the locals," Mia said. "He wants what's best to clean up the river and support the community."

The man in the cowboy hat tipped his hat and joined us with Loretta. "In case you haven't heard, my cows' manure polluted this river," he said sarcastically because he didn't believe it. "They want to eat steak, then complain that my cows caused this river trouble."

"Your cows are the scapegoat," Mia replied, touching his back. "Thomas intends to challenge the experts' assessment of your cows' manure."

"I'll be searching for truth," Thomas said, introducing himself. "Just because someone does research doesn't mean they are honest about the results."

Sarah suggested her friend's mother had designed and fudged the results of her science project and won first prize at the science fair when she was in middle school.

"That sounds like a good way to teach a bad lesson," Luke said because he was honest.

"People should research to search for truth," Loretta said. "Not to fudge data to prove the results they are looking for."

"Amen," Sarah agreed. "In a perfect world, it would always be that way."

"Some people don't like to make waves," Sue said, and Luke added that people make honest mistakes.

"I just want my private researchers to assess the pollution in the river and what we can do to reduce it," Thomas said. "Any researchers worth their salt to protect the river wouldn't mind having their results confirmed or disputed."

Phil Coleman stumbled into the party with his wife, Nella. He swayed side to side, clearly drinking heavily. "There's that jackass who tried to buy my farm," the cattleman said. "He carried a gun and flashed it at me as if it would make a difference to the sale."

I stood on all muddy fours and paid closer attention when the farmer mentioned the gun. Certain words were buzzwords in my vocabulary, and the gun was among the keywords that got my attention. I pricked my ears to listen as the conversation heated.

Loretta was fuming when she heard about the gun. I smelled her frustration turning to anger. "He threatened me with that insane silver-plated gun, too," she growled.

"I'm sorry, I had no idea he was threatening sellers with a gun," Thomas said, and Mia agreed it should never have happened as Thomas departed to speak to other guests, leaving Mia behind with us.

Gio and Val approached our growing circle of acquaintances. "Have you met Gio and Val?" Mia asked, and Loretta stiffened. "We've heard so much about you," she announced, and Val suggested she hoped it was all good.

I smelled Loretta's nervousness with my long, twitching nose when she lied about the couple she had been told wanted to purchase her clinic as a laundromat. Loretta always got nervous when she lied. "Nothing but the best," Loretta lied.

Sue reached out for her daughter's sweaty palm and changed the subject. "I'm so sorry about your daughter," she told Gio and Val. "Loretta is my daughter, and I can't imagine how I'd feel without her."

Tori had been gone for months, and her disappearance started sinking in for those who knew her well. "We funded the biggest search in Sweetwater's history," Val said. "They never found her body."

"We're holding out for her reappearance," Gio added. "Some people say Tori was murdered, but there's no murder without a body."

"It wasn't alligators that took my dear girl," Val said. "Our search and rescue team combed the wetlands with kayaks, Jon boats, and the land with search and rescue dogs. Not even a trace."

"Believe me, we know the right people for everything," Gio added. "Let me know if you need anything—anything at all."

"Tori was a wonderful advocate for the river," Sue said, biting her tongue about her encounter with their daughter on Mia's Run. If she didn't like her reappearance known, Tori would have to explain why she wanted Sue to keep it a secret. For now, she kept her promise. "The locals loved your daughter's genuine concern for their treasure."

"We don't believe people did so much to destroy the planet as the experts blame us for," Gio replied. "But we'd never let anything happen to Tori. If somebody hurts her, they'll be sorry."

Gio and Val shared the same distrust for experts and love for their families as Thomas and Mia. Their evolving friendship made more sense under the circumstances. Gio and Val knew people from every walk of life, and Thomas and Mia had the money to fund their research. This was the kind of stuff a dog can put together.

Phil stumbled closer to the group and opened his trenchcoat. "Nice piece," Gio said. "Grabs the attention, like a doggie in the window."

"It does a bit of good," Phil said, and Gio replied, "That's what I hire you for."

Looking at Loretta, he added, "This man is good at his job. You should listen to him."

"What does he do?" she asked, and Gio explained, "He buys properties for people."

"How did you find out about him?" Sue asked, and Gio explained, "Thomas Baldwin recommended him."

"We're thinking about spending more time in Sweetwater Springs," Val said. "We like to have work. "Gives us more money for the good times."

I could smell Loretta's fuming, but she held her tongue. "Has he ever bought a clinic?" she asked, and Gio assured her they had assets in every walk of life before Thomas called him away to introduce him to a friend on the other side of the tent.

Loretta glared at Phil with evil eyes, and he returned her stare. "Wanna touch my piece, Baby?" he asked with a sinister smile as he opened his trench coat.

"You are out of your mind," she said. "Get away from me!"

I could almost smell her blood boiling as Phil Coleman shifted his attention to Sue. "Maybe you can help her change her mind," he said, and Sue nearly raged before she turned to walk away. "You're evil," she said. "We will never sell you our clinic."

"You don't know what I want it for," Phil grimaced at his good fortune to intimidate them.

"We don't care," Loretta replied, shifting her heels to depart. "I've seen you for the last time, Phil Coleman," she hissed as the mayor approached with his wife. "Don't ever come looking for me again!"

The mayor neither liked nor respected Phil Coleman, a con and a shyster. "I wish I could say the same," he said, and his wife added, "Be thankful you don't live on the same street with him."

Chapter 13

The Dinner

I stood close to Sue when Mia rang the dinner bell. I later learned that it happened to be an old cowbell from a trip to Switzerland after she and Thomas married. The cowbell was a talking piece that reminded Mia to open a conversation with her guests about better times for cows when they lived on small farms with green pastures and dozed lazily in the sunshine between meals of luscious grass. It resonated deeply, sounding like a dong to dogs like me.

That said, I was the only dog in a tent full of 200 people from all walks of life. Some had small businesses, farms, and clinics, or taught the local schoolchildren. A few were entrepreneurs, realtors, or land speculators, and one was thought to be affiliated with the South Florida mob.

The smells were overwhelming—almost intimidating because they surpassed my limits of odor discretion. I focused on the evil or the uncertain—Phil Coleman, who played with intimidation, and Gio Pedri, who supported it.

I stood close to Sue because there were so many people, most of whom I had never seen before. I knew that Gio Pedri made Sue and Loretta nervous, and Phil Coleman made them angry. I had already observed that Phil had that effect on people for obvious reasons.

We were seated with Gio and Val for dinner, which made Loretta squirm. Thomas and Mia stood at the microphone, at the podium, in front of the dinner tables to deliver a welcome message to their guests.

"Please find your seat for dinner," Mia said. "I hope you enjoy your dinner partners and your locally prepared meals. Everything you see under this tent, including the ceramics, was made or prepared by a local chef, florist, friend, family, or artisan."

"We've invited you here tonight to share our dreams for a luxury hotel, a theme park, and a clean river," Thomas said. "Thank you so much for joining us."

"The river and its wonderful history mean everything to Thomas and me," Mia said. "I've lived here my whole life, and, as many of you know, Thomas found me in the card shop."

"I found every excuse to buy a card after that," Thomas admitted. "I finally convinced Mia to go out with me, and we were a match. She is the love of my life."

"We are nature lovers who want the best for the community," Mia said. "I've lived the river's changes and shared them with Thomas."

"I've loved springs more than the beach my whole life," Thomas said. "Finally, I can retire on the most spectacular spring-fed river in the world!"

"Everyone of us here is indeed blessed to live in Sweetwater Springs," Mia said.

"This is the perfect place to raise your families and grandkids," Thomas said. "We want to save the river and to provide jobs for them to live nearby."

"We plan to use locally grown or inspired arts and crafts for all our parties," Mia added. "Parents take note: We will be looking for workers in all trades, including artists, riders, chefs, craftsmen, scientists, actors, and showmen."

"I would be proud to inspire the first five-star steakhouse," Thomas added, and some people cheered. "Of course, we will have chicken, fish, and a vegetarian option for meatless lovers."

"I can't imagine a world without cows," Mia continued, inviting everyone to dinner. "They bring peace and tranquility to the countryside, yet they are villainized for polluting the river."

"Here, here," the cattleman said. "Smaller farms are part of the solution."

"In case you haven't heard, Thomas wants to start a laboratory and hire unbiased private scientists to assess the reasons for the river's pollution," Mia said. "We think we can correct it, but need unbiased facts to accomplish the cleanup."

"We are searching for truth, not trying to appease anyone," Thomas added. "We don't want status quo science, political results, or people trying to find results that support their beliefs; we want the truth."

Someone said, "There are too many people on the river." Thomas said they planned to address the issue.

I lay on my belly with my front feet extended between Sue and Loretta under the table, hoping a tidbit might fall. My greatest hope was for the fried chicken meal served with French fries. French fries reminded me of Cat Tails Pub, which reminded me of Tori. I miss Tori more than ever because she made me feel at home, as she did everyone who came to the pub.

I did not expect a morsel from the filet mignon Sue and Luke had ordered. Almost everyone at the table got the filet. It was the tiniest piece of meat I had ever seen, and it appeared its diminished size resulted from upscale food. I didn't look forward to a prime steakhouse, but I suspected it might become a hangout for Sue and Luke if they had a dog-friendly patio on the river. The thought made me long for Tori even more.

Loretta ordered the vegetable curry, but I turned my nose up at the curry. Yuk. It made my nose twitch. Finally, someone got the fried chicken. It was Gio.

"Those filets just don't fill me up," Gio said. "The best-fried chicken is a pleasure to behold."

"Maybe you could open a fried chicken restaurant in Sweetwater Springs," Loretta said, and Sue kicked her foot under the table.

"I'm an Italian food man," Gio said, and Loretta thought it might be so. "How about a Tratorria?" she asked, "I expect there could be lots of money from Tratorrias."

"I like the Italian diners," Gio replied, catching her drift and playing it. "Lots of cash."

Val looked at Gio, who dropped a French fry under the table. Truthfully, I don't think he dropped it. Gio liked to annoy people—or so it seemed. At the moment, it worked to my advantage since Sue was a stickler about my diet.

"These flowers are lovely," Sue said, and Val agreed. "I just love the ceramic cowboy boots."

"I wonder who made them," Val said. "Tori used to love to paint ceramics."

"Have you ever tried it?" Sue asked, and Val said she had painted crackpots with Tori when she was ten. "She had a crackpot birthday party."

It was hard for Sue not to tell Val and Giovanni that their daughter was still alive, but it was essential to Tori. Although they loved their daughter, Tori had her reasons, and Sue respected them.

"What's a crackpot?" Loretta asked, and Val explained it was a cute ceramic figure with big eyes and a cracked pot on its head.

"My daughter might like a ceramic painting party when she's older," Loretta said. "That sounds like fun!"

The diversion to more pleasant topics that some of the two-leggers called small talk momentarily released Loretta from the grips of her anger. Still, Phil Coleman was not far away and getting more drunk; now, he would say almost anything—and he loved to pick fights.

A beautiful young woman approached Phil's table and whispered something in his ear, flushing him.

"You're a Pig!" she screeched. "I can't stand you."

"You're in good company at this party," his wife, Nella, told the girl. "You've got many more enemies than I knew," she told Phil.

Mia stiffened under the table where I could sniff her feet. She was getting emotional—heated, scared? But afraid of what?

"That's Sarah," Loretta said to Sue.

"She was a friend of Tori back in Miami," Val said. "She was a call girl. Tori helped her get away from it."

"What's she doing in Sweetwater Springs?" Gio asked, and nobody answered.

"Why do you bring me to these parties?" Nella stormed at Phil. "You're an embarrassment to me, a jerk, or a joke to everyone else."

Phil grabbed his wife's hand and dragged her to a chair by the side of the tent. "Don't you get up again!" he bellowed. "Stay here and shut up."

"Don't tell me what to do, Phil Coleman!" she hissed. "I'll blow you away with your gun!"

"Maybe I'll do it for you!" the cattleman said.

"You're a jerk, and your gun is a joke!" Loretta screeched, leaping out of her chair. "I'll kill you myself before I sell you my clinic."

"We can't have a crazy man working for Baldwin Enterprises," Mia said, silencing the crowd that had grown louder with the chaos.

"Phil, you've got a lot of enemies, and you made more tonight. We'll talk tomorrow," Thomas said, ushering him to the back of the tent, away from his wife and the growing list of enemies. "Have a seat. I will call my driver to come get you and take you home."

After dinner, Thomas spoke once again from the podium. "I want this town to be as lovely as you do. I live here. I like the river sparkling everywhere like it used to be. Let's end this pollution once and for all!"

"Well, it ain't cows," the cattleman said.

"It's sewage," someone cried.

"It's less water flow," someone else said. "The aquifer has less water in it than it used to. It is being drained by increased population and political pressure for an agenda."

"Our scientists will find the root cause of the murkiness," Thomas replied. "We will fix this!"

"Enjoy the grounds. You're welcome to wander," Mia continued.

Meanwhile, Phil Coleman had wandered into the darkness. I could feel Sue's tension when she grabbed my leash and coaxed me from under the table. It hadn't been a lucrative evening for tidbits, but more to come. The night was young—and only just beginning.

Chapter 14

The Murder

A fter dinner, the guests explored the grounds of the Baldwin estate. As Sue pulled my leash to take me for a walk, I could smell the tension and nervousness of the people. No one had expected to come to a Baldwin housewarming party to hear the arguments and threats spewed from certain people, some of whom were usually in control of their emotions. I sensed that Phil Coleman was a source of great anxiety for them.

I had been looking forward to the walk all evening, especially when the fries were not forthcoming. Gio had only dropped one potato, and I was tired of lying between chairs under the table. Gio made Loretta tense and angry, just as Phil did.

Loretta was mad at herself. She had lost her temper in front of two hundred people, yet she was a pillar of stability in the community. I also knew she was just like her mother. She could process her thoughts with time alone.

"Mom, I want to take some photos of the estate," Loretta said after reaching down to pet me, but I noticed she was shaking. "I need some time alone."

"Are you sure you are okay, Honey?' Sue asked.

"Yes, I'm okay. "I can't believe what I said. I was just so mad at Phil, and it popped out. I'm never like that. I'll be all right after a walk."

"It's okay, Honey," Sue said. "Anyone can snap."

"I never do," Loretta said, donning a disposable raincoat. "I don't know why he's been so pushy and secretive about buying the clinic."

"Phil Coleman is a jerk," Luke said, and Sue agreed. "Everyone knows it."

"The secrets make him feel powerful," Luke said. "It's a game for him."

"Gio is a jerk, too," Loretta fumed. "His comment about an Italian diner having more cash flow than an upscale trattoria was uncalled for."

"You had been razzing him," Sue reminded her.

"About what?" Loretta asked, denying her role in the matter.

"As I recall, you said he should open a fried chicken restaurant."

"What's wrong with that?" Loretta asked, not willing to relinquish her pride.

Sue raised her eyebrows and lowered her head, looking at Loretta, who submitted to the evil eye.

"Back in the day, that's all my mother had to do," Luke said, watching the exchange.

"Sophie could scare anyone with the evil eye," Sue declared. "Maybe Sophie needs to meet Gio."

"We don't know anything about Gio and Val," Loretta said. "I know better than to assume anything."

"We know they are Tori's parents," Sue reminded her. "We know they are wealthy, know people, and don't talk about their work."

"You had every right to speculate," Luke said. "The mob loves to associate with legitimate business owners and use them as a front to launder money."

"Maybe that's what they are doing with Cat Tails Pub," Loretta said, and everyone agreed that no one knew which businesses in Sweetwater Springs or elsewhere might be fronts for the mob.

After Loretta departed to take photos, Sue and Luke meandered about the tent. I was on a leash, walking with Luke and sniffing everything, as I always did. Luke let me stop wherever I wanted, so it was a slow meander through the big tent.

Sue was less likely to let me investigate so much, so I was glad Luke had taken the leash. The clean-up crew had already come to carry plates and silverware off the tables. They dropped more tidbits than under the table, where I had been lying throughout the dinner party. I scarfed up a quarter of a filet mignon when Sue wasn't looking. It tasted good, and I thought better of the possibility of a steakhouse.

Someone accidentally, on purpose, dropped some meat off a chicken leg. She must have had a dog because she knew better than to give me the bone. Sue said cooked bones were the worst for splintering, and she never let me have them. The chicken was delicious, and I was hopeful for more, but Sue grabbed Luke's arm, and we moved onward.

Rain drizzled on the canvas top all evening. It was a light summer rain—just enough to cool things off. I was comfortable in my curly doodle coat. Most of my two-legged friends wore trenchcoats or raincoats when they meandered about the grounds after they left the tent.

We saw Nella by the edge of the tent, where Phil had left her. "Where's Phil?" Sue asked, recalling that Thomas was supposed to have someone pick him up after the screaming matches.

"He left," Nella replied without elaboration.

"Did someone pick him up?" Sue asked, and Luke added. "He was drunk. I hope he didn't drive."

"He left on foot," Nella said, "I don't know where he went."

"I'm sorry he treated you that way in front of everyone," Sue said, and Nella admitted she was used to it. "He's a mean man and a worse drunk," she said. "Excuse me, I must go to the ladies' room."

Mia joined us inside the tent where we had been talking to Nella. "I hope you didn't get the wrong impression tonight," she said. "Our parties are not usually so temperamental."

"The food was delightful," Sue said, and Luke agreed. "The rain is a pity, but I don't think it spoiled the mood."

"Phil did a fine job of that." Mia declared. "He's a Loser."

"I can't believe he slipped out of here," Sue said. "He's probably lying somewhere face down in the mud."

"There is no better place for him," Mia said.

"His wife would agree," Luke replied.

"I didn't know your daughter was so angry with him," Mia added.

"It's a long story that's been building over a short time," Sue replied.

"We should get together to talk about it," Mia said, and Sue agreed that the picture had many loose ends.

"Your dog is a Cutie," Mia said. "I hope she had a good time."

"She'd love a walk," Luke said. "She spent most of the evening sniffing feet under the table."

"Please, enjoy the grounds," Mia said. "I have some umbrellas in that vase in front of the tent if you need them."

I was glad to escape the tent after so long in confinement. Walks were my favorite activity, next to playing with my cousins at Loretta's house. It was delightful to explore the fenced-off grounds of the estate. The drizzle was nothing short of magic because it kept me cool.

Sue and Luke walked on the manicured lawns to keep me away from the wetlands, where the alligators could lurk. The massive lawns were perfectly groomed with mowed grass, colossal flower beds, and tall trees. It was much like Luke's estate, except bigger. Much bigger.

I don't care much about money, but Luke said buying a place like this takes big money. Not millions, but hundreds of millions. We walked past a spring with a wooden bridge and several cabins that guests could enjoy. Mia enjoyed entertaining guests.

I couldn't imagine how many cabins might be on the estate, which included woodlands, wetlands, forests, and lawns. Some of the cabins were on stilts. The stilt cabins were in the wetlands, where I couldn't smell much because my scent was reduced in water. I saw them from a distance since we didn't walk near them.

We walked through groomed areas with tall forests between them. "This is glorious," Sue told Luke as we passed a spectacular garden. "I am impressed."

"There are certainly many places to hide if one so desired," Luke noted.

"Why would anyone want to hide at the Baldwin estate?" Sue asked.

"Just a thought," Luke replied.

Sue tensed as she recalled her promise to Tori that she would not tell anyone she had been on the estate. I knew she hated lying to anyone, especially Luke, but this was a crime of omission.

"Who is Sarah?" Luke asked as they meandered back toward the tent.

"Who?" Sue reiterated.

"The pretty girl who called Phil a Pig?"

"I don't know much more about her than you do," Sue said. "According to Mia, she was a call girl in Miami."

"Interesting," Luke said without elaboration.

"What's interesting?"

"The mafia has ties to strip shows and adult entertainment—some of it is illegal."

"Where does Sarah live?" Luke asked.

"I don't know," Sue replied. "I only just met her."

"Have you seen her before?"

"Once," Sue said. "On Mia's Run."

Sue took my leash as we walked back towards the tent, retracing our steps but sometimes moving in a new direction. Now, there would be less dawdling as Sue was less prone to wait for me while I sniffed everything new. Here, just about everything was new. I smelled footprints, animal prints, and wildlife prints that I rarely smelled back at Sue's house.

I imagined there was wildlife in Sweetwater Springs that I had never seen before. Big wildlife. Little wildlife. Wild Boars. I had never seen them. How big were they?

When we heard the three gunshots, I imagined the wildlife by the river. Hunters? Protecting a guest?

This was the wildest party we had ever been to, but could it come to this?

Sue and Luke sprinted towards the gunshots, with me at Sue's side. We were faster than Sue, but Luke and I slowed down for her. We didn't want her to face whatever was out there alone. Someone or something had been shot.

In the distance, we could see someone lying face down in the mud, and another figure stood frozen beside him. As we drew closer, identifying one of the figures was easier yet more shocking.

Loretta was standing above Phil Coleman's dead body, with his gun at her feet. Her eyes were glazed, and her mouth was agape. She looked like she was in shock, although I had never seen a person in shock before. This was how I imagined it.

"Loretta, snap out of it," Sue said, shaking her daughter. "What happened?'

At first, Loretta did not speak. It seemed like a long time before she said anything, but Sue kept trying to make her talk. She put her arms around Loretta and held her tight. "Please, tell us what happened!" she cried, crying.

Luke splashed some cold water on her face, and finally, Loretta came around.

"What happened?" Sue asked again as Loretta's glazed eyes came back to reality.

"I don't know, Mom," Loretta said, looking at Phil's dead body. "It all happened so fast."

Loretta sounded like she was in a dream. She spoke softly but clearly. I had never heard her sound like that before.

"Someone came up behind me—someone in a black cape. They put Phil's gun in my hand and fired it."

"Do you remember anything else?" Luke asked, and Loretta muttered, "I didn't kill him."

Chapter 15

The Sheriff

I don't know how long it took the sheriff to arrive at the Baldwin estate—after all, I'm a dog, and we don't have a perfect sense of time. Just for the record, I spend most of my time sleeping. Have you ever noticed how fast time flies when you're sleeping?

Some people sleep a lot, but Sue is not one of them. Sue goes to bed early and rises early; I know that because I sleep with her. Sometimes, Sue has difficulty staying asleep, and she meditates. If you've never tried it, it's something like yoga. Technically, yoga is meditation. Dogs are experts at sleeping and stretching, but do not have a sense of time.

I digress. I was talking about how long it took the sheriff to arrive, but I don't know the answer because dogs don't care about time. Do you ever start talking about a topic and wish you had someone to remind you of it? Sue says certain two-leggers are good at that.

Sue says every amazing group should have someone who somehow re-members the orignal topic, a visionary who watches the nonverbal cues and avoids the nonsense, someone who talks too much, and others who enjoy the rambling. In Sue's group, Sue is the visionary; Jessie—bless her heart— talks too much about food, and Rita is good at recalling the topics that Sue never remembers.

Dogs are great observers and visionaries. We know a few words but are experts in nonverbal cues. Cats are even better at reading body language and nonverbal cues. Words and money cause most of the two-legged friends' problems, so I avoid them except in narration.

Loretta, for example, said things she never should have, and Phil Coleman was a con who was far too interested in money. Now, Loretta, one of my very favorite people in the world, was standing over Phil's dead body with his silver-plated gun at her feet.

While we were waiting for the sheriff, Sue asked Loretta. "Are you sure the person in the cape who put the gun in your hand made you fire it?"

"Yes, I fired it," Loretta replied. "Whoever it was put my hand on the trigger and made me fire the gun."

By now, a few people at the party had surrounded Loretta. Many had already left by the time the three gunshots were fired. Sue and Luke didn't know who had left early because we had explored the grounds more deeply despite the drizzle that had driven people away.

Some people tried to escape the trouble and avoided the scene, while others left after the dinner shouting matches. It had been an awkward party with good intentions and horrific side effects.

"Am I going to be arrested?" Loretta asked as they hovered over the dead body.

Sue took a deep breath and sighed. "I'm sorry, Honey, I think you will be."

"I've never been arrested," Loretta replied. "I'm scared."

"We know you didn't kill Phil Coleman," Luke said, and Sue added, "We are going to do everything we can to help you."

"Phil Coleman had a lot of enemies," Luke continued. "You weren't the only one to lose your temper with him tonight."

"Many people said things they shouldn't have," Sue reminded her.

"He was drunk and obnoxious," Mia said, and Thomas added they shouldn't have left Phil unattended after so much arguing and words that should not have been said.

"I'll never say anything like that again," Loretta said, and Sue reminded her of the heat of the moment. "You've been upset for days about his sales tactics and under duress."

"I was stupid—and I'm usually careful with words."

Sue's friends— Jessie, Rita, Stanley, and Peter— left early because of the drizzle. "Somebody must have heard something," Sue said. "We'll figure this out."

The sheriff arrived with his deputy, who marched toward the crime scene. I knew both of them from a visit to the jail once before when Sheriff Stone had started a program for dog-friendly visits with the inmates. I was, in fact, one of four dogs who had visited the jail in Sweetwater Springs.

Homer Stone and Bud Livingston were good people, but overworked and without a detective at the substation. Sweetwater Springs had little crime until now, but times were changing. Years ago, there had been chiefly traffic tickets and citations, but now there are prowlers, burglaries, and the occasional con man with a gun.

Last year, Sue had a Christmas tree stolen from her yard, and then the mayor lost a set of reindeer. Since then, the prowler crimes have shifted to cash and jewelry thefts from unlocked vehicles. Once, the local bank was robbed, but it became known as a water-gun heist, and the robbery status was demoted.

The murder of Phil Coleman was the first murder in over two decades. Deputy Bud Livingston was in charge of the arrest. He read Loretta her rights and handcuffed her in front of a small crowd of people and one dog.

Deputy Livingston's voice quivered when he read Loretta her rights. "I guess you can tell I'm nervous," he said after he finished the well-known speech.

"Do you have to handcuff her?" Sue asked, and Bud said it was protocol. "I'm sorry, Ms. Sue," he said, "This is as hard for me as it is for you."

The look on Loretta's face told me that it wasn't so. This was a serious charge that could take time to resolve. Despite the rain, Loretta had begun to sweat, and it was an emotional sweat that gave off a strong odor that even people, who aren't nearly as scent-sensitive as dogs, can smell.

"We're going to help you, Honey," Sue said as the deputy led her daughter to the squad car.

The sheriff stayed behind to question the remaining guests. By now, Mia was consoling Nella, who appeared to be distressed by her husband's murder and declined to stand near the body. At first, the questions were simple, but they would reveal much-hidden information in the coming days.

"Where were you when the shots were fired?" Sheriff Stone asked the woman who had called her husband a jerk and a joke and threatened to blow him away with his gun before Loretta mistakenly offered to kill him herself.

"I was in the bathroom," Nella said.

"Was anyone with you?" the sheriff asked.

"No, I was alone."

"Did anyone come in while you were there?"

"No, I told you, I was alone."

As his name might suggest, Sheriff Stone was much colder than Detective Livingston. Still, as he pursued the questioning, I smelled a game of good cop, bad cop. I wondered if they ever shifted roles, as he seemed like a man who genuinely cared about his southern town and the results of his investigations.

Sheriff Stone genuinely loved it when I visited the jail with the inmates. In truth, Stone was a Cat Man, but he recognized the merits of dog-friendly jail visits. His more significant concern was rehabilitation over incarceration. He believed inmates could overcome their issues with love—cats were, in fact, more unpredictable with how they doled love out than dogs, who loved unconditionally.

As much as Stone preferred cats, he had given me credit as a friendly dog. It was a big step for a Cat man.

The mayor had plenty of contact with Sheriff Stone, who already knew his history with Mia and the high school rivalries. He also knew he disapproved of Coleman's buying tactics on the Green Cove, which meant so much to Sweetwater Springs residents. The Green Cove was a sentinel for pollution since the river stagnated there. Still, the mayor had wisely held his tongue during the word battles and threats during dinner.

The cattleman, on the other hand, had not been so discrete when Nella had offered to blow her husband away with his gun. "Maybe I'll do it for you," he had offered.

"Where were you when the shots were fired?" Stone asked the cattleman.

"Walking the grounds of the estate," he replied.

"Were you with anyone?" he asked, and he replied he was with the mayor.

It wasn't a total win since both men could have covered for each other, but it was a start. Sue could pursue them for more information when needed.

"The third shot came after the first two shots," the mayor said, and the cattleman agreed.

Gio and Val disappeared early, as often happens with connected people. They disappear when the trouble starts. Sheriff Stone was not surprised but also pleased he didn't have to question them—for tonight, anyway.

Gio and Val knew Sarah, who had also spoken harshly to Phil Coleman when she called him a Pig. It wasn't a threat of murder, but it showed her anger at the con man.

"Where were you when the shots were fired?" he asked the call girl from Miami who had access to the black cape.

"I was getting a change of clothes from my car," she replied.

"Was anyone with you?"

"No, just me."

"Why did you need a change of clothes?" he asked.

"I had other things to do," Sarah replied. "My dress clothes weren't appropriate for walking the wet grounds."

"Nobody else changed clothes," Sheriff Stone said.

"Yeah, and many of them went home," she replied. "It was a rainy night, and my clothes were dry-cleaned only."

"That's a feeble excuse, don't you think, Young Lady?"

"No," Sarah replied, "It's the truth."

After the sheriff left, Mia approached Luke's car to talk to Sue before they left for home: "I have some information that may help," she said. "Please meet me at the guest house closest to the creek tomorrow. We can talk."

"I'll be happy to," Sue replied. "I have never been so nervous in my life."

"Me neither," Mia confessed. "There's a lot at stake here, and you're the only person I can trust."

"We don't know each other well," Sue said.

"We will when this is over," Mia replied.

I lay in the back seat as Luke drove towards his home. It had been an incredible night, packed with information. I thought I was going for steak and french fries, but I ended up with a caper.

Chapter 16

Luke's Mansion

W hen we returned to Luke's mansion, Sophie was waiting at the gate. "Mom, what are you doing outside?" Luke bellowed. "It's raining!"

By now, it was raining harder, but I didn't care. I loved rain on a warm night. It cooled things off after a hot day and made southern life bearable at the worst time of year. Nobody moved to Sweetwater Springs because of the summer weather.

I suspected Sophie felt the same way about summer rain, but it was different for an older woman to stand outside in the rainy weather than for a shaggy younger dog with a water-repellent fur coat.

"I'm waiting for you to come home!" she thundered as Luke reminded his mother she was ninety-four years old and needed to take care of herself.

"I am taking care of myself," she replied, noting her umbrella. "I'm worried about you! What happened at the housewarming party tonight?"

"It's a long story, Mom," Luke replied, stepping outside the vehicle to open the door for his mother.

"Jessie and Chris said some shots were fired near the creek when they picked up Beth," Sophie said as she climbed into the vehicle.

"Let's go back to the house and talk about it," Sue said, twisting her neck to see Sophie behind her.

While Luke returned to the house, Sophie sat beside me in the back seat. "I'm glad I stayed home tonight," she grumbled, ruffling my fur with her hand. "There's no telling what I would have said to that Con Man."

When we stepped inside the living room, which faced the river with floor-to-ceiling picture windows, Artemis was sleeping in his most enormous dog bed—he had many of them—at least one in every room. He got up to sniff me when I walked inside, and then we lay together on the floor. I never relaxed in his bed when he used it, but I sometimes tried sleeping there when he wasn't looking. It was the most incredible bed I had ever experienced, and I sometimes wished Sue would buy one for me.

Deep down, I knew Sue's much smaller house on the cove wasn't big enough for such a dog bed, but a dog could dream. I lay on the floor next to Artemis to listen to my people discuss the events of the evening.

"What on earth happened tonight?" Sophie asked as she sat on the couch facing two easy chairs where Luke and Sue were seated.

"Phil Coleman was murdered," Sue replied before Sophie immediately interrupted her.

"Good riddance," she spat. "Another dirtbag off the streets."

"Mom, you could never work undercover," Luke said, and Sophie replied, "I've earned my say in this life."

"You certainly have," Sue added, although Sophie had always been generous with her thoughts, which Sue admired. "I hope I'm as feisty as you in my nineties."

As he often told his mother, "You have the wisdom of age and experience," Luke said.

The words calmed Sophie as if she had earned their trust. "I told you I never trusted people who made deals in the corner of pubs," Sophie continued. "I'm not surprised somebody whacked Phil Coleman."

"Well, if you must put it that way, Mom," Luke said, "Loretta was arrested for whacking him."

It was one of the few times I ever heard Sophie at a loss for words. She rose to pour drinks from the bar—hard liquor, which she, or anyone else, rarely drank. "I'm so sorry for being blunt," she said, passing the cocktail glasses. "I had no idea Loretta was arrested."

"Loretta didn't kill him," Sue said before she tipped her glass for a sip of the liquor.

"Of course she didn't," Sophie replied. "Loretta is not a murderer."

"She's been very upset about the clinic," Sue said. "She got sucked into the heat of the moment when other people were arguing with Phil and lost her temper."

"She told Phil she could kill him," Luke explained, and Sue added, "Three other people said the same thing."

"Why was Loretta arrested?" Sophie asked.

Sue described the person in the black cape who came from behind her daughter and the gun she had fired, which was at her feet in front of Phil's dead body. "It was cut and dry," she said. "Motive, Weapon, opportunity. Deputy Livingston had no choice but to arrest her."

"Deputy Livingston?" Sophie spat. "He doesn't know the first thing about murder."

"He does know the protocol for arrest," Luke replied.

"Who's doing the investigation?" Sophie asked, and Sue replied, "The sheriff questioned us after the arrest."

"Homer Stone?" Sophie bellowed. "What does he know about murder? I'll bet there hasn't been a murder in this town in ten years."

"It's been over twenty years since the last murder," Sue corrected her.

"That's even worse," Sophie screeched. "Is there a detective in this town?"

"Nope," Sue said, and Luke added, "That's why we have to help Loretta," he said.

"Somebody framed her," Sophie thundered without hesitation. "I hope you know we have mafia in this town now. They like to frame people for their killings...I'm from Sicily," she added as she often did, pouring into her familiar monologue about her roots. "I know about the mafia."

"Mom!" Luke said, stopping his mother in her tracks. "We know your history."

"I know their tactics," Sophie said. "Extortion, racketeering, bribes, secrecy, fronts, frames, make murder look like an accident."

Sue was glad Sophie believed her, but it didn't prove anything. People would have second thoughts about her daughter's innocence, and the local law enforcement was slack in their experience with murder cases, let alone organized crime.

I was glad when the rain slacked because I needed to go outside. It wasn't so much that I needed to potty—although it had been a while—I needed to process information. Dogs spend a lot of time processing, much more than some people. Sophie made my head spin with her facts and assumptions. I knew almost nothing about the mafia because there had been nearly no crime in Sweetwater Springs, where people came to relax on the river and eat pub grub until now.

Did someone frame Loretta? If so, how and why? Did they plan it? Were they with the mafia, as Sophie thought? I had never heard the words frame or mafia before tonight, but I suspected they might become two of my buzzwords now that they had infiltrated Sweetwater Springs.

Artemis finished his duty quickly while I pondered the subjects and milled about with my nose in the grass. It was a good life if you didn't stumble. People needed our help. Sweetwater Springs had gone from a sleepy town when Sue first arrived to a boom town with rich people and organized crime, which Sophie knew more about than the sheriff.

When we returned inside, Sophie gave us homemade dog biscuits, and we settled in the living room. Artemis was uninterested in the conversation and fell asleep after chomping his biscuit. He was a good friend for a romp and a snooze, but not a good listener.

"Who threatened to kill Phil at the party?" Sophie asked as she poured Limoncello for the three of them.

"The cattleman," Sue said, and Luke explained he had threatened him with the gun when trying to buy his land, as he had threatened Loretta about buying her clinic.

"The man was crazy," Sophie said. "Who carries a silver-plated gun, anyway?"

Sue did not mention Theodore Roosevelt's engraved weapon or Phil's obsession with the Wild West theme park that Thomas Baldwin wanted to build. According to the folks at Cat Tails Pub, Phil was beyond odd—he was delusional. The handgun was an image statement, but it was also functional. "It must have been heavy, but it worked," she said.

"He liked to intimidate people," Luke said after he sipped his limoncello.

"He liked to look good," Sue added. "Phil was a show-off."

I noticed crumbles from Artemis' dog biscuit and scarfed them during his slumber. Artemis was spoiled, but not too spoiled. Despite his luxury lifestyle, he was lean and athletic. I was more interested in people and the smells accompanying their thoughts and emotions than guns. I occasionally drifted out of focus until the conversation shifted to my expertise.

"Who else threatened Phil?" Sophie asked, causing me to prick my ears.

"His wife," Luke said, and Sue explained that they had been bickering all night, as the mayor said they often did, and he had humiliated her by forcing her to sit down and shut up in front of everyone.

"My father was a man like that," Sophie said. "But my mother put up with him."

"Do you think your parents would have divorced during our times?" Luke asked, and Sophie said maybe. "My dad was wealthy, and my mother had a good life," she added. "She stayed out of his way."

"Times are changing," Sue said. "Couples are less likely to stay married now."

"For better or for worse," Sophie said. "I'm glad I stayed married to Luke's father, although we had differences."

Sophie met Luke's father when he was deployed to Italy during World War Two. It was a beautiful start to what later became a tumultuous marriage with her husband's two affairs. He loved her cooking. She loved his romantic gestures toward her but hated them towards other women.

"You mentioned a call girl named Sarah," Sophie said after she finished her limoncello. "Can you tell me more about her?"

"Sarah called Phil a Pig and insulted him," Sue continued, without mentioning the black cape that Tori had worn to disguise herself in public. Sarah knew about the cape because she visited the creek with Tori when she wore it. "Sarah is a new person in town, as anyone knows."

"How do you know she was a call girl?" Sophie asked.

"Val told me Sarah used to be a call girl, but someone in Sweetwater Springs was helping her find a new life."

"Who?" Sophie asked.

"I don't know," Sue lied, and I detected a strong scent of her nerves.

"Why was a call girl at Baldwin's housewarming party?" Sophie asked.

"The rich are different," Luke said to relieve Sue of his mother's grilling questions.

Sue said her son was cleaner and more wholesome than some men she had known.

"I may be rich, but I'm a country boy at heart," Luke said. "I'm not a playboy like some other men."

"Why didn't Thomas Baldwin buy his land himself?" Sophie asked, sensing the tension and changing the subject.

Luke explained that Thomas may have thought someone else could get a better price than he could because everyone knew he was rich. Also, sellers were less likely to ask what Phil wanted the property for, and some locals weren't keen on the hotel or the theme parks.

"That sounds reasonable," Sophie replied as Sue and Luke drained their limoncellos. Let me know if I can help. " She added, "It sounds like you've got a lot of work to solve Phil's murder."

"Thanks, Mom," Luke said, collecting me for the drive home. I jumped into the car's back seat for the short ride home as Luke called to his Mother. "Don't let me catch you in the rain again," he said, and Sue agreed, "We want to keep you around!"

Chapter 17

Sue's house

When we arrived at Sue's house, Toby awaited us inside the front door. "Hi, Little Man," Luke said, reaching down to pet the high-tailed cat. I remembered that Luke was a cat-loving man who also loved dogs.

"Let me get you both a treat," he said, walking into the kitchen, where Sue kept them under the counter. Toby followed him into the kitchen, jumping on the countertop for a morsel. He purred loudly, as he did when he was happy, and rubbed Luke on the face as he bent over and sprinkled the treats on the counter.

As dogs do, I followed them and waited on the floor for my treat. As usual, I was served second. Cats have an advantage when doling out affection from higher places and getting their treats first. Toby stomped around until he got what he wanted, but never pretended he didn't like it.

Zeke called while Luke fed us treats, and Sue put him on speakerphone. "Hi, Zeke," Loretta said. "I'm home with Luke, who's with me on the call. Have you heard the news?"

"They booked Loretta for murder," Zeke said. "She's in jail!"

"It was unbelievable," Sue replied, explaining the evening's events to her son-in-law.

"I'm shocked," Zeke replied. "What am I supposed to tell Lucy?"

"Tell her Mama is spending the night away, and she'll be home as soon as possible," Sue said. "Tell her Grandma is looking after her."

"Can I help you get an attorney?" Luke asked, and Zeke replied he did not want to represent Loretta, but was looking for one.

"She's scared," Zeke said. "I've never heard her so upset."

"She's innocent," Sue said. "She was in the wrong place at the wrong time. Somebody took advantage of the situation."

"She said something about a person in a black cape," Zeke said, and Sue replied that she knew someone with a cape and would talk to her.

"Should I hire a private investigator?" Zeke asked, and Luke mentioned that criminal attorneys had their private investigators, so not to.

"I'm going to talk to everyone I know who was at the party," Sue said. "Someone must have seen or heard something."

"Be careful," Zeke said. You don't know what you may encounter."

"I know," Sue replied. "Loretta is my only daughter, and I'd do whatever it takes to help her."

"I don't want you to get hurt," Luke said. "Ask questions if you must, but be careful who you talk to."

Everyone knew Sweetwater Springs was not as safe as it used to be. I would protect Sue if needed, but I was mostly an alarm dog who alerted her to unusual circumstances or untrustworthy people.

"I'll be careful," Sue promised. "I'll see Loretta at the jail tomorrow."

"Do you think they'll let you see her?" Zeke asked.

"I am her mother, and Daisy has visited the jail in the past," Sue said. "The sheriff and deputy know us, so it should help."

"They don't have to grant bail since this is a second-degree murder offense," Zeke said, and Sue replied she'd think about it if and when the time came.

"It's a scary thought," Zeke said.

"I don't plan on having it," Sue replied. "I will work day and night to discover what happened to Phil for you, Lucy, and Loretta."

"Thanks, Sue," Zeke said. "We'll keep in touch."

Sue made a pot of chamomile tea while Toby lay on the cat hammock, and I lay beside them. After a long day, I was comfortable on the cool tile floor. The air conditioner vent blew on my fluffy coat, which was dry after the rain.

Sue poured a cup of tea for both of them while they talked. "I have to find out who killed Phil," Sue said. "It's the only way to keep Loretta out of prison."

"Phil had a lot of enemies," Luke replied, adding honey to his tea. "There were more than spoke up at the party."

"I believe that," Sue said. "He's lived in Sweetwater Springs his whole life and liked to ruffle feathers."

"That trait seemed to be getting worse with age," Luke said. "He wasn't getting more mellow; he was getting meaner."

"Some of my friends sat with victims of his sales crusades during dinner," Sue said. "I have plenty of people to talk to."

"Where will you start?" Luke asked after he stirred his tea.

"Mia wants to meet with me at the Baldwin guesthouse tomorrow," Sue said. "I think she's a good starting person after I meet with Loretta at the jail."

"Agree," Luke replied. "If anyone has some behind-the-scenes secrets, it's Mia."

Sue sipped her tea. "I think Mia has a few secrets," she grumbled, not mentioning she was keeping one of her own from Luke.

"Is everything alright, Sue?" Luke asked, sensing her distress.

"How do you know me so well?" she asked, adding, "I can't tell you yet."

Luke put his arm around Sue and tried to kiss her, but Sue turned her cheek and avoided his lips. It wasn't my first time seeing evidence of the budding romance, but it was palpable, as always. I rooted for the consummation because I loved them both, but dogs have little say, and this wasn't the night.

"We're a good fit," Luke said, "even if you're not ready for us yet."

"You're a lovely man, and I like you a lot," Sue replied softly. "I like your mama, too."

"My mama likes you," Luke said.

"You've gone away from home too much for work, and I'm not up for a long-distance relationship," Sue replied.

"Are you looking elsewhere while I'm gone?" Luke asked, and Sue assured him she wasn't.

"I'm not looking anywhere else, either," Luke said. "I'll wait for you as long as you want me to."

Luke had a second home in Tampa and a third in Miami, where he spent weekdays on hotel development projects. He spent most weekends in Sweetwater Springs, where he planned to retire. Sue sometimes wondered why he didn't retire early, but he was a man with a plan, and she didn't try to talk him out of it.

"Mama would love to have you move into the Big House if you ever get tired of your little place on the cove," Luke said.

"I'll never get tired of my little house on the river," Sue said, although she was most likely the only woman in Sweetwater Springs who would choose a cottage over a mansion.

"That's what I like about you," Luke said, although he loved her already for hundreds of reasons, not the least of which were their shared love of pets, the same people, and nature.

"Let me know when you're coming home for good," Sue said, "I'd love to rock on the porch with you and watch the river forever."

When I was sleeping deeply, my breathing was shallower. Now, I was twitching and semi-awake in a dog dream. Luke was my favorite man, and Sue was my favorite woman. I loved it when they talked about love and dreamed of a future, possibly in a big bed like Artemis.

Tonight, they moved quickly from the subject of love to that of murder, which was also important because it involved Loretta. I cared deeply about Loretta, not just because of my cousins who lived at her house. Loretta was a good woman with a heart of gold for her friends, a head for medical treatments, and healthy living for dogs.

Sue knew how to keep me healthy, but Loretta had the clinic to take me if I got sick.

"Did you see anyone by the river when we heard the gunshots?" Sue asked, reliving the earlier nightmare.

"No," Luke said. "I didn't see a person in the cape."

"Maybe they took it off by the time we arrived," Sue replied. "Maybe they were already gone."

"A lot of people left early because of the rain," Luke said. "How could we know who left before and after the shots? We walked the grounds and went much further than most people."

"Jessie and Chris heard them," Sue said. "They must have been leaving at the time."

There were many questions and few answers, but Loretta needed our help, and she would get it. This was the most critical case in Sue's history living in Sweetwater Springs, or her life, for that matter. I was happy to have been to the jail before because it made it easier for me to visit again, and it was apparent that Sue needed a dog for direction and insights. I saw details that Sue missed because of the talking, and she needed all the help she could get.

"I'll sleep on it and see if I can come up with any more answers," Luke said. "You had better sleep," he added, departing for home.

"Tomorrow is a big day," Sue replied, walking him to the door. "Let me know if you think of anything."

"I won't forget," Luke said, pecking her cheek. "I won't forget about anything that happens between us."

Sue smiled as he departed for home. Luke was a hopeless romantic, but she loved it. She was asleep and dreaming in minutes with my furry body beside her. It was morning before we knew it.

Chapter 18

Loretta's in Jail

I've been to the jail, but never for family. A few months ago, Sheriff Stone read an article about how dog-friendly visits could benefit the inmates, who often struggled to have someone to love them. Having given it thoughtful consideration, the sheriff decided to try dog visits in Sweetwater Springs. The inmates, at the time, were being held for third-degree felonies, i.e., burglary of a parked car without a gun and arrest after a bar brawl.

I was especially interested in the bar brawl because it involved a dog that had jumped the fence and attacked another dog on a leash in the neighborhood. The inmates, who were neighbors, battered each other in the parking lot and were in separate cells. This could have happened to me since I walked with Sue every morning. I would have felt trapped and frightened and could have been badly injured. It was scary for me to think about it.

Sheriff Stone was excited to have Sue offer to bring me for the jail visits. Sue recommended a six-foot fence for the dog jumping the fence—or a rehome if that wasn't possible. Both inmates loved seeing a dog in jail and realized they loved dogs, but the fence jumper owner had to be responsible for keeping him confined to his property.

Sue believed dog owners should feel safe walking their dogs in their neighborhoods. "I wouldn't want Daisy to be attacked by a loose dog," she told the inmate with the fence-jumping dog. "Not every dog likes other dogs. Your dog was bigger and more aggressive than the friendly hound she attacked."

The jail visit had succeeded, with the burglar admitting that people who worked hard for life's bonuses didn't deserve to have them stolen. Sweetwater Springs was rich in spirit, but the luxuries and hobbies were hard-earned with blood, sweat, and tears. Nobody deserves to have a circle saw stolen by an addict who wants to buy a fix.

Dog safety and petty thefts were big deals for Sue and me. I made an impression on the sheriff, who was more likely to invite dogs to his jail for future visits. Who would have guessed that my next visit would be to see Loretta?

Loretta had been charged with second-degree murder, which carried much stricter protocols than thefts and bar brawls. Technically, murder inmates were confined without bail in Sweetwater Springs. Her attorney could make a case for bail because she was a hardworking, good citizen with no previous history of arrests. And the sheriff could choose whether or not to let her have visitors, two-legged or four-legged, like me.

Sue called Sheriff Stone first thing in the morning. "Can you please grant an exception for us to visit Loretta?" she asked.

Since she was charged with murder, Loretta was confined separately from other inmates. There was a chance she might be moved to other facilities before a hearing for bail, which may or may not be granted. Her best hope was her excellent reputation and clean history. Loretta never had a traffic ticket, let alone a criminal offense.

"Us?" Homer asked.

"I want to bring Daisy," Sue said. "You remember her, right?"

"Of course, I remember Daisy," he replied. None of the inmates has returned since your last visit. The dog owner doesn't let his dog outside without him, and the burglar got a job."

"That's good news!" Sue said.

"That's most unusual in Sweetwater Springs."

"What do you mean?" Sue asked.

"We have career criminals who return for the crimes and misde-meanors."

"Career criminals? In Sweetwater Springs?"

"Yes, but it didn't used to be that way here. They steal instead of work."

"Do you think Daisy made the difference?" Sue asked.

"You had good advice, yourself," Homer replied.

"It was simple," Sue said. "I made them think about how they'd feel if somebody did the same thing to them."

"Whatever it was, the jail is empty except for Loretta. You are welcome to visit your daughter."

"Thank you, Sheriff," Sue replied, "We'll be there shortly."

Since there were no other inmates, the sheriff let us mingle in the visitor room. Loretta was frantic. Her face was blanched, and her lips were white. Sue put her arms around her daughter and hugged her while I watched them from the floor.

"You're shaking," Sue said as she stood back to look at her.

"I've never been so scared," Loretta replied.

"I can only imagine," Sue said.

"This is surreal," Loretta replied. "Things like this aren't supposed to happen."

"You're right," Sue said. "You were at the wrong place at the wrong time. It's as simple as that."

"That could happen to anyone," Loretta said. "You just don't think about it until it does."

I leaned my furry body against Loretta's leg to console her. She was stiff, but no longer shaking. I wanted to jump in her lap when she sat in the hard chair behind a wooden desk, but there was no room for a lap dog, so I stood under the table.

"I'm glad you brought Daisy," Loretta said, rubbing behind my ears.

"She has a good reputation at this jail," Sue replied. "I might not have been permitted a visit without her."

Loretta took a deep breath and sighed. "I'm not sure if I'll get bail on a second-degree murder charge," she said. "There's no telling how long I'll be here."

"I'm thankful you're in Sweetwater Springs," Sue said. "It could be worse."

"I could get transferred to wherever they want to send me if the judge denies me bail," Loretta said.

"Zeke is looking for an attorney," Sue said. "I talked to him last night."

"How's Lucy?" Loretta asked, and Sue replied that her daughter was thinking about her, and Zeke had assured her she would be home soon.

"Don't get her hopes up," Loretta said. "I could be here for a long time."

"One day at a time," Sue said. "We're working hard to get you home."

"Who is going to run the clinic?" Loretta asked, and Sue replied that she'd find a relief veterinarian if needed.

"We don't know any criminal attorneys," Loretta worriedly continued. "No one in our family has been charged with a felony, let alone a murder."

"We'll find you the best attorney," Sue said, reminding her to quit worrying. "A lot of people are praying for you already."

I followed Loretta, four feet on the floor, as she stood and walked toward the jail bars in the visitor's room. She looked both ways and saw no one. I nudged her hand with my head, and she stroked my forehead.

"Do you think it's safe to talk?" Loretta asked, turning toward the wooden table.

"I don't think anyone is listening, and we have nothing to hide," Sue replied.

"I keep thinking about the black cape," Loretta said. "It looked like the one Tori wore the day we saw her at Mia's Run."

"I wondered about that," Sue said. "I'll talk to Mia later today."

"Does Tori have a motive to kill Phil?" Loretta asked, and Sue replied that she didn't know her well. "Phil spent plenty of time at Cat Tails before Tori disappeared," Sue said.

"He probably annoyed her customers," Loretta replied.

"He annoyed a lot of people, but that's not a motive for murder," Sue said. "Tori disappeared six months ago. Why wait?"

"Maybe she stumbled upon an opportunity," Loretta said.

"Still no motive," Sue said.

"What about Sarah?" Loretta asked. "She knew about the cape."

"Yes, and I've been thinking a lot about Sarah, too," Sue said. "Something doesn't sit right about her."

"She called Phil a Pig," Loretta said. "She must hate him for something."

"I don't know much about Sarah except she's a call girl—possibly retired— and Tori's friend from Miami," Sue said.

"That's right," Loretta said, "Val told us they used to do ceramics together. Tori tried to get her back into mainstream life."

"Maybe Sarah stumbled upon an opportunity to kill Phil for whatever made her call him a Pig," Sue said.

"And frame me?" Loretta belched.

"That might have been an impulse by whoever framed you," Sue said. "I'm going to investigate this myself."

"Be careful, Mom," Loretta said. "You're investigating a murder. Somebody out there is a killer, and they don't want to get caught."

"I won't rest until I get to the bottom of this," Sue said, taking me by the leash to depart for Baldwin's Mansion, where she would meet Mia at the guesthouse. "The only way to keep you out of prison is to find the real killer."

Chapter 19

Baldwin's Guest House

"You and I have a lot in common," Mia said, inviting Sue and me into the Baldwin property's guesthouse. I sat on the floor beside Sue, eventually relaxing and sniffing the familiar scents of people I had encountered recently—Mia, Tori, and Sarah.

Mia and Tori were presently in the guesthouse, but not Sarah. I knew Tori better than Sarah, whom we had only met at Mia's Run. Sarah had lost her temper with Phil at the housewarming party, and Sue wanted to know why.

Sue tried to take Mia's comment in stride—of course, she had oodles in common with the wife of the town's only billionaire. "That's good to know," Sue replied, becoming more skeptical about the company she kept.

"You'll understand when I'm finished," Mia said, catching her drift. "It's not the best thing to share in common, but I hope we can help each other."

"Please, go ahead," Sue said. "I'm listening."

Mia took a deep breath before the plunge. "Our daughters are both suspects in Phil's murder," she said, looking deeply into Sue's eyes. "Somebody framed Loretta and fired the gun in her hand. My daughter has an excellent motive and doesn't have a good alibi. It's only time until our well-intended yet unqualified law enforcement officers come looking for Sarah."

Sue swallowed hard and leaned toward Mia. "Sarah, the call girl, is your daughter?" she asked as I smelled the sweat from her palms.

"Yes, and we've only recently reconnected," Mia said. "I've been hoping to keep it that way."

Sue frowned as Mia continued. "Sarah was a love baby from high school," she explained. I was fifteen, and Phil was fourteen."

"Phil was Sarah's father?" Sue asked, her jaw agape as she was drawn more deeply into the family drama.

"My parents didn't want me to have the baby in Sweetwater Springs," Mia continued. "I left town for a year and had Sarah in a little town north of here. My dad was a prominent attorney and didn't want our family name tarnished. My mom didn't believe in abortion."

"Pregnant teenagers had a tough time in my era," Sue replied. 'When I was a teenager, two girls from my high school went to New York for abortions, while two others kept their babies."

"They still do," Mia, over twenty years younger, replied.

"My aunt and Uncle adopted Sarah," Mia said.

"I hope that worked out well for her," Sue replied, and Mia added that Sarah could explain later.

"Phil wanted no part of fatherhood," Mia said. He was a deadbeat dad who barely admitted Sarah existed, even as an adult.

"That explains why Sarah called him a Pig," Sue said.

"Have you told Thomas about Sarah?" Sue asked.

"No, Sarah doesn't want me to," Mia said. "This is my best life ever. Thomas is good to me, and we love Sweetwater Springs. She's afraid he won't understand."

"You have to be honest with him," Sue replied. "It's only going to get harder if you wait."

"I regret not telling him already," Mia said.

"Why doesn't Sarah live in the guesthouse with Tori?" Sue asked.

"She has her apartment. I pick her up and bring her to see Tori," Mia explained.

I could smell the tension as the secrets mounted. Finally, Mia dropped the bomb. "Thomas doesn't know that Tori has been living on the property," she said. "She doesn't want me to tell him, so proving Sarah's innocence is vital to her life and my marriage."

Mia had a perfect life with a man who dearly loved her. How would he react when he discovered she didn't trust him enough to tell him the truth about a secret daughter and a woman she kept hiding on his property?

Tori had a lot of explaining to do. She joined us in the living room, stroking my head before she sat on an easy chair across from Sue. "It's good to see Daisy," she said. "It reminds me of better times."

"Better times are around the corner," Sue said. "Life has ups and downs."

"I loved Cat Tails Pub," Tori said. "Dave was jealous of my happiness."

"That's sad," Sue replied. "You had so much possibility together."

"Dave was a poor kid from Miami with no future, but he wasn't afraid of me or my father," Tori replied. "A lot of the kids were afraid of me because I was a Pedri. He paid attention to me."

Sue shifted in her seat to examine Tori closer. "I can feel your struggle," she said. Your parents seem nice, but their lifestyle makes people uneasy."

"It wasn't easy to be the daughter of a man who was thought to be a mob boss," Tori replied. "I've been trying to separate myself from his reputation, so we moved to Sweetwater Springs, and now they have followed me."

"No one knew for sure," Mia explained. "They are sworn to secrecy."

"My parents bought the pub for us as a wedding gift," Tori said. "They put it in my name only in case we had relationship trouble and got divorced. Dave has been trying to get me to quit claim the deed in both of our names recently. I refused since we aren't getting along well."

"That sounds like a good plan not to add his name to your property under the circumstances," Sue said.

Tori replied, "Dave was furious. He said if I died, it left him with nothing."

"He still had the pub," Sue said. "It would go into probate."

"No, it wouldn't," Tori responded. "My parents insisted on a prenuptial agreement. "The pub reverted to my parents if I died."

Sue swallowed and groaned. "Too bad for Dave."

Mia asked, "Why haven't your parents taken the pub back?"

"No one can prove I'm dead."

Tori had made some good points, but many questions remained. Mia retrieved a pot of tea from the kitchen and set it on the coffee table with three cups. She brought scones for the ladies and a dog biscuit for me.

"Why are you hiding?" Sue asked after she put a dollop of clotted cream on her scone.

"I'm hiding from Dave," Tori explained. "He thinks he killed me."

"Your husband thinks he killed you?" Sue repeated after she swallowed the scone. "How does he think it happened?"

"He pushed me out of the kayak the night he left me at Mia's Run. I dropped and hit my head on the dirt. It knocked me out cold, but I wasn't dead."

"Did he check your pulse or something?" Sue asked, and I sensed that she was stunned.

"Nope, nothing. He just left me there for dead."

"That's horrific," Sue said. I can't imagine a person being so cold."

"He simply did not care," Tori said. "He kayaked away and left me lying in the dirt."

"Wow," Sue said. "I'm shocked."

"Mia found me later that night," Tori continued. "She hid me in the most remote cabin so no one would know I was there."

"I've seen it," Sue replied. "With Luke."

"My parents sent out search and rescue teams, but the dogs couldn't find me. The water from the swamps threw them off."

"It was an extensive search, but they didn't find her," Mia said after she sipped her tea. "I was sweating bricks because Thomas didn't know she was here, and I didn't want Dave to know she was alive."

"Mia told Sarah I was here," Tori continued. We were best friends in Miami after she left her uncle's house. We swim and make ceramics together. Sometimes we watch TV and play cards. If it weren't for Sarah, I'd go stir-crazy alone in this cabin."

"How long do you plan to stay?"

"Until this is settled. If Dave knew I was alive, he'd try to kill me again."

The scone, which came from the downtown teahouse, was delicious. I grabbed a crumble as it tumbled to the floor while Sue quickly processed the information coming at her. Still, it brought more questions.

"Why doesn't Dave move back to Miami?" Sue asked. "He could call it quits and start over."

"He needs to move forward with his life," Mia agreed.

"He's making more money than he has in his life," Tori explained. "The pub is profitable. If he returned to Miami, he'd work as a line chef, but here, he's the owner with hefty profits unless my parents take back the pub."

"Since there's no dead body to prove she's dead, Tori's parents can't take the pub from Dave until she's disappeared for years."

"If you pardon my asking, how long do you plan to play dead?" Sue asked.

"I hoped Dave would return to Miami when he made enough money as a nest egg to buy a restaurant there."

Sue digested the information slowly and carefully. She was concerned that Tori's parents had been left out of the information loop. Only five people knew Tori was alive, and she had not told her mom and dad.

"Your parents love you," Sue said. "Aren't you concerned about keeping them in the dark?"

"My parents don't know how much we fight," Tori explained. "They don't know how badly it was escalating."

"I'll do my best to keep your secret," Sue replied. "I understand your reasons, but I know how I'd feel if Loretta played dead for me."

"I don't want my parents involved. This is my problem, and I'll solve it myself. I'm proud of my business, and my parents are proud of me for making it successful."

After she learned about Tori's life, Sue thought about the murder that brought them together at the guesthouse. Loretta was in jail, and Sarah was a suspect for more reasons than Sue had known. I lay on the floor and waited for the final questions.

"What did you think of Phil?" Sue asked.

"He was a good customer," Tori replied. I stayed out of his business, just as the community stayed out of my parents' business."

"Do you know why Sarah hated Phil?"

"Yes, of course," Tori replied. "He was her father and a deadbeat dad. There's much more to her hatred of her father than you already know, but you need to hear the rest from Sarah."

"We need to stick together," Mia said. "Sarah didn't kill Phil, and she didn't frame your daughter for it."

The biggest questions remained. Who else might have fired the gun? And who was wearing the black cape when they thrust the gun into Loretta's hands? I could sense that Sue believed their stories, but she had to convince Loretta of her innocence.

"How do you know Sarah wasn't wearing the cape when someone grabbed Loretta from behind?" Sue asked Tori.

"Because I was with her when we heard the gunshots, " Tori said. Sarah told the sheriff she had gone to her car to change clothes because he thought I was dead, but had come to the guest house to see me."

"Where was the cape?"

Tori said, "I went swimming that morning and left it in a box by the river. I used to carry it with me, but it's been hot. Now, I only use it when I see someone coming, like when I saw you and your daughter."

"Interesting," Sue replied. "Anybody could have grabbed it."

Chapter 20

Sarah

"I'd love to introduce you to Sarah," Mia said as Sue approached her
SUV with me on a leash. "After you meet her, I think you'll believe
that she, like Loretta, lost her temper with Phil at the dinner party and said
things she should never have said. But she didn't kill him."

"The criticism was fueling itself," Sue said as I padded on all fours softly
beside her. "People are mad at Phil for different reasons—mostly valid."

"It was like a 'me too moment'," Mia agreed.

"Phil has that effect on people."

"He was a con and a show-off," Mia said. "It's never been any different
since I met him in high school, but it loses its charm as an adult."

I had never been in a vehicle like Mia's, but it was beautiful. It was a long
distance from the ground to the seat, and I was glad I was in shape for the
jump. Sue tried wiping my feet before I hopped onto the plush leather
seats, but Mia said the sand was easy to clean.

"You're a nature girl, like me," Sue said as Mia drove out of the long
driveway toward the main road.

"It took some time for me to know my loves," Mia said, "But I'm not a
woman for breast implants and facelifts."

"Never for me," Sue agreed. "I'm not sure why young and old women
distort what nature has given them."

"Men," Mia said, and Sue suggested they were attracting the wrong men.

"Pardon me for asking, but why were you attracted to Phil?" Sue asked.

"He was a handsome football jock in high school," Mia replied. "Lots of girls had a crush on him, but I landed him. I suppose, in some stupid way, it was a competition, and I won."

"Would you do it over again?" Sue asked, and Mia replied, "Never. I made a mistake. I should have waited for a better man with less hangups."

"Hangups?"

"Phil was in love with himself, and that was it," Mia said. "There was no room in his heart for anyone else. I didn't see it back in high school."

"You did very well for yourself in the long run," Sue said as I shifted positions on the comfortable seat to look out the window. "You are a remarkable woman."

"I suppose it took a big mistake, like Phil, for me to come to my senses. I stayed away from men for a few years after my dad sent me away to have Sarah. It was nearly unbearable to be rejected by my family."

"It must have been heartbreaking," Sue replied.

"After I realized what was happening to Sarah, I quit thinking about myself and focused on her."

Sue had an idea of what happened by now, but she knew Mia wanted Sarah to tell her story. I watched the familiar streets out the window as Mia drove toward Sweetwater Condominiums. We passed River Drive, where we saw my greatest fear—the big dog who had jumped the fence to charge at me. I will never forget, but it will get easier with time.

We crossed the railroad tracks and traveled to the other side of town. I had never been to the condos before, and I didn't know if Sarah had a dog, a cat, or any pets. I recalled that she seemed nice, but that was all. I mostly enjoyed meeting the pets on visits like this.

"That used to be my card shop," Mia said as we drove past a small green building that was now a beauty shop.

"Nice," Sue replied, recalling that Thomas had courted her there. "How long have you and Thomas been married?"

"Fifteen years," Mia replied. "It's his second marriage. I'm forty, and he's fifty-five."

"How old is Sarah?"

"Twenty-five. Sarah moved to Miami when she was sixteen. I didn't see her for years. "

"That must have been heartbreaking," Sue said.

"It happens in many families," Mia replied. "More than we know because some people make mistakes or have personal problems they don't discuss."

"Kids can be estranged," Sue agreed. "But if we're lucky, they come home again."

We climbed three stairs to reach Sarah's condo on the third floor. It was a hike, even for a conditioned dog like me. I couldn't imagine walking up and down those steps three or four times daily to relieve myself. Sue had chosen a house with a yard where I could step outside whenever necessary. That was much better for me.

When I saw a young man carrying a small dog down the stairs, I wondered how people lived like this. The lack of an elevator made this no place for the elderly, and my furry legs felt the burn of the climb. Although I was only four, I felt fourteen when we arrived at Sarah's door.

Sue was in shape from flat walks in the neighborhood and was huffing when we entered the living room. I was not breathing heavily, but I felt the climb. Mia seemed to take it in stride, and we decided she was conditioned from more visits.

"Thanks for coming," Sarah said, shaking Sue's hand and hugging Mia. "I'm sure Mom prepared you with my life history."

"Just the facts," Sue said. "Nothing too private."

"I'm usually private about my personal life," Sarah said. "One can't be too open without judgment, but many people know my history as a call girl in Miami."

"Agree," Sue replied.

"I tell my story only when it can help others," Sarah said, stroking my head. "I'm not ashamed, just careful."

"I understand," Sue said, "Please know that I won't judge you for your struggles."

A Mackeral tabby cat resembling Toby entered the living room and strutted past as if he were the most essential thing ever. "That looks like my cat," Sue said. "Is he an alley cat from the neighborhood?"

"Yes, I rescued him from the streets," Sarah replied. "His name is Tom."

"Tom seems very sweet," Sue said as he rubbed her leg, and I moved in on the territory. "Toby is one of the sweetest cats of my lifetime. People spend a lot of time helping the strays of Sweetwater Springs."

"He's a wonderful cat," Sarah said. "I haven't had a cat in fifteen years, but I used to have an orange cat I loved very much when I lived with my uncle."

"Pets can be our lifesavers," Sue said. "For many reasons."

"Has Mom told you about my Uncle?" Sarah asked.

"Only that you lived with your Aunt and Uncle for fifteen years after her family wouldn't raise you."

"I would never do that to my teenager," Sarah said. "If I made my teenager have a baby, I'd help her take care of it."

"People have different opinions about that," Sue said. "It depends on their experiences."

"Phil had nothing to do with me after I was born or ever again," Sarah said. "I hated him for abandoning me."

"I'm sorry Phil was a terrible father," Sue said, and Sarah corrected, "He didn't care about me at all—not ever. He never knew about my uncle."

"Thank you for sharing your story with me," Sue said. "I know this is difficult."

Tom sat on Sarah's lap while she told the story. She stroked his head and long body while she talked. Her story was devastating, but the cat soothed her.

"My uncle abused me from the time I was ten years old," Sarah began. "He threatened to hurt me if I told anyone, so I kept it a secret, even from my mom. She came to see me once a month back then. But I didn't know she was my mom until later."

"My uncle got me pregnant when I was fifteen years old. If I had the baby, it would have proven my uncle was the father, but I didn't think that was fair to the baby. I asked my mother to take me for an abortion, no questions asked. No shame on the family."

"I felt terrible shame to have left Sarah in that situation," Mia said, "but I had no idea my brother-in-law was abusing her until she became pregnant."

"Back then, some people blamed the victim, and I was ashamed of what happened to me," Sarah said.

"You were a brave girl," Sue said to Sarah.

"I couldn't return to my uncle's house, so I lived at my mom's house. We were getting close, but at the same time, Thomas fell in love with her. I was afraid of what he might disapprove of. Mom had a daughter at fifteen, and then her daughter had an abortion at fifteen. I moved to Miami to let her Mom and Thomas fall in love without a scandal in her background."

"I think Thomas will be alright with the truth," Sue said. "You should tell him."

"We will when this is over," Mia said. "We need to find Phil's killer to clear both of our daughters."

It was a horrific truth but full of bravery and courage. Sarah had been selfless in her determination to do the right thing. Her uncle had been a monster, and Mia had been in the dark. Phil had been the selfish, uncaring person he always was.

"How did you become a call girl?" Sue asked.

"After the abuse, I lost my compass. I moved to Miami, and then I met Tori."

"That was most fortunate for Sarah," Mia said.

"Tori was my best friend in Miami," Sarah said. I first worked at a food truck, making fish sandwiches. Tori came to the food truck, talking about her dad, his connections, and how she wanted out of the family business. We were both trying to escape our family histories."

"Not without good reason," Sue said.

"I spent much time with Tori's family, so I knew Gio and Val. They were kind to me and would have let me live with them, but I knew Tori wanted her independence, and I wanted my apartment. I got a fake ID that said I was 18 when I was only 16. I rented a room from an old lady who introduced me to a madam."

"I wish that never happened," Mia said.

"At first, I didn't tell my mom," Sarah continued. "I wanted more money and got the best gigs since I was pretty."

"As it turned out, Gio knew the madam. He tried to persuade me to live with Tori instead of becoming a call girl, but I refused because she was getting married and leaving Miami to run a pub in Sweetwater Springs. Since I was a friend of Tori, Gio told the madam to go easy on me. They gave me the gentlemen. I never got beat up like some of the other girls."

"You were lucky," Sue said, and Sarah agreed it wouldn't have happened without Gio's influence.

"I moved back to Sweetwater Springs to help Tori when Mom told me about Dave pushing her out of the kayak. I knew Tori and Dave were having trouble, but I did not know how bad it was."

"That sounds familiar," Sue said.

"After I moved back to Sweetwater Springs, I still got a few gigs in Miami. Usually harmless types. Lonely. Men who want to talk. The men choose the kind of date they want before the madam matches them with a call girl."

"Were you on a gig at Mia's housewarming party?" Sue asked.

"Heavens no. I was a guest."

"Phil and my uncle tried to ruin my life, but I'm overcoming it," Sarah said, and I could sense Sue and Mia's relief. "I'm ready to move forward into a better life."

I sat beside Sue, her hand glued to my warm and furry chest, while Sarah told her about her past, present, and future life. I could sense how much Sue appreciated the bittersweet story. Sarah had a kind heart. Bad things happen to good people, but she cares about people, and Mia and Tori care about her. She could turn her life around.

"By the way, I wasn't getting clothes in my car the night of the house-warming party," Sarah said regarding her statement to the sheriff. "I went to see Tori at the guesthouse."

"I believe you," Sue said. "You're going to make something of yourself when you find legitimate work and leave the madam and the call girl business behind," she said. "I just know it."

Chapter 21

Peter and Stanley's House

T he following morning, Mia met Sue at her house. They had decided
to work together to solve Phil's murder, as their daughters needed
their help. Both were potential suspects in a crime that would put Sweetwater Springs in the spotlight after twenty years without a murder. It was
a scary time for Loretta, who was in jail for a crime she didn't commit, and
a chance for Mia to do the right thing for a daughter she had unknowingly
left with a monster after Phil abandoned them in high school.

I was sitting on the couch, with my butt on the seat, more like a person
than a dog. My rear legs were on the seat, and my front legs were on the
armrest as I peeked out the sliding glass door onto the porch, where Toby
was focused on a lizard, as he often was. It might take him an hour to
pounce on it or not at all. He was the most patient cat I had ever seen, but
not consistently productive.

That said, I had not lived with that many cats—first, Boomer, who now
lives at Jessie's house. Then Toby joined us after Jessie and Beth moved
out. Toby loved to chase lizards, which, in my mind, was a waste of time. I
preferred relaxing between jaunts with Sue wherever she went. Now that
Sue had become an investigator, we had much better things to do than
chasing lizards.

Although I was not an expert on cats and found their pastimes silly, I noted that people enjoyed them. Sarah had enjoyed Tom sitting in her lap while she told her life story. It calmed her to stroke the cat while the details of her life emerged. Some of the details had been secrets for many years, yet the time would come when they had to unfold. Until they did, Sue and Mia had a better chance of getting friends and family to talk.

Sarah had good reason to hate Phil, but the sheriff had yet to assemble the pieces. Sue and Mia were ahead of the law in the town without a detective. The evidence was stacked against Loretta, but someone in the city must know more about the cape. Whoever donned a cape and framed Loretta with Phil's gun was the real killer. It was a matter of patience, diligence, and asking the right questions to find them.

Sarah knew about the cape and hated Phil. But did someone stumble upon it in the woods? Or did someone wear a raincoat that looked like the cape Tori had worn? Many people disliked Phil for apparent reasons, while others were yet to be identified. Several of Sue's friends had been at the housewarming party and may have talked to someone with more information.

Toby raced through an opening in the sliding glass door and flew down the hall when Sue opened the front door for Mia. Although he enjoyed Sue and Luke, he was not good with other company. Mostly, he preferred his own space in the bedroom when guests came over.

I accompanied Sue to the door, as most dogs would. "Good morning, Mia," Sue said. "Please come in."

"You have a cute house," Mia said, stepping inside to admire the photos of nature that adorned the walls.

"It's comfortable for Daisy and me," Sue replied, noting an alligator she had photographed on the river. "Toby likes it too, but is not brave with company."

"You mentioned you had a cat yesterday," Mia said. "A rescue?"

"Yes, Toby was a neighborhood cat from the streets," Sue replied. "I adopted him after Boomer left with Jessie and Beth. He's one of the sweetest cats I've had, but it takes time for him to warm up to new people."

"I'm glad Sarah has Tom," Mia said as Sue directed her to the back porch under the big fan. "You have a nice view," Mia said, and Sue replied that it was humble compared to Mia's Run, but she loved it just the same. "There's been a lot of activity with the wildlife in the cove," she added. "There's hardly a dull moment at my house between the bugs, birds, reptiles, and pets."

"I hear you," Mia said. "Frankly, I've never seen an alligator on Mia's Run," she added. "In some ways, you have the best views of wildlife."

"Dave claims an alligator took Tori," Sue reminded her, and Mia said they both knew better than that.

"I'll be glad when this is settled, and Tori can return to work," Sue said. "I don't like keeping her secret."

Sue and Mia sat on the back porch, sipping ice water while they talked. They planned to start the investigation by talking to Peter and Stanley, who lived at the end of River Drive. The couple had been at the housewarming party and may have heard something that could help.

"Peter has been a lifesaver for Tori," Mia said, "He manages the pub and does the cooking."

"He's the best chef on the street," Sue said. "We had dinner parties here for a year, but then Jessie moved away, and we didn't have so many of them anymore."

"How fun!" Mia replied. "I used to be part of a dinner party group."

"Jessie loves healthy food with bold flavors," Sue said. "She's my inspiration for healthy eating, and she's writing a cookbook."

"They are good people," Mia said, and Sue agreed.

"I'm taking strawberry banana Smoothies to Stanley and Peter's house," Sue said. "It's Jessie's recipe."

Sue grabbed my leash, collar, and the insulated smoothie container, and we stepped outside in the broiling sun for the short walk to Peter and

Stanley's house. I was excited to see my collar, which always meant an adventure. Peter and Stanley were good to me, and I missed seeing them more often.

"Stanley is a Criminal attorney in Miami," Sue explained as we walked. "He may know an attorney who can help Loretta."

"We may need a private investigator if it gets sticky," Mia replied, holding the container.

"We can talk to people we know," Sue said, "but we need to be careful with those we don't know."

"Sweetwater Springs isn't the crime-free mecca it used to be," Mia agreed. "When I was a girl, the sheriff used to say there was no crime in Sweetwater Springs, but no more."

"Pardon me for saying so, but your husband's developments may contribute to the crime rate," Sue said, and Mia agreed that the resorts would change the local flavor.

Stanley opened the front door and welcomed us inside their riverfront abode. The house faced the open river with a view of the bridge to the north and the wetlands to the east. Still, like Mia, they didn't see as many alligators as Sue did. I sat with my back to the people and looked out the enormous picture window while they talked.

"It's good to see you again, Mia," Stanley said, shaking her hand. "We've only just met, but I'm sure we'll see more of each other."

"My party was more eventful than I planned," Mia said. "I hope to clarify this and move forward to happier times."

"Good plan," Stanley agreed. "I'll do everything I can to help."

"Would you like to be Loretta's attorney?" Sue asked. "She needs someone to inspire the judge to grant bail."

"It doesn't always happen with a second-degree murder charge," Stanley replied, "but Loretta has an excellent reputation, and I'm sure we can convince him to grant bail. I'd love to be her attorney."

Sue breathed a sigh of relief when Stanley agreed to be Loretta's attorney. He was one of the best in the business, and Loretta was in good hands with him.

Sue poured smoothies into four tall glasses, and we walked to the back porch, where we sat at a glass table with our drinks. I sat on the floor between Sue and Mia while they talked. The river was low, and the sun was bright, enhancing the flowers on the stalks of the wetlands.

"Did you know that Tori and Sarah were best friends from Miami?" Mia asked.

"If you'll excuse my asking, who is Sarah?" Stanley asked.

"She's my daughter," Mia replied after she sipped the icy drink. "It isn't widely known, and I'd like to keep it that way until Phil's murder is resolved."

Stanley grimaced. "Why?"

"She's Phil's daughter, too, and it makes her a murder suspect since he abandoned her. She hates him."

"As I recall, she announced Phil was a Pig at the party," Stanley said.

"Phil was creepy," Peter said. "I hated how he sat in the back of the pub and made deals with the creepiest people."

Mia explained how Sarah was raised by an uncle who abused her and became a call girl. "Thomas doesn't know about it," she said.

"I can understand why you're not ready to discuss this," Stanley said. "We'll keep everything between us until you talk with him."

"We're working together since our daughters are both under the microscope," Sue said.

"I can help you," Stanley agreed. "Keep me informed, don't leave anything out, and always tell the truth."

Sue and Mia agreed to Stanley's terms while Peter's dog sniffed at my tail. Although he was sometimes an annoying little dog, he had helped look for Boomer's mother. It wasn't easy, but he had the nose for it. Eventually, Luke revealed the details, which had been a secret during their budding friendship.

"Who sat at your table at the housewarming party?" Sue asked.

"Phil and Nella sat with us," Peter said. "They bickered all night."

"Something was wrong between those two people," Stanley agreed. "Phil kept putting her down, and she finally exploded."

"What did they argue about?" Mia asked.

"He treated her like a second-class citizen," Stanley said, and Peter agreed that it seemed like a marriage of convenience for Phil, who liked a woman to come home to.

"She didn't want to come to the party," Peter said. "She was tired of his show-off style and embarrassed by the people he threatened."

"What did Phil want with the clinic?" Sue asked, and neither man had a clue.

"What was in the relationship for her?" Mia asked, and Stanley replied that they should ask her themselves.

"I suspect it was money," Peter said. "Phil must have been a good provider because he lacked a dollop of charm as a gentleman."

We boarded Mia's SUV to stop at Nella's house when they finished drinking smoothies. They were on a mission to discover the evidence they desperately needed to find Phil's killer. Their best hope was to prove their daughters' innocence, which was made better by recruiting Stanley to be Loretta's attorney. I lay on the back seat, excited for our next stop.

Chapter 22

Nella's house

It was a short drive to Nella's house on the green cove from Stanley and Peter's house on River Drive. I sat in the back seat on my haunches and looked out the window during the ride. Although it was a hot day, the breeze from the tiny crack in the window felt good on my furry face. I needed some fresh air at the moment.

Having Stanley as Loretta's attorney was good, but information and clues could be helpful. Nella was undoubtedly a suspect in her husband's murder. She had called Phil an embarrassment, a jerk, and a joke at the housewarming party and threatened to blow him away with his gun.

Sheriff Stone would question Nella further since she didn't have a good alibi. Being in the bathroom alone was not an effective alibi. Still, it didn't hurt for Sue and Mia to get to know her better. The best thing that could happen for their daughters was to prove someone else was guilty of Phil's murder. Whatever happened, it seemed like Nella may have been involved.

Mia drove past the mayor's house, a few doors from Nella's. "Do you know the mayor well?" Sue asked.

"A little," Mia replied. "He's been helpful for the meetings and transactions that clarify our position on cleaning up the river."

"Nobody knows its pollution better than him," Sue said. "Just look at the cove. It's green."

"This cove used to be one of the most beautiful places on the river when I was growing up," Mia said. "It turned green throughout the last ten years."

"Algae," Sue said, and Mia agreed. "Something is fertilizing the algae."

"What do you think fertilized the algae?" Mia asked.

"Mostly the same as the experts. Sewage, lawn fertilizers, lack of an adequate sewage treatment plant. More people on the river. Less water flow."

"What about cow manure?"

"It would be interesting to see what happens if we clean up the rest," Sue said. "It just doesn't make sense since the cows have been here for generations, and there are no farms on the river."

"Thomas wants to do his private testing," Mia said. Some people in academia don't like to rock the boat, and others fear losing their jobs."

"I understand that Phil got an excellent buy on his home because of pollution," Sue said.

"If that's the worst he ever did, somebody would be happy," Mia replied.

"Nobody killed Phil because he got a good buy on his house," Sue agreed.

When Mia pulled into Nella's driveway, a cat scampered from underneath a tree towards the house. "It looks like Phil and Nella had an alley cat," Sue said of the spotted furry creature.

"Even the worst people can have a soft spot," Mia said, and Sue agreed that sometimes pets softened the hardest of criminals.

"Is that why Daisy did dog-friendly visits at the jail?" Mia asked.

"Yes, but they were softcore criminals," Sue replied. "Loretta is the first murder suspect in two decades."

"This is crazy," Mis said. "She's practically a saint."

Sarah was not a saint, but Sue didn't mention it. "You're telling me," Sue said. "She's my favorite daughter on the planet."

When Sue let me out of the car, I tugged on my leash toward the cat hiding behind a flower pot on the front porch. Although I was now very familiar with cats because of Toby and Boomer, they still caught my attention at people's homes. This cat was lovely, with a face and body like Toby's and Boomer's. He was a small cat with short legs, a stocky body, and a round face.

Sue bent down to pet the friendly cat. "I'll bet Beth likes to see you," she said to the cat, who arched his back and purred. Looking at Mia, she added, "Sometimes Jessie's daughter, Beth, comes here to play."

"Nice," Mia said. "...I think," she added.

"Beth is friends with the mayor's daughter," Sue replied. "They usually play at the mayor's house, but Beth says sometimes they play at Phil and Nella's house."

"Interesting," Mia said.

Sue added, "Nella's daughter is embarrassed by her parents' chronic arguing and prefers to play elsewhere."

"Sounds legendary," Mia replied.

"At least in this neighborhood." Sue agreed. "Sometimes they heard the fights between Phil and Nella at the mayor's house."

Nella opened the door shortly after Mia rang the bell. "I hope we're not disturbing you," Mia said. "Do you have a few minutes to talk?"

"Mia Baldwin!" Nella exclaimed. "I'm honored. Please come in."

At this point, Nella hadn't acknowledged Sue or my four-footed presence. Sue seemed like a fifth wheel when Nella said, "I'm sorry, Sue. I didn't mean to ignore you."

"No problem," Sue replied. "Are you alright with Daisy in the house?"

"I like dogs, but my cat doesn't think much of them," Nella replied. "He's a street cat."

"I have a neighborhood cat, too," Sue said. "Daisy likes cats, but it takes time to warm up to new ones, and vice versa."

Nella ushered us toward the living room, leaving the cat outside. Sue and Mia sat on two chairs across from the couch, with a coffee table in between. I lay partially under the table, my head toward Sue, as I often did.

"Would you like water or tea?" Nella asked.

"No thanks," Sue said, and Mia agreed. "We had smoothies at Peter's house."

"I suppose you're here about Phil's murder," Nella grunted.

"That's right," Mia replied. "We are trying to find Phil's real killer to adjudicate our daughters."

"Both of them?" Nella asked. "I heard Loretta was in jail. I didn't know you had a daughter," she said to Mia.

"Her name is Sarah," Mia replied.

Nella was shocked. "The call girl?" she asked.

Now, it was Mia's turn to be unemotional. "Yes," she replied without judgment.

"The girl who called him a Pig?" Nella continued. "She seemed furious with Phil at the party."

"She had good reason," Sue replied.

"She was Phil's daughter, too," Mia declared.

Nella's jaw was agape as she gasped. I could feel the tension in the room, and it felt like the body heat increased the temperature. I slithered my long body out from under the table to sit by Sue while the conversation continued.

"I didn't know Phil had a daughter," Nella said, and Mia affirmed it.

"Did you have a good relationship?" Sue asked, and Nella said he was a good provider. "I cooked his meals, did his laundry, and stayed out of his way when he was angry."

"Pardon me for saying so, but maybe he had more than one child," Mia suggested.

"Did he know Sarah was his daughter?" Nella asked, and Mia assured her that he was aware of it. "He offered no support."

"Phil would never have wanted to spend money on a child out of wedlock," Nella said, and Mia reminded her that a judge could insist on it. "He'd leave the country and move elsewhere before he paid for a child."

"Did you want to have more children?" Sue asked because some men wanted a lineage when they grew older.

"Not with that man," Nella replied. "Frankly, I'm surprised it took someone so long to kill him."

Mia took a deep breath. "Do you mind if I use your bathroom?" she asked, standing up from the chair. Nella said, "Of course not."

Sue talked to Nella while Mia carried her purse to the bathroom. "Is she pregnant again?" Nella grunted. "I can't believe Mia Baldwin had a child with my husband."

"It was a long time ago," Sue replied. "They were in high school, and you weren't married then."

"She's the wealthiest woman in Sweetwater Springs," Nella said as Mia returned and sat down.

"I'd appreciate it if you could keep Sarah our secret—just for a little while," Mia said. "Thomas doesn't know I'm Sarah's mother yet. I plan to tell him after we settle this."

"I'll try," Nella replied. "I'm flabbergasted. My stepdaughter is the heir to a billionaire's wife."

Mia did not mention that she was hardly a stepmother since they had no relationship and never lived together. Sarah was a grown woman with a house and money of her own. Mia did not support Sarah, except only rarely.

"Oh, by the way," Sue asked. "Did Phil have a will?"

"Yes, of course," Nella said. "But there wasn't much money. The house was mortgaged, and he spent everything we had. We lived well, but he was a ten-cent millionaire."

"I haven't heard that phrase in a long time," Sue said. "My husband used to say it when somebody skipped out on a bill after they requested a premium service."

"Do people do that?" Nella asked, and Sue assured her it was true. "My husband passed away years ago, but not a day goes by that I don't think of him."

"Thank you for your time," Mia said, leaving. Sue and I followed her to the front door. "We'll be in touch," she said as we departed.

When we were safely in the car and out of earshot, Sue asked, "What was that bathroom bit about?"

Mia said, retrieving a small glass from her purse. "I got a DNA sample. Whoever killed Phil got DNA on Loretta when they grabbed her from behind."

"That's good thinking," Sue said. "I suppose you also have a DNA lab to test it?"

"Thomas is connected," Mia reminded her. "Remember Val and Gio?"

"Of course," Sue said. "Tori's parents."

I stared out the rear window while Sue changed the subject. "Do you think Nella will keep your secret about Sarah?" she asked.

"Not for long," Mia said. "But unless I miss my guess, we'll solve this caper by the time she spreads it."

"Why did you tell her?" Sue asked.

"A secret is a good connection," Mia said. "I hoped to gain her trust so she'd feel comfortable confiding in us."

"We may need her in the future," Sue replied. "You're smooth, but I like it. We'll make a good team to solve this crime."

After Mia dropped Sue off at home, I lay on the tile floor for a long nap. It had been a long and productive day. Tomorrow, Mia will join us in visiting Loretta at the jail.

Chapter 23

Jail

S ue awoke in the middle of the night to the sounds of dogs barking in the distance. It sounded like a lot of dogs—like a kennel. The strange thing was that there was no kennel nearby. Sweetwater Springs had an ordinance that only four dogs were allowed per household.

"Dogs," she said aloud, causing me to stir on the blanket beside the bed. "Nobody has that many dogs. Where is that barking coming from?"

I groaned and readjusted to a balled-up position. It had been a positional adjustment night for me, as well. The room fan, which Sue used to cover up the noise, was broken. Instead, she put her phone on a white noise fan beside my bed.

I had inadvertently covered the phone with the blanket when I made a nest, dulling the white noise. I was a sound sleeper, so the noise didn't bother me. Without it, Sue heard the barking and sat up in bed.

I jumped on the bed when Sue looked for the phone. I could hear the dogs in the distance, but wasn't alarmed. My job, as night watchdog, was to alert Sue to danger. There were just a jolly lot of dogs barking, but it didn't sound like they were roaming the neighborhood.

"I have no idea where those dogs are," Sue said aloud. Now she was wide awake, with no fan and white noise from a phone that didn't cover the barking.

As everyone knows, dogs have different barking habits depending on what they are barking at. This sounded like cousins barking at a mouse running through the yard. Sue said it continued for three hours, almost every fifteen minutes. I slept through it while Sue readjusted her phone to cover the noise, unsuccessfully.

It was not a good night for sleeping but a good night for thinking. Now that Sue was wide awake, she thought about Loretta, who she and Mia would meet at the jail in the morning. What had Mia said about working backward?

I slept belly up on the bed while the dogs barked somewhere up the hill. The following day, Sue talked to herself while she made coffee. I was well-rested and sat beside her in the kitchen while she reflected aloud, as people do when a dog follows them around day and night.

Whoever grabbed Loretta and put Phil's gun in her hand to fire it grabbed her from behind. The sheriff had taken the weapon and Loretta's clothing into evidence when they booked her at the jail. Sue and Luke were the first to arrive at the scene. Mia and Thomas were second on the scene.

What had Loretta been wearing? Could something have been left behind? It was dark, late, drizzly, and warm. Had the killer torn away clothes in the struggle?

Sue recalled the disposable raincoats available to guests for the walking tour of the grounds. Loretta had taken one of them but wasn't wearing it when they found her in the woods. Where was it?

Could there be a hair or a skin cell on it? Maybe a hair. Since it was drizzly, it could have washed off. It was a shot in the dark for a needle in the haystack, but maybe it could be worth the trouble.

We learned much from our daily travels. I ate brown dog kibble on the floor while Toby snacked on the counter. I was ready to ride when the doorbell rang. It was Mia.

Shortly after the coffee was brewed and the bagels toasted, the two women sat at the kitchen table and discussed the evidence.

"What did you mean about working backward?" Sue asked Mia.

"Oh, you mean getting a DNA sample from the cup I took from Nella's bathroom?"

"Yes, that's it," Sue said. "What good is a DNA sample to us if the sheriff has Loretta's clothes in evidence?"

"The sheriff has her clothes," Mia said. "But what about her disposable raincoat?"

"Do you know where it is?" Sue asked.

"Not exactly," Mia replied. "But I found four disposable raincoats in our dumpster."

"Not exactly evidence," Sue said, and Mia agreed no one knew who had worn them.

"I told the sheriff about them, but he didn't want them," Mia said. "We can check all four of them for DNA."

"It's a long shot," Sue replied, and Mia mentioned that they had already found Loretta's hair.

"If we don't find Nella's DNA, we can presume she's innocent," Mia said. They both agreed it wasn't proof, but it could be helpful.

"Or that she didn't lose skin cells or hair during the struggle," Sue added,

"We might find somebody's DNA we don't expect," Sue added. "We have to know who we're looking for."

"We can check for a match when we have a suspect," Mia agreed.

I jumped into Mia's SUV before she drove to the jail. Since it was early, Mia opened the window a quarter of the way down. As she drove, the wind ruffled my fur coat. It was a feeling I loved and would never grow tired of.

Summer was not my favorite time of year for riding in cars, but it was best done before the scorching heat. Sue and Mia had the front air conditioners on, but I preferred the breeze. Sue never opened my window over a quarter, so I couldn't fit my head through it, which she didn't think was safe.

Deputy Livingston was seated behind the front desk when we arrived at the jail. "Good morning, Ladies," he said. Loretta will wait for you in the visitor's room.

Sue walked closer with me on a leash so Bud could say hello. "We miss our visits with Daisy," he said as I rested my head on his lap.

"How's Loretta?" she asked.

"Improving," he replied. "She had a better night's sleep than her first night. I think she's getting used to the cot."

"Hopefully better than me," Sue replied. "My fan is broken, and the dogs up the hill barked until 3:00 am."

"I've heard about them," Bud said. "The owners sleep all day and let them play all night."

"It was a first experience for me," Sue replied. "The fan drowned out the barking before it broke, and Daisy slept right through it."

When we arrived in the visitor's cell, Loretta greeted us. She stroked my head as I rested it against her leg. "I miss my dogs," she said, referring to my cousins at her house. "I miss my family, too."

"Any word on when you may have a court set for bail?" Sue asked.

"Stanley is coming to see me this morning," she replied. "He thinks he can get the judge to release me on bail."

"I hope so, for everyone's sake," Sue said.

"We're doing our best to find Phil's killer," Mia added. "People aren't afraid to talk to us. Something will leak, eventually."

"Stanley has a Private Investigator that may come from Miami," Sue said, and they agreed he could handle the dangerous investigations.

"Homer is going to talk to Sarah today," Loretta said, "I heard him talking from my cell. He knows she's Phil's daughter."

"Word spreads quickly in Sweetwater Springs," Mia replied. "We're working quickly to resolve this."

"We talked to Phil's wife yesterday," Sue said. "It was a good connection that may prove useful."

"We don't think she killed her husband, but she liked us," Mia added. "It can't hurt to build some rapport with people."

Loretta ruffled my fur while they talked. I was glad to calm her, but we had a long way to go to prove her innocence.

"What were you wearing the night of the murder?" Sue asked, and Loretta reminded her of the ensemble. "Sheriff Stone has it in storage," she said. "He has it stored until forensics can use it."

"They need a suspect for DNA testing," Sue agreed, and Mia explained their plans.

"I found four disposable raincoats in my garbage container," she said. "We also found two kinds of hair, some had roots to test for your DNA."

"I didn't think of the disposable raincoat," Loretta replied. "Whoever grabbed me ripped it off of me."

"And threw it away in my dumpster," Mia added.

"The same DNA will be on your clothes in storage," Sue said. "The raincoat doesn't prove anything to them, but it's helpful for us."

"Could you tell if the person who grabbed you from behind was a man or a woman?" Mia asked.

"They could have been a man or a strong woman," Loretta said. "They wore a black cape, making it hard to see."

"How tall were they?" Sue asked, and Loretta said, a little taller than herself.

"Did they wear any perfume or cologne?" Mia asked, and Loretta said it happened too fast to know.

"How did you break free?"

"It must have been hard to hold me after they fired the gun and dropped it. I must have slipped away when the raincoat ripped off."

"Then what happened?"

"They ran away."

"Then what?"

"You and Luke found me standing over Phil's dead body."

They talked until Deputy Livingston said it was time to prepare for the next visitor. Mia had found the disposable raincoat in the garbage, but who was wearing the cape? I looked forward to sniffing out the evidence that would solve the crime. For now, I jumped into Mia's SUV for a ride to Rita's house.

Chapter 24

Rita's House

I jumped back into Mia's SUV when she drove to Rita's house. She did not roll down the back window, as she had before, leaving me to the rear air-conditioning to cool my snout. There was a bit of a breeze from the vent, but I passed up lying on the floor, where the best air was, to lie on my belly stretched across the back seat, as dogs do to keep cool.

It was a hot summer—one of the hottest on record. Already, it was shaping up to be a hot day—too hot to crack the windows for a fur-ruffling breeze, as I liked it best. Lying on my belly was second-best, but it was better than cracking open the window on a scorching day. The only relief from the relentless heat was the afternoon and evening rain showers.

There was no such thing as a perfect raincoat for a Sweetwater Springs summer. Still, certain raincoats covered the subject better than others. Some guests brought their rain attire, while others used disposable rain jackets to explore the grounds at the housewarming party. Some of the best disposables were plastic capes, like Loretta's, that allowed more airflow.

My kinky fur coat repelled the rain, broke the wind, and protected me from summer sunburn and winter cold snaps. Humans were not so fortunate in matters of temperature control. I was lucky to be a dog; however, my two-legged friends had a wide range of weather-regulating attire.

Someone with a grudge may have worn a black Trench Coat when they encountered Phil, wearing a disposable, in the woods. But whom? And where did they leave it after Phil's murder? Indeed, it was doused in bloodstains, but color could conceal them, especially after being washed. Forensics could detect washed blood, but not everyone knew it.

"Maybe Phil's killer wasn't wearing Tori's cape," Mia said as she drove towards Rita's house.

"It doesn't make sense to wear a cape on a wet summer night," Sue agreed.

"It's too hot to wear, and there's no rain protection," Mia suggested. "It would be soaked."

Sue suggested the killer could have stumbled upon Tori's cape in the woods and wanted a quick disguise.

"That's unlikely," Mia said. "Tori's cape was in a box. Not easy to find or wear."

"Agree," Sue replied. "A black Trench coat is more likely. Non-descript. Readily available. Lots of people have them."

"And could look like a cape from behind Loretta when the killer grabbed her," Mia added.

"We need to find a guest who brought a black trench coat to the housewarming party," Sue said, and Mia agreed there were a few of them.

Sue and Mia refined their ideas as Mia drove. They had the best motive in the world: to find Phil's killer and protect their daughters' innocence. I had my work cut out to help them uncover the clues and discover the evidence.

Visiting Loretta at the jail brought some good news. Stanley may convince the judge to grant bail despite Loretta's second-degree murder charge, which usually results in incarceration for the accused without bail. Still, the judge could go easy on citizens in excellent standing with no prior arrest. Loretta was a good citizen with a sterling reputation in the community.

Loretta's friends and family adored her, and her clients appreciated her. Her daughter needed her at home, and she wasn't a murderer. Sue and Mia planned to speak with everyone they knew at the housewarming party.

They wanted to discuss what their friends learned from their table mates. As they grew closer to the killer's identity, it could be a dangerous mission, but they were eager to question their friends. Rita could be an excellent source of information, but there was no threat to their safety.

"Have you been to Rita's house?" Sue asked as Mia pulled into her driveway.

"No," Mia replied. "I knew her from school, as a teacher. Not as a friend."

"She remembers you well," Sue replied.

"All good?" Mia asked.

"Nothing too wild and crazy," Sue replied. "Just a few unanswered questions."

"She remembers I was away for a year in high school?" Mia asked.

"She remembers the mayor and Phil both had a crush on you," Sue said, and Mia agreed she had some explaining to do.

"You'll like Rita," Sue continued, "She's happy you found Thomas, and she wants the best for everyone."

I jumped out of the back of the SUV to land with all four feet on the ground. It had been a short drive and with a new directive. Sue and Mia wanted to know who their friends sat with at the housewarming party, what they talked about, and whether they brought a black trench coat.

Five black trenchcoats of unknown ownership were hanging on the rack inside the dinner tent. Some guests had trench coats hanging on the back of their chairs. Not all trench coats were black, but it was a start to the unanswered questions.

"Hi, Ladies," Rita said, opening the door for us to step inside. "Please come in."

She led us to the sunroom, where her husband, Fred, was sitting and watching the sun ascend the sky to the east. "You have a beautiful view," Mia said, admiring the picture window. "Every home on this river had something unique and different about the view."

"At least the river's not green on the run down from the bridge like it is at the Green Cove," Fred grumbled.

"We visited Nella yesterday," Sue said. "The cove is green, but Mia doesn't see much algae where she lives on the springs."

"That's nice for Mia," Fred replied. "That hotel your husband wants to build will make the cove worse for Nella and the mayor."

"Oh, honey. You don't know that for sure," Rita said. "The council is doing everything it can to correct the pollution."

"The mayor can't fix the algae," Fred replied.

"We need a new sewage treatment plant," Sue said. "Thomas suggested one at the housewarming party."

"My husband is championing a new state-of-the-art sewage treatment plant," Mia said. "It will improve the water clarity."

"That takes politics and money," Fred argued, and Mia agreed it was a slow process. "This town has little of either."

"Take my word for it. It will happen," Mia said. "It's been approved already."

I sat near the window, looking out, when Sparkles passed through and swatted at me. Sparkles was the least friendly of the neighborhood cats adopted by the families on the street. Sue thought he might have been traumatized when Miami Cat escaped Peter's house and chased him through Fred and Rita's house during a clean and wholesome love story.

Today, Sparkles looked at me with an evil eye but did not swat. According to Fred, her manners were improving.

"Can I get you ladies some tea?" Rita asked, and Sue and Mia politely declined while I stared at the floor before the cat.

"We came to ask a few questions about the housewarming party if you don't mind," Sue said. "It won't take long."

"Fire away," Rita replied. "I'm not sure we will have the answers, but it's worth a try."

"Who did you sit with?" Sue asked, and Rita replied the mayor and Dave were at their table.

"Did either of them have a black trench coat?" Mia asked.

"What difference does that make?" Fred asked. "I brought a black trenchcoat to that party!"

"I hung it on the coat rack inside the tent," Rita added. "Fred's not one for hanging up his clothes."

I shuffled on my haunches at the window while they spoke. Talks with Fred could lead off in many directions, but he was grumpy in most of them. Sue wondered how a kindhearted woman ended up with such a grumpy man, but we saw much of it in Sweetwater Springs. Fred was a thorn, and Rita was a peach.

"The mayor had a black trench coat hanging on his chair," Rita said, softening the conversation.

"The mayor?" Mia replied, surprised.

"Yes," Rita said. "As I recall, he had a crush on you in high school."

Mia described the conflict between Phil and the mayor as something everyone knew very well, including Sarah's birth and her exile to another town where her abusive uncle raised her.

"I'm so sorry," Rita said. "I knew you left Sweetwater Springs for a year but had no idea you were Sarah's mother."

"I'm Sarah's mother, and Phil was her father," Mia explained. "Please don't spread the news because I haven't told Thomas yet."

"Well, then you should tell him he has a stepdaughter!" Fred declared, and Mia said she would shortly.

"Phil was a user, an opportunist, and an untidy neighbor with a messy house and a bad temper who yelled at his wife," Sue explained. "The mayor didn't like him, but we don't think he killed him."

The cat continued to taunt me as I looked out the window at the river. I could not excuse his attitude as a one-time experience with an escaped cat from Miami, but I felt pleased Toby was more friendly. I was being patient, but this cat could get on my nerves.

"Who else sat at your table?" Sue asked while Sparkles paraded past.

Rita replied that Dave had sat with them.

"He didn't have a trench coat on his chair like the mayor did," Fred grumbled. "I remember that much."

"Do you remember what he talked about?" Mia asked.

"He talked about Tori and how much he missed her," Rita recalled. "He said it's tough to run the pub by himself."

It wasn't news to anyone, but we had places to go and people to talk to. Tori was alive, but Mia couldn't tell Rita because Dave had left her for dead on the creek, and Tori wanted him to believe it until he made enough money at the pub to move back to Miami, where he belonged.

"I don't want Dave to kill me twice," Tori had said.

I was happy to move on to our next destination and leave the annoying cat behind. Sparkles pranced to the front door while Sue and Mia said goodbye, and then I hopped into the back of her SUV before Mia drove off into the sunlight.

Chapter 25

Jessica and Chris

When we arrived, Chris pruned the hedges at their upriver house across from Mia's Run. He spent most of his time pruning, mowing, planting flowers, and enjoying the shade under the enormous oak trees in summer. I loved the shade, as Chris did, but I mostly enjoyed digging holes in the yard to stay cool.

Sue let me dig one hole in the yard, and I made it a doozy in the shade. It didn't take long to realize that Sue would fill additional holes with concrete blocks. Dogs are intelligent about things like that. Sue explained that I would get the message if she filled the extra holes soon after I dug them.

Chris had no holes in his yard because Redman was past the digging years. His lovely yard was perfectly groomed, with flower beds and vegetable gardens. Chris grew the flowers while Jessie and he worked together in the vegetable gardens.

Jessie insisted on fresh vegetables in summer since they were becoming too expensive to purchase at the store. She was fond of tomatoes, fresh herbs, and jalapeno peppers, which she found easy to grow. She grew the vegetables in raised containers to control the nutrient-rich soil.

"Hi, Chris!" Sue said, stepping out of the SUV and opening the rear door so I could lunge out to greet him.

Chris was one of my favorite people in Sweetwater Springs. I raced full speed ahead, rear legs nearly touching my front legs as I flew in great leaps across the yard.

"I've never seen Daisy run so fast," Mia said, impressed by my warp speed.

"She doesn't get much opportunity to run in my little yard, Sue replied, but she does love it."

My stop beside Chris was as impressive as my run. He reached down to pet me, pulling a dog treat out of his pocket.

"It's good to see you, Mia," Chris said while I devoured the biscuit. "I don't know if Daisy loves me or the treats more," he said, and Sue assured Chris it was him.

"How's Loretta?" Chris asked as we walked towards the house.

"Doing better," Sue replied. "She's sleeping better at night."

"I can't imagine what it must be like to be whisked off to jail as an upstanding citizen," Chris said. "Loretta is the gold standard of veterinarians near Sweetwater Springs. People drive for miles to take their pets to her."

"Hopefully, the judge will consider that when he decides whether or not to set bail," Sue said.

"What happened to Loretta could happen to anyone," Mia added. "I'm ashamed it happened at my housewarming party."

"Loretta was framed," Chris agreed. "She didn't murder Phil Coleman."

"We don't think it was premeditated," Sue said. "She just happened to be at the wrong place at the wrong time."

"Somebody jumped her from behind, put the gun in her hand, and fired it," Mia said. "Phil was already dead."

"Why would Loretta kill him?" Chris asked, and Sue explained he had been pressuring her to sell the clinic. "We don't know why he wanted it."

"Phil pressured everybody to sell everything," Mia added. "Nobody liked him."

We walked toward the house, with me in the lead. I could feel the pressure mounting as we climbed the steps. What would anyone do if they were unjustly faced with a murder charge? This was a brutal injustice for Loretta.

"Sue, I'm so glad to see you," Jessie said when she greeted us in the kitchen. "Please let us know if we can do anything to help Loretta."

"We are trying to find Phil's killer," Mia explained. "If we find the real killer, it will free Loretta."

"Isn't that the job of the sheriff's office?" Jessie asked.

"Well...., yes and no," Sue said. "There's no detective in Sweetwater Springs. The department could use our help."

"Be careful, Sue," Jessie said. "You are looking for a killer who also framed your daughter."

"He's a dangerous person," Chris agreed, and Mia explained it could be a man or a woman.

"Loretta said the person who grabbed her was short and strong," Sue explained. "It happened very fast, and she doesn't remember much."

"Do you have any leads?" Chris asked.

"Phil's wife, Nella, and Sarah have motives without an alibi," Mia replied.

"Sarah, the call girl?" Jessie asked.

"She used to be a call girl," Mia explained. "Sarah is my daughter."

Jessica and Chris shared the same jaw-dropping expression as Mia described the familiar yet horrifying experiences Sarah had endured as a child and later as a young woman. I could feel their shock and Mia's pain, as dogs will do with their two-legged friends.

"I feel awful for her," Mia said. "This is my fault."

"It's your parents' fault, too," Chris said, and Jessie agreed. "If they were going to insist that you have a baby as an unwed teenager, they should have adopted her."

"My dad didn't want his reputation damaged," Mia explained. "He had political aspirations, and a family scandal would have hurt his career."

"That's pathetically narcissistic," Jessie said, and Chris agreed.

"My father was a selfish man," Mia said. "Sarah paid the price for it."

"Is Sarah a suspect?" Jessie asked.

"She could be," Mia replied. "She hated Phil for abandoning her and leaving her with his brother. She was at the housewarming party with a weak alibi, and she knew where her friend kept a black cape that could have disguised her."

"We've seen someone on Mia's Run wearing a black cape," Jessie reminded them, but to protect Tori's safety, they did not reveal Tori's secret.

Jessie walked to the stove to stir her tomatoes in a bold and spicy tomato sauce for a pasta dinner. I recalled that she had spent much time in the kitchen when she lived with Sue. I had spent much time on the kitchen floor awaiting a morsel to fall.

"Remind me to give you some tomatoes," Jessie said while she stirred the pot. "We have a solid crop this year, and I don't want them to go to waste."

Sue recalled how Jessie insisted on controlling the ingredients in her home-cooked dishes. "I'm dead set against processed food," Jessie said, "Now, more than ever."

"Your sauce smells delicious," Sue said. "I miss you and Beth living with me."

"People should be rewarded for healthy living and eating," Jessie said. "Tax credits, insurance discounts, rewards for a job well done."

"It's the first step to lowering our chronic disease epidemic and health insurance costs," Mia agreed. "I've been trying to encourage Thomas to lose weight."

"That's how my mother raised us," Sue agreed. "I tried to pass that philosophy down to Loretta and my granddaughter."

"How is Lucy?" Jessie asked, and Sue replied that she missed her mother, but Zeke had taken good care of her.

"Loretta must miss Lucy," Jessie said, and Mia said she hoped the judge would grant bail.

Jessie was writing a cookbook called CHEWS—Food for Fitness. The recipes were Cheap, Healthy, Easy, Wholesome, and Spicy. She donated the recipes to the parents of schoolchildren, including Rita's classroom, to inspire them to cook healthier.

"Some parents don't know what's in their children's food," Jessie told Mia. "If you have a recipe you'd like to share, please let me know."

"I'm the easy recipe person," Sue explained. Rita is the cheap-recipe person, and Peter is the spicy-recipe person. Everyone believes in Wholesome and Healthy recipes, but Fred and Stanley aren't always cooperative."

"Imagine that!" Mia said. "Fred is a bit surly."

"Rita is just the opposite," Sue said, and Mia mentioned she had noticed.

"It's going to take a few generations to educate the public on healthy living," Jessie said. "Processed food is easy, but it's not healthy."

"I'd love to be in your cookbook," Mia said. "I'll remember your recipe book if I make something you might enjoy."

"Vegetables are expensive," Jessie added, " but not so much when you grow your garden."

"What can we do to help solve the murder?" Chris asked while Jessie cooked fresh vegetables and herbs in the simmering pot.

"We think Phil's murderer was wearing a black trench coat," Sue said, and Mia added they had been asking around if some of the guests were wearing a black trench coat or had one hanging on their chairs.

"Now that you mention it, the Cattleman had a black trench coat on his chair," Jessie said, and Chris agreed he openly despised Phil for threatening him with an atrocious silver handgun to sell his property.

"The same thing he did to Loretta," Sue agreed. "Eventually, she convinced herself Phil wanted it for Gio to launder money."

"Gio and Val are becoming closer to Thomas and me now that Tori is missing," Mia said.

"Why?" Chris asked, and Mia had no specific answer except possibly to honor her memory by protecting the river.

"Who knows?" Jessie said, and Chris agreed it was worth looking into.

"According to Loretta, the person who assaulted her was short, and the cattleman is tall," Sue said, and Mia agreed it left him out of the list of suspects.

"Sarah sat at our table," Chris said. "But we had no idea she might be a suspect."

"I'm trying to clear her name forever," Mia replied. "When this case is resolved, I plan to tell Thomas she is his stepdaughter."

"Thomas will welcome Sarah with open arms," Chris said, and Jessie agreed he was a good man who would love having her in his life with Mia.

Jessie poured two bowls of freshly made tomato sauce for Mia and Sue to take home, with instructions on how to eat or freeze it. When we walked to the car, Chris gave them each a bag of tomatoes and a container of fresh jalapenos. He gave me a dog biscuit to munch on for the ride to Sarah's house. It was a productive visit with no new leads but one more black trench coat accounted for.

If nothing else, Mia got to know Jessie better and might one day join the cookbook club that brought joy to healthy eating for the families of Sweetwater Springs.

Chapter 26

Sarah

I was extra tired the following morning when Toby extended his striped
leg under the door to greet Sue. I was still lying on the bed, stretched in
a comfy repose next to Sue, when his paw clunked under the door, causing
the wood to bang against the doorjam like a pack of rats in the rafters. Toby
often made noise during the night, making me think of rats, although I
couldn't always figure out what new mischief he had gotten himself into.
It was silly of me because we didn't have rats at the river house.

Toby was full of mischief at night but slept most of the day. Unlike
Toby, I sleep day and night unless Sue takes me on a mission, as she has
been doing more often since Loretta was arrested. Today, I was tired when
Toby awakened us because of where we went and the people we met to find
Phil's killer. Toby, on the other hand, had stayed home and slept all day.

"Hi, Toby!" Sue said, opening the door to pet the cat, who arched his
back in agreement with her friendly affection.

I was barely awake when I peeked out underneath my furry eyebrows,
head furrowed, to see him racing to pounce on the bed. I have never
understood why Toby races to jump on the bed nor why he springs a foot
above it for the landing. He's old enough to gauge his landing without
the extra effort of the high jump, but he still acts like a kitten on a mission
when he greets me on the bed.

I stretched my front legs forward when Toby nuzzled against my neck. It was an act of love that would wake me up for the day. Before long, I was off the bed and headed to the door for my morning potty break before my breakfast of dog kibble.

Mia arrived shortly after I had breakfast. She met Sue for coffee in the dining room. Sitting on the porch and watching the alligators over their cups of steaming brew was too hot, so they stayed indoors for coffee.

"I miss the rain," Sue said, and Mia agreed it was a relief from the summer heat.

"It hasn't rained since my housewarming party," Mia replied. "And I didn't expect it to rain that night."

"Lately, it's been a drought or a deluge in Sweetwater Springs," Sue said after she sipped her coffee. "There's no in-between."

"We used to have daily afternoon rain showers," Mia agreed. "The weather is changing and less predictable. I can't imagine living in Sweetwater Springs before air-conditioning," she added.

"When my family came to Florida, my schools had no air conditioning," Sue explained. "We had big fans and hot classrooms."

"That wasn't so long ago," Mia replied. "It's hard to believe my husband's generation was amongst the first to have air conditioning in their classrooms."

"And their homes," Sue added. "Air conditioning and color TV were two of the biggest changes in my lifetime."

I stretched on the cool tile beside the dining table while they talked. Back then, dogs lived outdoors and dug holes in the shade, as I still loved to do.

"I enjoyed visiting Jessie and Chris yesterday," Mia said, and Sue agreed they were good people. "Did you try Jessie's fresh tomato marinara sauce?"

"Yes, it was delicious with the jalapeno peppers for a kick!" Mia replied. "Thomas liked it too."

"Jessie loves spicy flavors. When this is resolved, we should plan a dinner party with them," Sue said. You'll enjoy their company."

"They are some of my closest neighbors," Mia replied. "I'd love to get to know them better."

"They live close enough to have seen someone wearing a black cape on Mia's Run," Sue reminded her. "But they don't know it was Tori."

"How well do you know Tori?" Mia asked, and Sue replied, mainly from the pub. "We never did anything socially."

"She seems like a good person who cared as much about the river as most locals," Sue added. "Her husband is a different story."

I lay my furry head flat against the tile while they talked. I'd be ready to start the day if I could get in a few more Z's. It didn't take much to refresh me. Soon, I'd be rearing to go.

"Sarah knows Tori best of all," Mia said. "Now that we know more, we should see her again."

Sue agreed that it was a worthy visit. Sarah was a suspect with a weak alibi—actually untrue since she was with Tori— who needed justice as much as Loretta. Sue cleared the dishes, and we hopped into Mia's SUV to drive to the condominiums.

I led the way up the stairs to Sarah's third-story unit, with Sue in tow and Mia following. This time, I was prepared to be a stair master while Sue and Mia were huffing and puffing.

When they reached the unit and Sarah invited them in, Mia asked, "How do you do this daily?"

"I do it several times a day," Sarah replied, "It's good exercise."

"It should be illegal," Mia said, and Sarah said they were getting an elevator.

"You're getting soft, Mom," Sarah said, inviting us to sit in the living room.

The sun shone in from the east through Sarah's big front window. Sue, Mia, and Sarah gathered around a coffee table with a driftwood base and a glass top. I lay under the table on a furry carpet while they talked.

"We think Phil's killer was wearing a black trench coat," Mia said, and Sue agreed that it may have seemed like a cape to Loretta, but it was more likely a raincoat.

"That makes sense," Sarah said. It was drizzling, and a cape would have been soaked.

"We are trying to figure out who had a black raincoat the night of the housewarming party," Sue said.

"We know there were five of them hanging on a rack in the tent," Mia added. "But we don't know who they belonged to."

"We know Phil and Loretta both wore a plastic disposable cape," Sue added. "We found them in Mia's dumpster and found hairs on them, and the lab tested the roots for their DNA."

"How did you get a laboratory to do that?" Sarah asked, and Mia reminded her that Gio and Val were connected to people who could do it.

"We think someone, short wearing a black raincoat, grabbed her from behind."

"I'll try to think of someone who may have brought a black trench coat to the party, but I'm drawing a blank for now," Sarah said.

"My dad was deadbeat," she said, "but I'm over it. He was a con, a cheater, and a liar. Maybe another woman had his baby, just like my mom had me."

"Nella wouldn't be pleased about that," Mia said. "It enhances her motive to murder him."

"Maybe she's asked him for money for child support," Sarah suggested, and Sue agreed it could happen.

"We know he cheated on Nella," Sue said, and Mia said they called it an open marriage.

"I'll think about the black trench coat," Sarah said, "Maybe I'll think of something."

Sue and Mia digested the information with Sarah. The DNA lab had required connections, but they knew little about Gio and Val. Gio was Tori's father, but they knew little else about the history.

"How did Tori and Dave meet?" Sue asked.

"They met in middle school," Sarah replied. "Most kids didn't want anything to do with Tori because they feared her dad's reputation, so it was hard for her to make friends."

"I can believe that," Sue said.

"She couldn't wait to move away and start a new life where nobody knew her," Sarah added. "I was happy for her to come to Sweetwater Springs when she married Dave."

"It was a fresh start for Tori," Sue agreed.

"Tori was Dave's meal ticket," Sarah said. "She was the best chance he had for a better life, but he still had to work hard at the pub."

"Gio and Val were very kind to me, but I didn't want to impose on them, nor Tori's chance to move away, so I stayed back until recently when Dave started mistreating her."

"That's understandable," Mia said. "That's what friends are for."

Chapter 27

Luke's Mansion

I was excited to go to Luke's house on Saturday night. I missed running with my cousins at Loretta's house and barely had a chance to stretch my legs at Chris and Jessie's house. I had enjoyed racing across the yard to greet Chris, but their senior dog, Redman, was no match for a younger, spirited Doodle as an exercise partner. We spent most of our time lounging indoors while Sue and Mia talked to Jessie and Chris.

On the other hand, Luke's Hound Dog, Artemis, had the youth and the drive to romp around Luke's enormous yard. Please forgive my lack of humility; Artemis has his strengths, just as I do. He has a stronger sense of smell—Luke claims he could follow his nose off a cliff. I am a faster runner, and I don't shed.

Artemis covers Luke's house in a short-haired dog shed, which gives his mother, nonagenarian Sophie, something to complain about. According to Luke, his mother accounts for her ninety-something years by pursuing her three favorite activities: complaining, giving advice, and caring for her family, which accounts for many superior niches.

Sophie follows Artemis around with a hand-held vacuum and a wet sponge. She claims the damp sponge is better for removing fur from the furniture than roller tape. I don't think it has occurred to Sophie that I don't shed, but she does enjoy sharing fur-removing advice with Sue, who lets her ramble and rant to her heart's content.

It's a nifty thing I don't shed since I'm a 50:50 Doodle. My mother was an Australian Shepherd, and my father was a Poodle. Poodles don't shed, but Australian Shepherds are shedders of soft fur that bundle in clumps. My parents were both fast runners, but you never know which side of the shed or shed-free ticket a 50:50 mix will generate.

I was happy to see Artemis in the big yard when Luke drove through the gates to his mansion—as most locals call it- and parked. I could feel my heart pumping for the vigor of the run I had been missing with Loretta in jail. I happily launched out of the back seat onto the soft grass to play with my four-footed friend.

"Look at Daisy, go!" Luke said as we sped in great circles, and Sue replied, "It looks like Artemis has been missing their play dates, too."

Sue and Luke chuckled to watch us playing in the grass. Sometimes, I would stop and lie on my belly to feel the soft blades. When Artemis passed, I launched into the race from a puppy pose before one of us dropped belly down for another rest.

"They're getting tired," Luke said before we'd start up again.

"Daisy needed this," Sue replied as they watched another round.

Sophie's grandson, who happened to be Jessie's daughter's not-so-secret crush, joined us to watch the races' fits and starts. "They're having fun, Nonni," the young man said. "I wish Beth could see them."

"How is Beth?" Sue asked since she hadn't seen her at Jessie's house.

"Great!" he replied. "She was here a few days ago."

"Nice," Sue said. "I saw her Mom a few days ago, too."

"I haven't seen Jessie in a while," Sophie said. "We should get together sometime."

"Jessie and Chris would enjoy that," Sue said, grabbing a large basket of tomatoes from the front seat. "She asked me to bring these tomatoes for you," Sue said. "She had a bumper crop this year, spreading the love."

"The only thing better than Jessie's tomatoes is a Sicilian tomato," Sophie replied. "I know just what to do with these beauties."

Some experts believe the Mediterranean diet is the healthiest diet on earth. The Mediterranean region is known for the quality of its vegetables. An area of Sicily was known for some of the longest-lived people, as Sophie happened to be in Sweetwater Springs. Sophie believed in the benefits of whole foods before most Americans recognized the chronic illnesses related to processed food.

"I don't eat anything from a bag or a can," Sophie said. "I make homemade bread and freeze my fresh homemade sauces."

"That's good," Jessie said. There are no artificial ingredients or ultra-processing to increase shelf life. We now know the body doesn't recognize certain chemicals, and they can cause health problems."

"In Sicily, we didn't have to learn that," Sophie had said. "We went to fresh markets every day."

"As we should do," Jessie said as she pondered how we had gotten so far off course with easy cooking rather than healthy living.

Sophie lived and ate as Jessie did her entire life. Still, healthy cooking took a long time to catch on in Sweetwater Springs with the onslaught of fatty fast food choices and bagged chips. "We don't have such foods in Sicily," she said. "I wouldn't call it food!"

Sophie moved to Sweetwater Springs in the fifties. During World War II, she married Luke's father, an American soldier. She remembered when Patton's troops marched through Palermo during the war in Sicily. She remembered seeking shelter in bomb shelters.

"It was like a tornado," she said. "Hit or miss, with one building destroyed and the next left untouched."

Sophie had first-hand experience with the history of World War II, which she divulged as requested rather than on a podium as she did with food and advice. "The Americans liberated us from the tyranny of Mussolini, who threatened to destroy our freedom. For that, we owe them thanks. According to Sophie, the mafia's organized connections were an asset in relaying information about the enemy during the war.

"The mafia was helpful with Patton's march to liberate Sicily," she had said, "but it was also a criminal organization with various divisions of racketeering."

She was open and transparent about her life. She had first-hand experience with the Sicilian mafia and knew its history. She considered herself the foremost expert on the mafia and its newest associates in Sweetwater Springs, Gio, and Val.

Luke invited us to dinner to indulge Sophie, who wanted to know the details of the murder investigation. She had little to offer regarding the black trench coat since she hadn't been at the housewarming party. However, she stayed engaged in analyzing the suspects and her favorite, offering her advice.

We walked inside the house and settled at the dining room table. Artemis and I sat beside Luke, who was more likely to toss us a treat than Sue.

Sophie offered us coffee because she rarely drank alcohol, except on special occasions.

"Mom, I"m half Italian, and Sue is part French; how about opening a bottle of red wine tonight?" Luke suggested.

"Of course, Honey," Sophie said, and she brought a bottle and glasses from the wine cabinet. "This should be delicious with my lasagna," she said as she poured the drinks.

"I understand you have been talking to suspects," she said, and Luke added, "Be careful...one of them is a killer."

"Who do you think killed Phil?" Sophie asked bluntly as she sliced and dished the lasagna.

"We don't know," Sue replied, taking the first plate. "We are closer to a list of who didn't kill him."

"Do share!" Sophie said.

"The cattleman and the mayor had black trench coats at the party, but the cattleman is too tall, and the mayor has a shabby motive," Sue said. "Phil was a con, an opportunist, and a lousy neighbor, but that doesn't account for murder."

"Continue!"

"Loretta was framed by someone who knew Phil wanted to buy the clinic," Sue said.

Why would someone want the clinic?" Sophie asked, and Sue reminded her it could be used as a laundromat.

"Lots of businesses could be used as laundromats," Sophie replied. "The book cookers can push more money through struggling and cash businesses. It's possible, but not likely."

"Sarah had a secret alibi," Sue continued. "She wasn't truthful about her whereabouts during the murder."

"Was she with a married man?" Sophie asked, and Sue said no, she was trying to protect a friend who needed her help.

"Seems to me that girl needs help," Sophie said. "She's a call girl, for heaven's sake."

"She used to be a call girl," Luke reminded his mother as he stabbed a forkful of lasagna. When this is over, she's getting into a more legitimate business back in Sweetwater Springs."

"Good for her!" Sophie said, "I'd like to meet Sarah."

"That can be arranged," Luke replied.

"Nella doesn't seem the type to murder her husband, but Sarah suggested Phil might have another baby by another woman."

"Good point!" Sophie said. "Maybe Phil was paying child support, and Nella didn't like it."

"Nella mentioned they didn't have much money," Sue said. "Phil spent everything he made,"

"You should revisit Nella," Sophie said, and Sue mentioned they had taken a glass with her DNA on it if something turned up as evidence to compare.

"DNA?" Sophie asked. "You're not a forensics laboratory!"

"Yes, but Gio and Val have become closer to Thomas and Mia since Tori disappeared. "They know people who can get things accomplished."

"Interesting!" Sophie replied.

"We found three different types of hair, with roots attached, on disposable raincoats in Mia's dumpster," Sue explained. "One from Phil and one from Loretta. When we have a third suspect, we'll compare the evidence."

"You should compare the third hair to Nella's DNA on the glass."

Luke and Sue finished a bottle of wine and a slice of tiramisu for dessert. The dinner was delicious, with bites of bread and morsels of lasagna falling for Artemis and me. The company was informative. By the time they were done eating, Luke was becoming concerned about Sue's safety during her investigations.

He knew a private investigator from his travels who could help them protect themselves.

Chapter 28

Val and Gio

G io and Val had been visiting Sweetwater Springs ever since Tori disappeared. Like me, their fluffy little dog, Jelly Bean, attracted attention because he was warm and fuzzy. Jelly Bean was confident and harmless and loved no one but Gio. He didn't especially like Val, who had her dog, a yappy pup, who would bite the fingers of the mailman if he could.

Since I am an only dog, my loyalty is to Sue—but I like most people—unlike Jelly Bean, who couldn't care less. I can quickly tell good people from bad people, but sometimes, my good sense is diverted by people who let me get away with things that Sue would disapprove of. For example, Gio let me jump on him.

Gio would lean down, get in my face, hug me, and let me jump on his chest. Sue would tug on my leash, make me get down, and give Gio a dirty look.

"I don't want Daisy jumping on people," she would say to Gio. "It could be dangerous if she jumped on older people, like Sophie."

"Who's Sophie?" he would ask, and he had never met her, but Sue would explain she was Luke's Sicilian ninety-four-year-old mother.

"Aww, you mean Sophie is my cousin!" Gio would say, and Sue would grunt. Not every Sicilian had mafia ties, but every Sicilian knew more about the organization than the average local in Sweetwater Springs.

Gio saw—or pretended to see— no one's point of view but mine, and he knew I loved to jump. "You're a big man, and she doesn't hurt you, but she's strong enough to knock a small person down," Sue would say, but it got her nowhere.

Quite frankly, I knew better than to jump on people, but sometimes excitement got the better. I was so happy to see Gio that I forgot my manners. Gio wasn't used to saying no to me, and he loved encouraging the jumping interaction, so Sue avoided him on dog walks in the neighborhood.

"I think he does it on purpose," she had confided in Luke, but he didn't answer. They were good neighbors, but it was better to avoid conflict.

Gio and Val rented a series of bed and breakfasts on the riverfront, some of which were in Sue's neighborhood. Recently, they had rented a big brick house two streets away for a month, but they still traveled back and forth between Miami and Sweetwater Springs.

Sue wrestled with keeping Tori's secret from her family, but she understood her motives. When Dave had enough money, he'd leave on his own, but for now, she was in danger of a second murder attempt if Dave knew she was alive. It was safer to surface after he left Sweetwater Springs and could start fresh.

"Do you want to go for a walk?" Sue asked Mia while eating watermelon and toast for breakfast on the back porch.

"Sure," Mia replied since she had arrived early and the heat hadn't intensified to its full fury. "I'll make ice water for both of us."

"I'll bring a collapsible water dish for Daisy," Sue said. She can also have some ice water."

When I heard the word "walk," I lunged into motion. Certain words were buzzwords in my limited vocabulary. Walks were good, wherever they took us if we started early.

Ice water was the second best option to lying on my belly in the cool river, which I preferred to many summer activities. Sue had a fantastic cup with a handle that kept the ice frozen throughout our walks. I liked ice, whatever the occasion, but it was best on a hot walk.

Sue and Mia walked onto the front porch with two insulated steel cups and me on a leash. "I heard Val and Gio are back in the neighborhood," Rita called from across the street, and Sue cringed.

"Don't you want to see them?" Mia asked, and Sue explained the nearly impossible jumping ritual.

"Gio likes to razz people," Mia said, "But his contacts have been beneficial."

"Should I ask if he wants to buy the clinic to launder money?" Sue cajoled, and Mia suggested the negative, although it had caused Loretta much trouble to speculate.

"How's Loretta?" Mia asked, and Sue said the judge had granted bail, and she should be released shortly."

"I'm so happy for her," Mia said. "It's one thing to be falsely accused and quite another to be falsely incarcerated."

Sue reminded her they were still looking for proof, and Mia agreed they weren't out of the woods. "We're making progress," she said. "One step forward, two steps backward."

We followed the shadiest path up the hill and turned right towards one of the cat colonies Peter had transported for spays and neuters at the rescue. "I didn't see Toby this morning," Mia said, and Sue explained he was one of the most affectionate cats of her lifetime, but he had to get to know you before he felt comfortable.

"They are all so different," Mia said. "I'm happy that Sarah is enjoying Tom."

"He's good for her," Sue agreed. "This is a major stepping stone in her life, as she plans to leave Miami behind and settle in Sweetwater Springs."

"The two cities are like night and day," Mia replied. "Exciting and busy versus slow and steady and personal."

"Why do you think Dave prefers Miami?" Sue asked.

"Maybe he's jealous Tori fit in better than he did," Mia said. "Or maybe he has another woman, and Tori was in the way."

We walked along a riverfront street in the next neighborhood where Gio and Val had rented the house. When I saw Gio, the familiar heartthrob pulsed in my chest. With most people, I could control my excitement, but not him. Shortly after that, I stood nearly as tall as he was.

"Dave was using Tori, and he's using us," Gio said, bending over for a dog kiss, followed by a standing ovation on my rear feet. "We bought them the pub but didn't think they would last together."

"We buy you a business, and you're one of us," Gio added, resting my front paws on his chest. "We're like family."

Sue scowled, but she didn't chastise Gio as she had before. Scolding Gio would likely make him worse, and I was already finding my way to four paws on the pavement. Avoidance could work another day when they weren't searching for clues.

"In Dave's case, you're out of here," Val said. "That's why the pub reverted to us after Tori's death in the Prenup."

"If you don't like Dave, why don't you fire him?" Mia asked.

"Until they find Tori's dead body, it's still his pub," Gio said, and Val agreed they were praying for a miracle. "There's no murder without a body," Gio reminded her.

"What will you do if they find her body?" Mia asked, although she knew Tori was in the guesthouse with Sarah.

"We want to join Thomas in his hotel business," Gio said. "Saving the river is the least we can do for Tori."

"Thank you for connecting us with people in the DNA laboratory," Mia said as I chewed an ice cube from my collapsible water bowl. "It's helpful to rule out suspects."

"One day, we hope for a match," Sue added.

"Some people think Sarah may not be Phil's only baby," Mia said, and Val agreed they should follow up on the lead. "Sarah is over Phil, but who knows what happened to the next girl.'

"Phil is a deadbeat," Val said, and Gio agreed he was a pig.

"Sarah was a good friend to Tori," Val said. "It's not easy having Gio as a father."

"We asked her to live with us, but she didn't want to interfere with Tori's romance with Dave."

"That's Sarah," Mia agreed. "Always thinking of someone else first."

"That's a dying virtue," Val replied, and Sue said it shouldn't be.

"Gio kept Sarah from getting hurt," Val added, and Gio said it was a rough line of work.

"I hope she stays away from it forever," Mia replied.

Chapter 29

The Guest House

T he following morning, we had to stealthily go to Baldwin's guest house. Few people knew Tori was alive, and almost no one knew that the house was occupied. A few people may have begun to suspect her presence, or someone else's presence, after the walks to Mia's Run that helped her keep her sanity.

By now, she had begun to shed the black cape more often. Swimming in Mia's Run rejuvenated her. The cold water was refreshing and renewed her spirits. She felt like a new woman when she emerged from the springs-fed run. I remembered the exhilarating feeling from my dog paddles across the creek and downstream.

After Phil's murder, Tori still tossed the cape whenever she could. Tori was convinced someone had worn a black trenchcoat to frame Loretta with the gun. Still, it was a ubiquitous look. Anyone with the appropriate physique and features—short, muscular, and dark-haired—could have worn the trenchcoat at Phil's murder.

Tori knew the third hair on the disposable raincoats was dark, so the laboratory analyzed it to compare the DNA sample to Nella's hair. Since many people in Sweetwater Springs had dark hair, there wasn't much to go on. Finding the killer by a hair sample was like finding a needle in a haystack. The odds weren't good, but ruling out people who weren't Phil's killer was also helpful.

Most of the hired hands at the Baldwin mansion had dark hair. One day, Tori thought she may have seen one of them watching her at the creek when she took the cape off. There was only so long Tori could keep her whereabouts a secret. One day, someone would reveal her hideaway to whomever they pleased.

Dave, who had left her for dead, would not be pleased to know she was alive. The alligator hoax would make him and the sheriff's office look stupid. The search had cost a bundle of money, mostly from her parents.

Tori had been living in near seclusion for months. It was almost like solitary confinement, except for her friend and her mother's visits. Sarah always brought something fun to do—like a new game or a painting project. Finally, after yoga, Pilates, and meditation, Tori started asking for yarn, and she began to knit.

Mia drove through the gates of their property with Sarah in the front and Sue and me in the back of the SUV. I watched out the window as one of the gardeners couldn't keep his eyes off the vehicle. He followed the SUV with his eyes as it forked off into one of the most remote locations on the expansive grounds.

"That one's been watching us," Mia said. "I've seen him following us with his eyes before."

"That's scary," Sarah said. "He could be a whistleblower about Tori's whereabouts to Dave or anyone else."

"Do you think he knows where the cabin is?" Sue asked.

"Yes, but he may or may not know that Tori is living in the cabin."

"She thinks someone has seen her at the creek," Sarah said, and everyone agreed she needed to batten down the hatches until this was over.

"I wonder if he's the same gardener who lost a wildlife camera at the creek," Sarah said under her breath, but Mia heard her and made her repeat it.

"What?" Sue asked.

"A wildlife camera," Sarah repeated. "One of the hired hands hung a wildlife camera in a tree by the creek, but it disappeared."

"Before or after Phil's murder?" Sue asked, and I felt her skin turn hot.

"Months before Phil's murder," Sarah replied. "It wasn't on video if that's what you're thinking."

"Yes," Sue agreed, Phil's murder isn't on video, but whatever Dave did to Tori that night he left her at the creek could be.

Mia drove to the front of the cabin and parked in the driveway. If anyone asked, the story was that Sarah wanted a new place to live, and the cabin was available. Mia ascended the stairs, followed by Sarah and Sue, with me padding along on all fours in front of her.

The stairs were not as tall as the steep ones to Sarah's apartment. When the time came, it would be a good move for Sarah to be closer to her mother. First, Mia had to prove her daughter's innocence and inform Thomas about his stepdaughter.

When we arrived at the top of the stairs, Tori did not come to her door. Instead, Mia unlocked the door as if she were a realtor showing it to Sarah, who gushed at the inside of the luxury cabin.

"I love it!" she exclaimed as if someone were listening. "When can I move in?"

We walked inside the cabin without groceries, which Sue and her friends could bring later. The SUV had food and snacks, but it didn't fit the setup after we saw the gardener watching the vehicle.

"What's going on?" Tori asked before we settled in the living room.

"That gardener has been watching us again," Mia whispered, and we sat on the couches.

I pretended to watch squirrels out the window while the ladies talked. It's remarkable what a dog can get away with, and people would be suspicious if other people did the same things. I could watch for the gardener—or anyone else—out the window for as long as I pleased without drawing a scrap of unwanted attention.

Sometimes, I barked for the heck of it. Sometimes, I raced between windows, barking at flies—or appearing to be. Sue would nod in disgust and tell me to be quiet, but it did no good.

I am smarter than Sue thinks I am. Don't get me wrong, Sue thinks I'm smart, but I'm smarter than she knows. I acted as a decoy to distract the peeping Tom, but Sue didn't know.

"What happened here that night when Dave and you kayaked up Mia's Run?" Sue asked when I was quiet.

Tori summed it up without embellishment: "Dave pushed me backward out of the kayak. I hit my head on a rock, and it knocked me out."

"You're lucky it didn't kill you," Sue said, and Tori reminded her that Dave thought it did.

"Did Dave ever hit you?" Sue asked, and Tori replied that he shoved her more often, and she fell. "We both thought he would love it in Sweetwater Springs, but he didn't like it."

"You could have tried living somewhere else," Sue suggested, but Tori had no interest. "This is my place, my river, and my people," she said. "I want to live here forever."

"Forever is a long time," Sarah said, but Tori didn't budge.

I lurched in a wild bark at the window when I saw the gardener hiding in the bushes, causing the man to retreat. Sue joined me in investigating the scene, but he was gone.

"What's that about?" Tori asked.

"That's how Daisy barks when she sees a person," Sue says. "She's being protective, although she's mostly an alarm dog."

Tori took a deep breath before she spoke. "Lately, I've been thinking about that night Dave and I paddled up Mia's Run," she said. "If he thought I was dead, he'd want to destroy the evidence."

"What evidence?" Sue asked.

"One of the hired hands at the Baldwins' mansion kept a motion camera in the tree by the creek," she said.

"How do you know that?" Mia asked.

"He used to come to the pub and talk to Dave about the wildlife he recorded on the camera," Tori replied. "Dave usually hated to talk about the river, but he was interested in hearing about motion cameras."

"You mean Dave was actively listening?" Sarah asked, surprised.

"Yes, Tori replied, "Dave was all ears when he talked about the videos on the motion camera."

"How was it stored?" Sue asked, and Tori replied, "On a memory card."

"Where is the camera now?" Sue asked, and Tori said it had disappeared about the same time Dave pushed her out of the kayak.

I stared out the window quietly after the gardener disappeared into the wetlands. Now, I sat on my furry haunches without a yip. The man was gone, and it was safe to walk downstairs.

"If Dave thought I was alive, he'd try to kill me again," Tori reminded us as she donned the black cape for one of the last times ever. "My parents would never forgive him for leaving me at the creek."

When the coast was clear, we walked downstairs to get the groceries out of Mia's SUV. Four people were descending the stairs now, whereas there had been three, but no one seemed to be watching. I could feel the eyes upon us without seeing a person. Dogs are much more insightful about watchers than people.

"Dave's safest bet was to make enough money to leave Sweetwater Springs and start over," Sarah said. "Tori was too nice to him."

"Maybe so," Tori agreed. "But I remember better days when life was a dream, and he was a better man."

The ladies, now becoming better friends in the murderous fiasco, carried the groceries upstairs and filled the cabinets and refrigerator with fruits, nuts, and vegetables. The pieces unraveled one step at a time, but not everything fit together in a neat puzzle. A motion camera was missing; it seemed like something Dave would want to review.

Maybe Dave came back for the camera after he left Tori behind. If it belonged to the gardener, perhaps he told him Tori was still alive.

"Let's walk in the woods," Sue said. "I want to review the locations where the camera was, and Dave pushed you out of the kayak."

"That's a good plan," Mia agreed after they unpacked the groceries.

I had not been barking because no one was watching, but the evidence was mounting. Everyone wanted to know who knew what, how much had already been shared, and with whom. Sue attached my leash to my collar, and the ladies prepared for a walk in the woods.

Chapter 30

A Walk in the Woods

W hen Sue was sure the gardener was gone, she attached my leash to my collar for a walk in the woods. We descended the stairs, with me in the lead, followed by Sarah, Tori, and Mia. It was a familiar walk for Tori, who had visited the creek often during her months in captivity.

"How did you live alone in the woods for so long?" Mia asked as they trudged down the trail toward the creek.

"It wasn't always easy," Tori replied. "But it gave me time to think."

"It must be scary to think your husband would try to kill you," Sue said.

"I never thought I'd have thoughts like that," Tori agreed. "But, I don't think he was trying to kill me when he pushed me out of the kayak. I think he left me for dead after it happened."

"That's cowardly of him," Sarah reminded her, and Tori said her family could be intimidating.

"It's worse if he came back for the camera after he thought he killed you," Sue said, and Mia agreed that it was cold and incriminating for Dave to remove the evidence that could be on the memory card.

It was quiet, hot, and humid in the woods. The grounds were sopped with water from the wetlands, making it harder for a dog like me to detect smells. Although it hadn't rained since Phil's murder, the wetlands surrounding the creek were soggy, as they should be when nature is in balance.

I could smell blood on one of the trees where a branch had been torn away. Blood smells like copper, but I wasn't familiar enough with the scent to detect one person's blood type over another. I was familiar enough to know someone had been cut and bled in the woods.

I stopped to sniff the torn branch, alerting Sue to the location. She examined the broken limb and saw the frays from a torn shirt.

"Somebody has been here," Sue said, examining the micro-cloth. "It must have been recently because this tiny fabric would have washed away."

Mia sighed to think someone could have been on the Baldwin property without her knowledge, but it wouldn't have been difficult. There were many ways to enter the majestic estate without crossing the fence line. It wouldn't have been difficult to enter by the river, but the dogs guarded the property at night and would have detected someone on the groomed lawns. The land closest to the house was protected by cameras and monitored by a 24-hour staff.

Closer to the river, it was different. Some staff members placed wildlife cameras in those locations for personal interest. Some of the men were deer hunters, while others had a personal interest in alligators.

"His name was Carlos," Tori said, without explanation.

"Who?" Sarah asked.

"The man who used to come to the pub and tell Dave about the wildlife camera he kept near the creek."

"I haven't seen a motion detection camera since I've been going to the creek," Tori said. "Someone must have taken it."

"Carlos doesn't make a lot of money," Sarah said. "He must have been mad when someone took his camera."

"He was always talking about it," Tori said. "Anyone at Cat Tails could have heard him."

"What did he see on the camera?" Sue asked, and Tori explained Carlos was particularly interested in the alligators. "He watched them hunt for their prey on the night vision camera."

Alligators were known to hurl their bodies high above the water to grasp their prey and spin it beneath it to drown it. While the prey varied, it could be larger, like the deer that roamed in the woods or, occasionally, the wild boar that roamed the river.

"Carlos had a video of an alligator taking a deer," Tori said. "Dave was mesmerized by watching it."

"That must be why he came up with the idea of an alligator taking you when the search and rescue teams couldn't find you," Sue said.

"Maybe he believed it," Tori replied, and Mia said that the locals knew an alligator would have stored some of the remains for later. "Pardon me for saying so, but the search and rescue teams would have found them."

"If Dave had taken the camera, he also knew Mia and Sarah would have saved you the next morning," Sue reminded her, and Tori agreed he wouldn't have wanted her parents to know he had left her there.

We walked past the location where Phil Coleman had been murdered. The crime scene tape still surrounded the oak tree closest to where he had been shot. I could smell the blood that had spattered outside the tape, but Sue didn't let me wander to sniff inside the tape.

"Do forensics have all the evidence they need?" Mia asked as we passed the scene.

"I think so," Sue replied. "Stanley hired his private investigator to collect evidence, as well."

"It sounds like they've covered the bases," Sarah said, and everyone agreed it was better than leaving the investigation to the sheriff and his deputy in a substation without a detective.

"How is Loretta?" Mia asked.

"She's happy to be home with Zeke and Lucy," Sue said. "The judge released her from jail to her home and work."

"Too bad she can't join us," Mia said, and Sue agreed she'd be good at the investigative work. "Maybe next time," she said.

We walked past where Tori buried an extra cape in a box. "Aren't you hot with that on?" Sue asked, and Tori said she'd be thrilled when she could take it off, once and for all, forever. "It's been stifling," she said. "A dip in the creek has been the only way to make it bearable."

Everyone agreed the water was refreshing. I tugged at the leash to take a swim, and Sue let me dip my belly in the river.

"Daisy loves the cool water on a hot day," Sue said as I laid down with my head above water.

"Back in the day, people thought the springs had health benefits," Mia said, and Sue agreed they were probably right.

We found the tree where the motion-detection camera had been hung on the opposite side of the creek. A nearly hidden hook was the only thing left of its past presence near the river.

"This is where Dave pushed me out of the kayak," Tori said, pointing to a location in range of the camera's hook.

"I never saw a camera hanging there," Sarah said, looking at the hook.

"That's because it's never been there since you came home from Miami," Mia said.

"Someone must have taken that camera within a short time of Dave pushing Tori out."

"Someone who wanted it real bad," Sarah said. "Someone who wanted to alleviate the evidence."

We walked back to the cabin in thought-provoking companionship. It had been a productive walk with much to know and digest. When we returned to the cabin, Tori alerted us to something we had never heard before.

"I've been hearing footsteps around my cabin for the last two nights," Tori said. "Somebody knows I'm here."

'That's frightening," Sarah replied. "I'll stay with you."

"Thanks, Sweetie, I'll be all right," Tori said. "I wouldn't want anything to happen to you."

"What do you mean you'll be all right?" Sarah screeched. "You have zero protection in these woods and wetlands."

"You need a bodyguard," Mia said, and Sue agreed we were close to finding the solution.

"Someone is running scared," Sue said, and Mia decided, "Somebody may not want you alive."

Tori agreed that she didn't feel as safe as she used to in the cabin. Today, we were followed by a gardener who seemed more interested than he should have been in the current occupants. They could have told Dave or anyone if someone knew Tori was there.

"Do you mind if I share your secret with Luke?" Sue asked. "He may know a bodyguard."

"Yes, I'd appreciate that," Tori replied. "I've been in the woods for six months. I'm ready to come back to work at the pub."

We were getting closer to the truth, with a few details remaining. I was happy to stop at Luke's house for a romp with Artemis before the end of the day. Whoever was onto Tori's disappearance, she needed a bodyguard, and Luke was the best man in town to find one.

Chapter 31

Luke's Mansion

It was a short drive from the Baldwin's guesthouse to Luke Wilson's estate downriver. Mia was excited to visit Luke's house, as she had never been inside the home closest to hers. Luke's house had direct access to the river, unlike the Baldwin estate, which was connected by a spring-fed creek. Luke and his family enjoyed the connectivity to the people, kayaks, and boats on the river, while Thomas preferred the seclusion of the creek and the wetlands.

Tori stayed behind at the cabin while we went to talk to Luke. She gave me a beef stick from the cabinet as we were leaving. "I miss seeing you at the pub, Daisy," she said as I clenched the dog treat in my mouth. "You were one of my favorites."

"You should have a dog to keep you company," Sue said, and Tori agreed.

"My family always had dogs," Tori said. "My mom enjoyed training them, and my dad loved them."

"We saw your parents walking a dog in the neighborhood," Sue said, "They rented a house near mine for a month."

"My dad loved the little dogs because they reminded him of his softer side," Tori said. "Jelly Bean is his pride and joy."

"I'll bet your mom was the strict one, and your dad let them get away with—murder— whatever they wanted," Sue said, and Tori smiled. "My dad never said no to any of his family," she said, but he had a frightening reputation amongst people who crossed him."

"Will he be mad that we helped you deceive him about your disappearance?" Mia asked, and Tori assured her that he would understand everything after she could explain it.

"They will probably own a second house in Sweetwater Springs when this is resolved," Tori said. "I caused my family a lot of grief when I married Dave, but it seemed like the right thing to do at the time."

Sarah agreed she understood Tori's reasons for the marriage, but Dave had changed with the times. "He's not the same person anymore," she said. "You're not safe with a man who would leave you for dead beside a creek."

"Luke will know a good bodyguard," Sue said as we loaded into Mia's SUV. "We'll help you through this, and you can return to work."

I sat beside Sarah in the back seat of Mia's SUV. Although Sarah was more of a cat lover, she seemed to like me. I placed my head on her lap while she stroked the fur on my forehead and between my ears.

Sue seemed preoccupied with looking out the window at the wetlands, but I knew she was thinking as she often did when she looked through windows. She had been friends with Luke since they met her at the park, and he helped her and Peter treat the cat colony on Cypress Street for fleas. Luke had been her guest at Beth's birthday party and for Christmas.

Sue met Luke's mother later at his estate. Recently, she has confided in her more and more. Sophie could be a source of helpful information, but you had to get used to her.

"Have you met Sophie?" Sue asked, and Mia and Sarah replied they had not.

"She's a nonagenarian character straight out of Sicily," Sue said. "She thinks she's an expert on vegetables, cooking, and the mob."

"She sounds like fun," Mia said. "I didn't know Luke's mother was Sicilian."

"Yes, and she'll never let you forget it," Sue said.

"Does she like cats?" Sarah asked because she had heard Luke was fond of them.

"I believe she does," Sue said, "but she's also fond of Luke's hound dog. His name is Artemis, and he's Daisy's best friend at Luke's house."

When we arrived at the estate, Artemis was waiting at the gate. Sue called the guard who manned the cameras, and he opened the gates for Mia to drive inside. After we had entered, Sue set me free to run with Artemis.

I leaped out of the vehicle to race circles with one of my best four-legged friends. I loved walking with Sue, but I missed lunches with Loretta when I was allowed to run free in the yard with my cousins. It was exciting to run with Artemis.

"I didn't know Daisy could run like that!" Sarah said after we flew in great leaps together toward the river and returned to greet them.

People who have not seen Poodles or Australian Shepherds run would be impressed by an Aussie Doodle's running skills. "Daisy loves to run," she said before we raced off again. "I'm unsure if she prefers running or dipping her belly in the river."

After three races around the estate, Artemis and I joined Sue and her friends for a visit indoors. "That was impressive," Mia said, and Sue replied that she looked forward to returning to Loretta's for regular exercise instead of intermittent romps with Artemis.

Luke met us at the door and invited us into the sunroom, where we could see the river through the tall trees that bordered it. "You have a fabulous view," Mia said, and Luke smiled. "I enjoy the activity," he said. "There's always something happening on the river."

"There's always something happening in Sweetwater Springs," Sarah said, and Luke replied life was better with people who love you.

"I assume you've heard about my previous profession," Sarah replied, and Luke said he was sure she could rise above it. "One day, you'll fall in love with a good man and never look back again," he said.

"I was lucky Gio kept me away from bigger trouble," Sarah said as Sophie popped into the room.

"You're that Call Girl I heard about, aren't you?" Sophie said, and Sarah nodded.

"She's my daughter," Mia explained. "I failed her as a mother when she was younger, but I'm trying to do better for her now."

"You don't look old enough to be Sarah's Mama," Sophie said, and Mia explained the details of her teenage pregnancy with Phil Coleman and their reluctance to tell Thomas until his killer was identified. Sarah's and Loretta's names were cleared.

"Thank you for telling me," Sophie said. "I might have been more likely to judge you if I hadn't known."

Luke looked surprised by the confessions but not shocked. He's been around long enough to know about people's scandals, far and wide. He mostly tried to stay out of the drama, but it helped to learn about their history. "Thanks for trusting us," he said. "It means a lot to Mom and me."

I followed Sophie into the kitchen, where she prepared an antipasto with fresh homemade bread. She fed me a bite of sausage, which Sue would have declined, but I couldn't resist the temptation. Sophie—and almost everyone else— was not nearly as strict with my diet as Sue. Sometimes, a dog likes to sneak when the boss isn't looking.

When we returned to the living room, Sophie set the tray on the coffee table between the guests. "That looks delightful," Sue said as Sophie poured sparkling lemon water for everyone. "You shouldn't have," Mia said as she sampled an olive from the platter.

Luke popped a slice of salami into his mouth, "It's nice to see you," he said. "To what do we owe the pleasure of your visit?"

Sue chased a bite of cheese with a swallow of sparkling water. "There's something I haven't told you," she said, and Luke frowned after hearing the previously untold stories.

"Tori Pedri is alive," she exclaimed without softening the blow.

"What do you mean, Tori Pedri is alive?" Sophie screeched before Luke could speak. "She's been missing for over six months."

"Yes, and her parents put out the biggest search and rescue mission in the history of Sweetwater Springs," Sue agreed.

"How long have you known?" Luke asked, furrowing his brow.

"We found out just before Mia's housewarming party," Sue replied. "We accidentally saw her at Mia's Run when she was swimming with Mia and Sarah."

"She's been hiding in one of my guest houses," Mia explained, and Sarah told the story of finding her after Dave pushed her out of the kayak.

Sophie was shocked at the descriptions of Tori's hiding in a guest house after her near-death experience. "You're an accomplice," she said.

"I was an accomplice in trying to save her life," Sue replied. "There's been no fraud, just a disappearance and people who helped her."

"Why have you kept this a secret?" Luke asked, and Sue explained that Tori wanted to give Dave a chance to make money at the pub before he moved back to Miami.

"That's lame!" Sophie said. "He tried to kill her."

"He didn't try to save her," Mia corrected, and Sarah agreed that Tori saw it that way.

"Now we are afraid he might be trying to kill her," Sue said. "Someone has been stomping around her cabin for the last two nights. She's been hearing footsteps."

"Someone followed my SUV to the cabin today," Mia explained. "We saw him hiding in the bushes behind the driveway. He could have told anyone if he saw Tori."

Sophie was so upset that she fed me a slice of salami in front of Sue. "You can't keep secrets like this from men like Gio!" she said.

"It won't be for much longer," Sarah replied, and everyone agreed it wasn't a secret for much longer.

"What can I do to help?" Luke asked, strained by the explanations and the potential misconceptions about Sue's involvement in sheltering the daughter of a suspected mob boss.

"We think Tori needs a bodyguard," Sue said. "We were hoping you might have some contacts."

Luke replied that it wasn't his typical territory, but he knew people to ask about people who might do such things.

"It's only for a little while," Sue said. "We want to protect Tori until this case is solved."

"You girls, Be Careful!" Sophie said as they rose to leave. "I'm afraid you've cut off more than you can chew!"

"We did it for the right reasons," Sue replied. "Thank you for caring about our safety. We'll be OK."

I could feel the tension in the room from my two-legged friends. Sue was acting calm, but I knew she was worried. Someone was following Tori, and she had kept his daughter's hiding place a secret from Gio. This could have potential repercussions if he didn't give them a chance to explain. She hoped Luke could find a good bodyguard, but now he was involved in the cover-up.

"If this isn't solved in a week, I'll talk to Gio," Luke said before he looked for a bodyguard for Tori. "I couldn't stand it if something happened to you."

"Don't tempt fate," Sophie called as Mia drove away, and Luke added, "Be careful."

I lay my head in Sarah's lap as they planned their next visit to Nella's house. Tomorrow was another day, but it couldn't come soon enough. Sue had a week to reveal Tori's whereabouts to her parents; I had a lot of sniffing to do between now and then.

Chapter 32

Nella's House

The following morning, Toby was sleepier than usual. A lizard had gotten into the house, and he'd spent the night bustling across furniture to reach him. It was a foolish pastime that had resulted in some disarray of Sue's seasonal knick-knacks on the sofa table. After a busy night, he was tired.

I was tired from a busy day at the Baldwin's guesthouse and Luke's estate. I had encountered someone watching Tori at the guesthouse, run between windows to bark, and taken a walk in the woods, where I'd sniffed blood near Tori's hideaway. Later, I'd romped with Artemis at Luke's estate and eaten forbidden food in Sophie's kitchen. It was both revealing and exhausting. I was tired, but it was a good tired.

Toby slept all day and chased a lizard at night. This morning, Toby was too tired to stick his paw under the door to greet Sue as usual. He did not jump on the bed to greet me or chase the flowers on the bedspread. I believed his work was irrelevant compared to my investigations, but I missed him. It was Okay to be lazy in a cat's world.

"I hope Toby's all right," Sue said when she came out of the shower to dress.

Sue talked to herself when no one was home to talk to. She seemed to enjoy the discussions, and I liked to listen to her light banter, which usually revolved around me, Toby, or something she couldn't find.

This morning, she found Toby sleeping in the living room, where he had captured and beheaded the lizard. She took the body and disposed of it, grumbling about the kill as she removed it to the waste basket. Afterward, she fed us breakfast while she made a large pot of coffee for three people.

Mia and Sarah arrived shortly after our breakfast. Since Toby had never met Sarah, he quickly escaped into the bedroom to hide in the interfacing under the bed. Toby loved the people he loved, sharing loud purrs and gentle affection, but he was not a connector cat with strangers he had never met before.

Although Sue lets Toby be Toby— a loyal and affectionate cat with only a few people—she knows I'm social with everyone unless I don't trust someone. In that case, I'll crouch on all fours and back away. Or sometimes, I crouch and sniff. Sometimes, but rarely, I bark to alert Sue that something is wrong.

"I understand you have a neighborhood cat," Sarah said after she sipped her coffee.

"Yes, Toby is a delight," Sue replied, sharing the creamer with Mia. "He makes me smile every day."

"I've never met him, but I've seen him," Mia said, and Sue explained that Toby was shy. "He comes out a few minutes after the guests leave," she said. He likes Luke, Beth, me, and Daisy— a petite group guy."

"I've heard Luke is a cat man," Sarah said, and Sue explained his role in saving Boomer, Beth's cat, from the rainstorm and the alligators. "Luke is one of my favorite people," Sue said. "He has a big heart."

"He sounds like Thomas," Mia said. "A developer with a soft spot," and Sue agreed Thomas had a soft spot for Mia, whom he named everything after.

"He wouldn't be happy if he knew you were risking your life to help Tori and me," Sarah said, and Sue reminded them it had started with Loretta, who was happier at home since the judge released her on bail for home and work.

"Do you think Luke found a bodyguard for Tori?" Mia asked.

"He called to let me know the bodyguard is stealthily on his way to your guesthouse," Sue replied. "He'll arrive by kayak in Mia's Run later this morning to avoid alerting your camera security closer to the house."

"I feel better already," Sarah said. "I wanted to stay with her after she told us about hearing footsteps at night."

"I can't imagine living in that remote guesthouse, with someone outside, without protection," Mia said. "Especially now that we know that motion camera has been missing since Tori disappeared."

The clues were assembling quickly, but something was missing. Luke turned on the heat after Sue told him Tori Pedri was alive. For their safety, they had one week to solve the evolving questions. You didn't mess with men like Gio. Luke and Sophie—above all—- knew about people like him.

I jumped into the back seat of Mia's SUV for the short drive to Nella's house. Sue wanted to clarify a few details, and Mia had the results from the DNA sample from the bathroom glass. It didn't match the hair from the disposable raincoat. They wanted Nella to know her position on the suspect list for her husband's murder was downgraded.

Mia drove across the bridge where the polluted lake, the Green Cove, was in view.

"I don't know how anyone can stand to live here," Sarah said, and Sue explained the pollution—an overgrowth of algae— in the river. "It didn't used to be this way," she said, and Mia said it had been crystal clear when she was a teenager.

"The locals think a hotel will contribute to the pollution," Mia said, "But Thomas thinks he can correct it much sooner than anyone thinks."

"Excuse me for asking, but why would anyone believe him?' Sarah asked, and Mia said he needed a chance to prove it.

"Phil didn't buy a house on the Green Cove thinking the algae would last," Mia said, and everyone agreed he might have known something they didn't.

I looked out the rear window of Mia's SUV and noted a black sedan behind us. Green Cove was a small subdivision with few homes, so I didn't think much of it. Since it might have belonged to an owner, I etched it on my memory for future reference.

Mia drove past the mayor's house, who had lived through the turmoil of the cove turning green. Sue reminded Sarah, "The mayor and Phil both had crushes on your mother in high school," and she laughed. My life could have been so much different," she said.

"You wouldn't have been born," Mia reminded her.

Sarah agreed she was lucky to be born despite her struggles. "Thank you for having me, Mom, and for coming back for me."

"Pardon me for asking, but would you have a child if you knew she would be abused like you were?" Sue asked.

"No, I wouldn't want anyone to go through my experience with my uncle or anyone else," Sarah said. "It was a painful childhood for me. Men like him need harsher punishments and children need to know they'll be safe without their abusers."

"I wanted you to live with me," Mia said, and Sarah softened. "I know you did, Mom, and I love you for that."

Sue attached my leash to my collar when we arrived at Nella's house. I jumped out of the car behind Sue and followed the three women to the front door. After Mia rang the doorbell, Nella ushered us quickly inside.

Nella seemed nervous—more nervous than I remembered her. We followed her to the living room, where she directed Sue and her friends to the couch while I sat on the floor beside them. "Somebody tried to break into my house last night!" Nella screeched.

"Have you told the sheriff?" Sue asked, and Nella confirmed. "I don't know what good it will do."

"Sheriff Stone is more experienced with detective work than he used to be," Sue assured her. "He's learning."

"Do you have any valuables?" Mia asked, and Nella said no. "Phil was a player and a cheapskate," she said. "If he bought valuables, he didn't buy them for me."

"If he had a mistress, he might have bought something for her," Sarah suggested, and Nella frowned. "Who are you?" she asked.

"I'm sorry for the late introduction," Mia said. "This is Sarah. She is my daughter."

"Phil was my father," Sarah explained, and Nella's jaw went agape. "You are Phil's daughter?"

"Yes, I am one," Sarah replied, and Nella ignored the inference that there could be more.

"You are a call girl!" Nella said. "I remember you from the housewarming party."

"I used to be a call girl," Sarah replied. "I'm looking for honest work in Sweetwater Springs."

I sniffed the floor for unusual scents, but there were none. The house smelled the same as before—clean but musty. It was older and had not been updated. After the cove turned green, Phil bought the house for speculation but had no intention of flipping it quickly.

"We have good news," Sue said after she stroked me behind the ear.

Mia continued, "Did you notice a missing glass from your bathroom after we visited you before?"

"Yes, as a matter of fact, I did," Nella said. "I thought you might have broken it and forgot to mention it."

"I took it for a DNA sample," Mia confessed.

"We wanted to compare it to a third hair we found in Mia's dumpster on the disposable raincoats after the housewarming party," Sue said.

"Who did the other two hairs belong to?" Nella asked.

"Phil and Loretta," Sue replied.

"What did you learn?" Nella asked.

"It wasn't your hair," Mia said.

"That doesn't prove anything," Nella said.

"No, but we're one step closer to proving you weren't involved in Phil's murder," Sue said.

"Phil wasn't a good husband, but I had a good life. I cooked his meals, did his laundry, and was his party companion," Nella replied. "He criticized me, insulted me, humiliated me, and gave me a stepchild out of wedlock from long ago."

"That's enough for some people to stay together," Sarah said.

"And enough for other couples to break apart," Mia added.

"I didn't love him, but I didn't kill him," Nella replied.

"We didn't think you did," Sue said.

After a pause, Nella said, "Let me know if I can help with your investigation. A lot of people will be happy to discover the truth about Phil's murder."

I followed Sue and her friends out of Nella's house and loaded into Mia's SUV to drive to Chris and Jessie's house. Now, two houses were being watched by prowlers—one with an attempted break-in. Somebody out there wanted something. Were there two prowlers or one? What did they want?

When Mia drove out of the Green Cove subdivision, I couldn't help but notice the sedan that seemed to be following us into the subdivision on the drive to Nella's house. Now, the black sedan was back again. This time, the driver drove closer than before, as if not to lose us.

"Somebody is following us," Mia announced, and I barked in agreement as the sedan rolled behind.

Sweetwater Springs was small enough that if a tail lost us, it wouldn't be difficult to find us. The driver didn't know his or her way around and followed too closely to compensate. "Can you lose him?" Sarah asked, and Mia stepped on the gas to accomplish the task.

As I watched from the back seat, the sedan was lost quickly. Mia took the long way to Chris and Jessie's house, pulling into an alley in the historic district as the driver continued past. I sat and watched out the rear window of the SUV rather than resting my head in Sarah's lap as I had before. When we finally arrived at Jessie's house, no one had seen the sedan again.

Chapter 33

Chris and Jessie's House

When we arrived at Jessie's house, Beth stood in the yard with her mother's Doberman, Redman. I was excited to see Beth, who loved her cat Boomer better than any other animal, but gave Redman and me attention despite her cat preference. Redman was old and stiff and didn't have play left in him, but he was Jessie's beloved pet who would live out his years in peace. I knew better than to run close to him, so I moseyed to greet them carefully without disturbing his rickety posture.

"Hi, Daisy!" Beth said as I sniffed her shirt, which smelled like Nella's house.

I snuggled my head under her hand so Beth could rub it behind my ears while Redman watched without moving his body except for a twitch. I doubted he could see or hear well, but he enjoyed senior living by the river. One day, I made the mistake of running towards him and accidentally knocked him off the seawall into the river, where Chris had to retrieve him from an unexpected dog paddle. After that, I learned to walk more slowly around Redman so he didn't lose his balance.

Mia and Sarah followed Sue over to the tree where we were standing. Sue hugged Beth and introduced her to Sarah, adding that she may become a resident of Sweetwater Springs.

"My mom said she met you at Ms. Mia's housewarming party," Beth said. "It's nice to meet you."

"And you as well," Sarah said. "Sue told me you and your mother used to live with her."

"Yes, we did," Beth replied. "We had a lot of fun living at Aunt Sue's house. It's where I met Mr. Luke and found Boomer. He was a street cat who wandered to Sue's home as a tiny kitten during a rainstorm."

"I have a neighborhood cat, too," Sarah said. "His name is Tom."

"Alley cats are the best!" Beth said Sarah agreed, and Sue added, "They are fortunate to find good homes with people like you who love them."

"I'd like to meet Boomer," Mia said, and Beth replied she would introduce them. "Do you have a cat, Ms. Mia?" Beth asked.

"It's been a long time since I've had one, but I'd love to have another one," Mia said.

I lay on the soft grass, with my legs stretched behind me while Sue and her friends talked. "I'm so happy my Aunt Loretta is finally out of jail," Beth said. "It must have been scary for her there."

"She's glad to be home with her family," Sue replied, and Beth said she missed seeing Lucy.

"She'll be back to Sweetwater Springs before you know it," Sue said, stroking her hair.

"Does Lucy know her mother was in jail?" Beth asked, and Sue said that Lucy knew her mother was detained in Sweetwater Springs to answer questions after the housewarming party, but nothing more. "Loretta will explain what happened when Lucy's old enough to understand."

"I'd be terrified if my mom went to jail," Beth said. "There's no way Aunt Loretta killed Anita's father."

"Of course she didn't," Sue said.

"Who's Anita?' Sarah asked.

"She's Mr. Phil and Ms. Nella's daughter," Beth replied, adding, "She's Nella's daughter now that Mr. Phil is dead. We play together sometimes."

"When was the last time you played together?" Sue asked, and Beth replied yesterday.

"Were you at Anita's house?" Sue asked, and Beth cringed. "Barely," she said. We usually play with Missy at the mayor's house."

Sue recalled that the mayor and his wife did not like their daughter going to Nella's house any more than she or Jessie wanted Beth at the recently widowed woman's house. Nella and Phil fought a lot when he was alive, embarrassing Anita. Now that Phil was dead, she must have felt more comfortable taking her friends to her mother's house.

"How is Anita?" Sue asked, and Beth replied that she seemed alright, almost relieved that her father was gone.

Beth walked towards her house, followed by Redman, Sue, and her friends. I walked beside Sue, feeling her tension. Jessie would never have approved of Beth going to Nella's house under the circumstances. A prowler—or someone—had tried to break in just last night.

"You must not go back to Nella's house until this is resolved," Sue said after Mia and Sarah walked ahead. "It's too dangerous."

"What do you mean, Aunt Sue?" Beth asked. "Why is it dangerous?"

"Somebody tried to break into Nella's house last night," Sue said, and Beth asked, "Why wouldn't Anita have told me?"

"Maybe her mother didn't tell her about the prowler, Sweetie," Sue replied. "Maybe she didn't want to frighten her."

Not all children had an open relationship with their parents. It was likely that Nella and Anita shared secrets from each other. Although Phil embarrassed Anita by yelling at her mother, she buried her shame. She loved her mother and didn't want to hurt her feelings.

It was unlike Beth keeping secrets from her mother, but possibly Anita's predicament affected her judgment. "Is there something you're not telling me?" she asked.

When Beth choked up, Sue said, "Please confide in me, Sweetie," she said. "You can trust me."

"Do you promise you won't tell my mother?" Beth asked.

It was Sue's turn to cringe. I could feel her body stiffen against my furry chest. "I can't promise you that, Honey," she said. "If it might keep someone from getting hurt, I'd have to say something—but I'd be conscientious with whom I shared it."

Mia and Sarah walked ahead while Sue and I stayed behind with Beth, who seemed like she wanted to cry. I nuzzled my furry body against Beth to console her, feeling her distress. Beth was about to break with a secret—and she wanted only Sue to know.

"Anita showed me something yesterday," Beth said before she burst into tears. "She told me to keep it a secret."

Sue hugged her for a long time, feeling her pain. "You're not betraying her if it helps her," she said.

"I'm telling you this because you said someone tried to break into Anita's house last night," Beth replied. "I may know why."

Sue looked Beth in the eyes and wiped away her tears. "What did Anita show you?" she asked.

Beth swallowed hard before she spoke. "Her father kept a safe behind a picture in his office," Beth said. "It had money in it."

"How much money?" Sue asked, and Beth said they didn't count it. "A lot."

"Why didn't Anita want anyone to know about the safe?" Sue asked.

"She was afraid her father was keeping the money to spend on another woman," Beth said. "She didn't want to hurt her mother by telling her about it."

"You did the right thing by sharing the secret with me," Sue said, and I knew she was processing the information. It was a lot to digest quickly, but Sue would figure it out. "Thank you for trusting me."

When we reached the house, I raced ahead of everyone to greet Jessie and Chris. I could almost feel Sue's wheels turning as she quietly stepped inside. She stayed in the background while the ladies discussed Jessie's cookbook and Mia's desire to contribute.

"That sounds like fun!" Sarah said. "I love how you share healthy recipes with kids and their parents in the classrooms."

"We used to live across the street from Rita," Jessie explained. "Her idea was to share CHEWS— Food for Fitness with the students' families."

"Rita is a school teacher," Mia explained. "She's been here since the beginning of time."

Beth laughed. "I won't tell her you said that," she said, and Mia replied, "I meant that she knows everyone in Sweetwater Springs and how they grew up."

"Like you?" Beth asked, and Mia smiled softly, "Yes, like me."

"Does Rita know about me?" Sarah asked, and Mia said, "I told her you're my daughter."

Beth gasped. "You are Mia's daughter?" she asked.

Mia covered her mouth as if to keep it quiet. "Please keep it our secret for now," she said. "There are some people I'd like to share it with privately before it's open."

"I can keep a secret," Beth said, and everyone agreed it would come out eventually.

It was impossible not to notice that Sue kept quiet in the background, although she was everyone's best friend and the person who had brought them together. I knew she was digesting information, but not everyone knew her as well as I did. She kept Beth's secret about the safe but wrestled with keeping it from her mother.

"Is something wrong, Sue?" Jessie asked.

"You're quiet," Mia agreed.

Sue looked out the front window as a diversion. "Do you remember that sedan following us?" she asked.

"Yes," they agreed.

"The driver found us," Sue replied, pointing across the front lawn. "The car is sitting on the berm before Jessie's house."

Jessie suggested that Beth find Boomer so they could talk privately. "Who would follow you?" she asked after her daughter was gone.

"I have no idea, but someone tried to break into Nella's house last night," Sue said, revealing the story they had come to tell.

"And someone has been traipsing around one of my guest houses at night," Mia added without revealing Tori's secret.

Beth returned from the house search with Boomer in her arms. I sniffed the cat that used to be my housemate and sniffed Beth's shirt again. The scent of Nella's house was profoundly noticeable. Beth exchanged looks with Sue before she confessed the story.

Sarah and Mia petted the friendly mackerel tabby cat while Beth talked. Boomer was no longer shy like Toby, who hid under the bed. He enjoyed the strokes and caresses, arching his back while they spoke.

"Mom, I've kept a secret from you," Beth said as her mother raised her eyebrows. "I know I was supposed to stay at Missy's house yesterday, but I went to Anita's, too," she said.

Jessie took a deep breath. She was proud that Beth dared tell her she had made the forbidden trip to Anita's house, but she didn't want to deter her from talking. Beth told her mother and friends about the wall safe behind the picture and the money. She explained that Anita had not told her mother about the safe because she didn't trust her father and did not want to upset her about the purpose of the money.

"Thank you for telling me, Sweetie," Jessie said, nodding.

"I'm sorry I went down to Anita's house and didn't tell you," Beth replied. "Her mother was nice the last time I was there, and Anita wanted to show me something."

"You mustn't go to Anita's house again until this case is solved," Jessie said. "Do you understand how dangerous it is to know the secrets of criminals and hidden money?"

"I'm sorry, Mom," Beth said. "I didn't know what she was going to show me."

"I couldn't bear it if something happened to you," Jessie said, hugging her daughter. "I don't want you in the Green Cove neighborhood until this case is solved," she added. "You can stay home with me, Chris, and Boomer until this is resolved."

"Anita didn't think she was endangering me," Beth said, and her mother agreed that she had shown her the wall safe before she was ready to tell her mother.

Sue smiled at Beth for bravely sharing the story that could have gotten her in trouble. It was hard to do, but it was essential to know about the safe.

The friends collected their belongings and left for a stop at the Baldwin Mansion to assemble their thoughts before proceeding with their plans. The truth was in sight, but staying safe and getting the details right was crucial. I followed them to Mia's SUV, noting where the sedan had been parked following us. The car was no longer there, but its mission was a mystery soon to be solved.

Chapter 34

Baldwin Mansion

The following morning, Sue met Mia and Sarah at the Baldwin Mansion. I hopped into the back seat to accompany her on the drive, seated on my rear haunches and watching out the window as before. It didn't take long to notice the black sedan was following us. The car met us on Main Street, at the shopping center, where we turned right to go to Mia's house.

"There's that car again," Sue said under her breath, but I heard her as always. Dogs have acute hearing for their favorite humans, and I had noticed the car already.

I shifted to watch the driver behind the dark windshield. He wore dark sunglasses and a hat—most likely a fedora like Sue's, but dogs are not experts on hats.

"What's with this guy?" Sue asked, pulling into a parking space on the side of the road to force him to pass or call in his game if he stopped behind her.

The driver passed Sue and drove across the bridge, probably hoping she would follow. He turned into a parking lot and waited, where she passed him again shortly after that. She was down the road before the driver pulled out and attempted another tail that took him to the unpopulated road where Thomas and Mia lived. This time, he did not follow when Sue turned left.

By now, he must have known that only a few houses were sitting on the street dead-ended at the Baldwin mansion. The owners of the houses were not friendly when people drove past. One chased Sue's car with a broom before she explained who she was. She identified herself as a friend of Luke and Sophie, who lived closest to the Baldwin Mansion.

"I lost him this time," Sue said aloud, but I remembered that he had found us at Chris and Jessie's house yesterday. It was hardly a shot in the dark to see Sue at a friend's house if the driver knew anything about her. He appeared to know a great deal already.

I hopped out of Sue's car when we arrived at the mansion at Mia's Run headwaters. The house was the newest and most prominent in Sweetwater Springs, tripling the size of Luke's estate. It was served by a staff of gardeners, groundskeepers, housekeepers, a butler, a driver, a chef, servers, and twenty-four-hour security near the main house.

Guests of the mansion were directed to one of twelve guest houses scattered across the property. Tori's guesthouse was the most remote and least utilized of them. Sometimes, close relatives stayed in the main house where Thomas and Mia lived.

Two guest vehicles were parked in the driveway today. "That's Gio's truck," Sue said aloud as we walked closer. The old truck was perfectly maintained and easy to recognize. Val claimed Gio liked it because he could tinker with it since it came before computers and sensors. The car belonged to Sarah, who was meeting Mia and Sue for breakfast.

The butler directed us to the enormous verandah overlooking the main spring of Mia's Run. "This is fabulous!" Sue said as I followed closely beside her to the white wicker table overlooking the spring-fed run. Mia and Sarah sat at the table and waited for Sue and me.

"Thank you," Mia replied. "It's refreshing to watch the creek under the big fans. When it's sweltering, we have outdoor air conditioners. Today, the fans are good enough to keep us cool."

"It's supposed to rain later," Sarah said, noting the rain clouds to the west across the river.

"It's been a long time since we had a shower," Mia said, and Sue agreed it hadn't rained since the housewarming party.

"Did you bring an umbrella?" Mia asked, and Sue said no. "I have umbrellas and raincoats by the front door if we need them for our travels."

"I have a doggie raincoat for Daisy," she continued, stroking my curly fur. "There's a new dog store in town, and I wanted to buy something."

"Thank you, that's sweet," Sue replied. "You should save it for another dog. Daisy hates to wear clothes and loves getting wet in a summer rain-shower."

The server brought yogurt, black pepper biscuits, and fresh fruit and set them on the table beside the coffee server and orange juice. "That looks delicious," Sue said, admiring the spread.

"I love to cook," Mia said while the server poured beverages. "Sometimes I send everyone home and cook for Thomas and me."

The server said, "Ms. Mia is an excellent chef. "She went to cooking school in Italy."

"That's impressive," Sue replied as the server returned to the kitchen. "You didn't tell me."

"Mom has some great recipes for Jessie's cookbook," Sarah said, covering her mouth when she caught her mistake.

"Nobody heard you," Mia said, squeezing her daughter's shoulder. "We don't have cameras on the verandah. You can speak freely here."

I felt Sue stiffen against my chest as she did when she was concerned about eavesdroppers. Mia must have noticed the tension because she added, "It won't be a secret much longer."

"Isn't that where Dave pushed Tori out of the kayak?" Sue whispered, pointing to a location past the bridge over the spring.

"It's a little further down," Mia replied. "You can't see it from the verandah, or the security cameras would have detected it."

"One of the staff kept the old motion camera in the woods to watch the wildlife at night," Sarah said. "Everyone knows it's been missing."

"The whole staff knew about the wildlife camera," Mia said.

"Nobody but Tori knew what could have been on it," Sarah added. "It went missing shortly after she disappeared."

"Wildlife cameras go missing all the time," Mia said. "It was just a loss or a petty theft to the staff, but the gardener kept accusing other people of stealing it."

"If your gardener talked about the missing camera at Cat Tails Pub, Dave knew where it was," Sue said.

"Phil knew where it was, too," Mia added, and Sarah agreed, "According to Tori, Phil did most of his business at Cat Tails Pub."

"Both of them could have known there was a camera across from the site where Dave pushed Tori out of the kayak," Sue said. "Either of them could have returned for it the next day."

"Dave would not have wanted Tori's parents to know what he'd done," Sarah said. "I wouldn't want Gio mad at me."

"If both of them came back for the camera, one of them found it missing," Sue said.

"Beth said there was a lot of money in Phil's safe," Sue added. "According to Anita, Nella didn't know her dad had a safe. We need to find out what's in it."

"That sounds like a dangerous mission," Mia said. "Thomas would be mad if he knew I went alone."

"We're getting so close to solving this case," Sarah said. "We need to finish."

Sue and her friends agreed to visit Nella once again after breakfast. They decided to alert Sheriff Stone to the increasing clues after the visit, because his presence might make her nervous. The contents of the safe could be incriminating—or not. For now, they knew someone might have tried to break into Nella's house to retrieve them.

"Are you ready to tell Thomas about Sarah?" Sue asked after she chased a bite of biscuit with coffee.

"No, not yet," Mia replied. "Sarah is still a suspect."

"We need to prove who killed Phil, and we're getting closer to the truth," Sue said.

"After that, I'll tell him about Sarah," Mia replied.

"Beth was a big help when she told us about the safe yesterday," Sarah said, and Sue agreed that sometimes kids don't know when they are on to something important or dangerous. "I'm glad she told her mother about the safe, so I didn't have to," Sue said. "Beth is a good kid."

I stood up from my favorite spot under the table where the crumbs fall and walked towards the rail on the verandah. I could see people standing on the bridge that crossed the big spring at the headwaters of Mia's Run. One of them looked like Gio, but a sniff would have been helpful for identification.

Sue stood up closer when she saw me wagging my tail at the rail. "Isn't that Gio and Val with Thomas?" she asked.

"Yes, Gio has been visiting Thomas for the last few days," Mia said. "I think he may invest in the hotel."

"He knows people," Sarah said, and Sue agreed he knew people who could test for DNA."

"Gio knows people who can test for about anything," Sarah said. "He trusts his people to do things but is reluctant to trust anyone else."

"What do you think of Val?" Sue asked, and Sarah replied she had always made her feel welcome.

When Sue and her friends finished breakfast, they agreed it was time to leave for Nella's house. "I'm nervous, but Thomas will know it," Mia said. "I don't want him to see me before we go."

"Does he wonder why you spend so much time with Sarah?" Sue asked.

"No, he doesn't ask," Mia replied. "He knows she had a rough start, and I'm sure Gio and Val put in a good word for her."

"Have you heard anything from Tori?" Sue asked.

"Her bodyguard arrived by kayak, and she's doing alright," Sarah replied. "I don't want to go to the guest house again now that someone knows someone is living there."

"We drew a lot of attention last time," Sue agreed. "It's best to lie low for a while."

The server came to retrieve the dishes while we were leaving. As we walked through the house to Mia's SUV, she reached down to pet me. "I love dogs," she said. "She's a Cute Dog."

I was used to being called "Cute Dog" when someone didn't know my name, but it had been a while. "Thanks," Sue said. "Her name is Daisy."

We piled into Mia's SUV and drove to Nella's house before Thomas and his friends arrived at the mansion. While I looked out the window, rain drizzled on the windshield beneath the wipers. I could sense the tension in the vehicle, but it seemed to be under control. This was the most critical mission yet, but it could be dangerous.

"Oh, by the way," Sue said as we passed a sedan on the side of the road. "That car has been following me again today."

All would become clear shortly, but for now, it was drizzling. Sue and her friends had much to prove and a short time to get there. I would be with them every step of the way, but my reputation as a Cute Dog did nothing for my reputation as a crime solver. It was good to go stealthy when solving crimes in Sweetwater Springs, and for now, that worked to my advantage.

Chapter 35

Phil's Safe

The black sedan didn't follow us immediately, but it did appear after Mia turned the corner to drive to Nella's house. I watched the car from the back seat, snuggling with Sarah, who also thought of me like a Cute Dog. It was alright with me. Being cute helped me be stealthy as a crime solver since few people knew my abilities like Sue did.

"The driver is trying to be sneaky," Mia said as I rested my head on Sarah's shoulder and watched through the window.

"That's not an easy task in Sweetwater Springs," Sarah replied. "It's hard to hide from us and easy to find us."

"I wonder why someone would follow us?" Sue said.

"Somebody who thinks we're getting too close to solving the case," Mia replied.

"Do you think the driver is the same person who tried to break into Nella's house?" Sarah asked, and Mia shrugged. "If so, they want the contents of that safe badly."

"We know there's money in it," Sue said, and Sarah added, "Lots of money."

When we arrived at Nella's house, Sarah had me leashed and ready to walk through the drizzle. It was the kind of light rain that lasted all day, soaking the dry lawns with precious water. Sarah dodged the raindrops with me while Mia and Sue followed with umbrellas.

"I hope this isn't a trap," Sarah said after she rang the doorbell.

"We'll find out soon enough," Sue replied calmly, and Mia said she didn't think it was.

Anita answered the doorbell, followed by the cat, safely tucked indoors for the rainshower. "Hi, Dr. Sue," she said. "Come in. I didn't know you were coming over."

"Thank you," Sue replied as we followed her to the sunroom. "Beth and I had fun playing together," she said. "We had a birthday party for my cat."

"Did you bake a cake?" Sue asked, and Beth replied that they had baked and eaten one. Mom had some, too."

"Beth says your mom likes tea parties," Sue replied.

"My mom loves tea parties," Beth said. "She used to own a tea house in town."

"I remember her tea house," Mia said. "It was close to my card shop."

"I heard that's where you met Mr. Thomas," Anita replied, dropping her head. "My mom didn't get so lucky."

"I'm sorry about your father," Sue said, "Are you doing alright?"

"My dad wasn't the best dad," Anita replied. "He wasn't nice to my mother."

"You love your mother a lot, don't you?" Sue asked softly.

"I love her to the moon and back," Anita replied. "I'll go get her for you."

We could see the rain sprinkle on the Green Cove from the sunroom. Without sunlight to penetrate it, the cove looked darker. The drizzle made me want to snuggle on the loveseat next to Sue while she sipped hot tea. Although it was summer, the rain made it feel colder.

"I had no idea the algae was this bad in the cove," Sarah said.

"People don't realize it unless they come here," Mia replied. "It's not nearly so green where the river flows."

"The water stagnates in the cove," Sue added. "There's not enough water flow to move it downriver."

"The water comes out pure from the spring upriver, then the algae grows in summer, but most of it washes away on the main river."

"The cove was clear when I was growing up," Mia added.

"What makes the algae grow more than it used to?" Sarah asked.

"That's the sixty-million-dollar question that Thomas wants to find the answer to," Mia said.

"He thinks Gio can help him," Sue added.

"My mom is making a pot of vanilla chai tea," Anita said, popping her head back into the sunroom.

"That's kind of her," Sue replied.

"I hope you like it," Anita said.

"Your mother's tea was always delicious," Mia replied. "I liked every-thing she brewed."

"Missy's mom is here to pick me up," Anita said. "I'm playing at her house today."

"Have fun!" Sue said, sighing in relief that Anita wouldn't be present during the upcoming ordeal, which would expose the safe's contents.

By now, Missy's father, the mayor, had to know about the prowler who tried to break into Nella's house. The mayor was in close contact with the sheriff, who told him everything in Sweetwater Springs.

It was unlikely Anita had told anyone but Beth about the safe. But the prowler was a different story. If a random break-in occurred, everyone who lived in Green Cove could be affected. Regardless, the likelihood was that Nella's prowler was on a mission regarding the safe.

When Nella entered the sunroom with the tea set, she looked tired. Mia and Sue rose quickly to assist her while I stayed on the floor close to Sarah, who kept her arm around my chest. I knew Sarah was worried about the recent events, and my presence comforted her.

"Pardon me for saying so, but you look exhausted," Sue said.

"I've had a lot of visitors since Phil died," Nella replied. "Some offer condolences, but some ask questions, including the sheriff."

"You had to report the prowler," Mia said.

"I'm not sure the sheriff believes I didn't kill Phil," Nella replied. "The mayor knows we fought all the time because he heard us. Phil wasn't the best husband, as everyone knows."

"We believe you didn't kill him," Mia said, and Sue reminded her of the DNA from the hair root that didn't match the glass.

"Someone else killed my father," Sarah said. "We hope you can help us discover the truth."

The ladies sipped their tea while I sniffed the rug for unfamiliar smells. With so many people coming over, there would be many of them, but a dog could stumble upon something important now and then. I always kept sniffing despite the odds.

"Beth enjoyed playing with Anita," Sue said, breaking the silence.

"Beth is a sweet girl," Nella replied. "She loves cats."

"Yes, she does," Sue said. "She loves cake, too. Her mother never lets her have sugar, but I won't tell her about the birthday party," she winked.

"I'm sorry. I didn't know."

"Don't be sorry. I love Jessie, but she can be strict with Beth's diet. I'm glad she can branch out now and then."

"We don't always eat healthy, but having tea parties with the girls is fun."

"Everything in moderation," Sue said. "It's about eating whole fruits and vegetables in the rainbow colors, but it's also about portion control when we branch out into sugar and unhealthy fat."

Sue sipped her tea before she breached the topic they had come to discuss. After she swallowed, she looked Nella directly in the eyes. They were moving into unfamiliar territory Nella had most likely been unaware of.

"Can I ask you something personal?" Sue asked, and Nella cringed.

"Are you aware that Phil has a safe behind a picture in his office?'

"How would you know that?" Nella asked.

"Anita showed it to Beth when she came over to play. It has money in it."

"Do you mean she opened it?"

"Yes, she opened it."

"I've never opened that safe," Nella said. "Frankly, I haven't thought about it since he was killed."

"I wonder how she knew the combination," Nella said.

"She found it on a piece of paper inside his change box in his closet."

They sipped their tea in companionable silence while everyone digested the information. Meanwhile, I continued to sniff the floor without finding anything, but it gave me something to do. I could feel the tension in the room, making me nervous.

"Do you mind if we look in the safe?" Mia asked after a silence.

"I think we should look in the safe," Nella replied. "I'm sorry. I'm flabbergasted."

"You've had a lot coming at you in the last few days," Sarah said. "I'd be flabbergasted, too."

Nella looked at the woman who was her stepdaughter from her deceased husband. "Let's look inside that safe," she said, directing us to Phil's office. "I'll meet you here after I find the paper with the combination."

Nella returned to Phil's office with the combination and opened the safe on the first try. When they looked inside, they saw the wildlife camera from Mia's Run sitting behind a pile of cash. Mia recognized the box immediately.

"That's the camera our gardener put in a tree to monitor the wildlife," Mia said.

"He's accused many people of stealing it," Sarah added.

"The gardener told Dave and Phil about the camera when he saw them at Cat Tails," Sue said. "Both knew exactly where it was hanging in that tree."

"Anyone could have taken that camera, but now we know it was Phil," Sarah said, and everyone agreed they should review the video.

I felt nervous tension from Sue and her friends when Nella popped the memory card into Phil's computer. They almost forgot to breathe as the digital story from the incident over six months ago came to life.

The entire chilling event was captured in the imagery: Dave pushed Tori out of the kayak. She fell on her backside and was motionless. Dave paddled away and left the scene of the fall without checking to see if Tori was alive.

"He didn't check to see if she had a heartbeat or if she was breathing," Sue said, and everyone agreed it was horrific.

"Dave just left her lying there," Sarah said. "She could have died."

"Tori lay on the ground for hours," Mia said. "He didn't check on her."

"Gio and Val would have been furious if they knew he left her for dead," Sarah said. "They would have killed Dave if they knew what he did."

After looking at the images, they counted the $50,000.00 in cash.

"Phil must have been bribing Dave not to tell Gio and Val about pushing their daughter out of the kayak," Nella declared, and everyone agreed she was right.

The cash was bundled in five stacks, each of $10,000.00. "Dave must have been paying Phil by the month not to share the images with Tori's parents," Sue said.

"Tori has been missing six months," Sarah noted. "Phil spent some of the earnings."

"Dave must have been embezzling cash from the pub to pay Phil," Mia added, and everyone agreed Dave could only take so much from the business without drawing attention to the loss.

"Tori was convinced her parents would kill Dave if they knew what he did," Sarah said. "No one had any idea that Phil was the only person who could prove it."

"Dave must have killed Phil to end the payoffs and save his life in case Gio and Val saw the images," Sue declared.

"Both men knew that camera was hanging in the tree by the creek," Mia concluded. "It was a matter of who got there first."

"I think Dave tried to break into my house to retrieve the camera and the money," Nella announced. "He killed Phil at the housewarming party and wanted to destroy the evidence for his motive."

"Where did the intruder try to break in?" Sue asked, and Nella noted the window to Phil's office.

I looked out the window and saw the black sedan pass by Nella's house. Whoever had been following Sue and her friends was back again, but he didn't stay. There were a few details yet to prove the case, but first, it was time to alert the sheriff to the evidence. I pawed at the front door for a walk and sniffed around the outside of the house with Sue.

Chapter 36

Sheriff Comes to Phil's House

Mia stayed inside with Nella while Sue and Sarah took me for a walk around the house. The drizzle made it hard to sniff wet evidence, but taking a dog walk gave them an excuse to get outside to discuss their findings. We walked to Phil's office window, which was partly pried open, and searched for evidence.

"What made the intruder leave?' Sarah asked, noting that he didn't finish the job.

"Nella sounded an alarm inside the house when she heard the damage to the window," Sue replied. "It wasn't connected to the sheriff's office, but it scared him away."

"Are you sure she reported it?" Sarah asked.

"Nella said she would call the sheriff after we last visited her house."

"As I recall, she said she didn't know how much good it would do," Sarah said, and Sue mentioned she had reassured Nella he was improving at detective work since Phil's murder. "He'll be here shortly when Nella calls to report the contents of the safe."

The rain decimated any shoe prints under the window. Since there had been no break-in, there was no crime tape. Sue and Sarah searched the area for anything he may have missed.

I stood on my hind legs and sniffed a corner of the window, detecting the scent of blood. I was particularly good at smelling blood but had no idea whose blood it was. I pawed at Sue to alert her to the potential evidence.

"Do you see anything?" Sarah asked when Sue shifted her head under the eave to examine it closer.

"No, but Daisy smells something," Sue replied. "We'll tell Sheriff Stone to swab the area for DNA when Nella reports the safe."

"Hopefully, he's already done so," Sarah said.

"Has Dave ever been arrested?" Sue asked, and Sarah was uncertain but doubted it.

"He may not be in the DNA database," Sue said. "That will change when Sheriff Stone sees the images of Dave pushing Tori out of the kayak and the money in Phil's safe."

"Dave will be arrested," Sarah agreed. "He'll be in the DNA database before you know it."

I looked toward the street where the black sedan made another pass by Nella's house. Since Sue and Sarah were busy with the window, I tugged at my leash to alert them.

"What's with that car following us?" Sarah asked when Sue pointed it out.

"I don't know," Sue replied, waving to the driver. "I want him to know I'm not afraid of him."

"It's just weird to be followed," Sarah replied. "It's like we're being stalked."

"You're assuming he's a bad guy," Sue said. "I'm not sure what he's up to, but he isn't very discreet."

"He may be reporting to someone what we're up to," Sarah said, and Sue smiled in agreement.

When they were finished inspecting the window, Sarah pulled me close to her leg and snuggled my damp fur. She turned to Sue and looked her in the eyes.

"I want to update Tori about the camera," she said. "She deserves to know that Phil has been bribing Dave not to tell her parents about pushing her out of the kayak."

"We don't have all the evidence to prove that," Sue replied, "but Tori may be able to help us."

"Tori was trying to give Dave a chance to start a new life," Sarah said. "Going to prison isn't the life she expected for him."

"Maybe she'd like to say a few words to him before Dave is arrested," Sue said.

"Do you know where Dave is?" Sarah asked.

"I'll make a phone call," Sue said. "A friend of mine works at Cat Tails Pub. If Dave is there, he can confirm it."

Sue called Peter, who confirmed that Dave was working the afternoon shift and would be there until 8 p.m. "Let's give Tori a call," Sue said. "She can meet us at the pub if she wants to join us."

"Tori has been waiting for this moment for a long time," Sarah replied, pressing Tori's number from her contact list.

Sarah put the phone on speaker while they spoke. Dogs like me don't understand why they can't see people who talk on speaker phones. But I recognized Tori's voice on the small box and could sense everyone's excitement.

"We have good news!" Sarah exclaimed. "I have Sue on the line, too."

"Did you find out who has been stalking my cabin?" Tori asked. "I'm tired of living with a bodyguard," she whispered. "He eats me out of house and home and snores like a freight train."

Sarah laughed, and Sue chuckled. "I'm sorry about that," Sue said. "I'm afraid bodyguards are not Luke's expertise."

"He's a Big Man," Tori said softly. "He takes up a lot of space, but I'm unsure if he's any help."

"Have you heard anyone prowling around the cabin?" Sarah asked.

"No, not since I talked to you last," Tori said. "The big man spends a lot of time watching movies on his computer. I'm not sure I could hear anyone prowling,"

"I'm glad you're safe," Sarah chuckled.

"Where did you find the Big Man?" Tori asked.

"Luke knows people who know people," Sue whispered.

"I've heard of them," Tori replied. "My dad knows people like that, too."

"We saw Gio and your mom at the Baldwin estate this morning," Sarah said. "They didn't see us."

"Imagine that!" Tori said. "My parents at the Baldwins!"

Sue and Sarah were unsure what she meant, but Tori appeared to be having a brainstorm. It had only been a short time since we met Tori at the guesthouse, and she told us about the prowler. I recalled barking between windows while someone watched from below. Someone who knew Tori was there.

"What's the good news?" Tori asked.

"We're standing in the drizzle at Nella's house," Sarah explained. "Somebody tried to break into her house this week."

"If that's good news, I wouldn't want to hear bad news," Tori said.

"We think it was Dave," Sue said. "Daisy found some blood for DNA testing on the window."

"It wouldn't be hard to find a cup with his saliva on it at Cat Tails," Tori replied. "Why would Dave want to break into Nella's house?"

Sue described the story of Phil's safe, the missing motion camera, and the images of Dave pushing her out of the kayak. "We think Dave was paying Phil not to tell your parents about the kayak pictures on the memory card."

"I can't believe it," Tori said. "It explains almost everything."

"Yes," Sarah replied. "Almost. There's a few pieces left to fit together."

"You've been an amazing friend," Tori said, and Sarah said, "Don't thank me, thank Sue and your mother."

I could feel the love between friends, as dogs do. It was an incredible moment for my two-legged friends, and there were more to come.

"Sheriff Stone will be at Nella's house shortly to review the evidence in the safe," Sue said. "We thought you might like to meet us at the pub to talk to Dave before he arrests him."

"That would be lovely," Tori agreed. Can you pick me up for the liaison?"

"We thought you'd never ask," Sarah replied.

"I'm looking forward to it," Tori said.

"We'll be there in fifteen minutes," Sarah replied, and Tori said she'd be ready.

Sue and Sarah walked back to the house with me on the leash. I had not pottied, but it was only an excuse for them to get outside, and I didn't have to go. I would have pulled on the leash if necessary, but for now, everyone wanted to get started on the next mission.

"Have you called Sheriff Stone to report the evidence in the safe?" Sue asked when we found them making brownies in the kitchen.

"He's on his way," Nella replied.

"You took your time, and we got hungry," Mia said. "Nella is teaching me her recipe. I've always loved her brownies; I used to buy them at her tea house."

"Save some for us," Sarah said.

"What do you mean, 'Save some'?" Mia said. "Where are you going?"

"We just talked to Tori," Sarah replied. "We told her everything, and she wants to go with us to share the evidence with Dave."

"Won't he be surprised to see Tori alive?" Nella exclaimed, and Mia chuckled.

"You betcha," Sarah said, "He's going to think he's seeing a ghost!"

"Be sure to tell the sheriff Daisy found evidence for the break-in on the window," Sue said, and the desert chefs chimed they'd be glad to.

"Can I borrow the keys to the SUV, Mom?" Sarah asked, and Mia replied, "I'd be honored to let you use it to chauffeur Tori to her pub."

ele

I jumped into the back seat of the SUV while Sarah drove to Baldwin's guest house to retrieve Tori. Sue waved at Sheriff Stone as we passed his car while driving to Nella's house. Deputy Livingston followed the sheriff's car in another vehicle.

"Do you want to stop?" Sarah asked, and Sue said Mia and Nella would be fine sharing the evidence.

This was the most prominent case ever solved in Sweetwater Springs. Any law enforcement officer would have been honored to participate in the arrest that cleared the names of innocent people at a housewarming party. Loretta would soon be a free woman again, free to go where she pleased. Sarah and Nella would no longer have their reputations tarnished by suspicion.

"Sheriff Stone won't be far behind us at the pub," Sue said. "He has just about everything he needs to solve the case."

Sue waved at Anita and Missy, who watched the sheriff through the window of the mayor's house, while I sat at the rear window watching the girl who had shared the most important evidence of the case.

"Anita is a good kid," Sue said. "Beth will be excited to know when it's alright to play at her house again."

We didn't see the black sedan on the drive to the guesthouse, but the driver was lurking somewhere. I sat on my haunches and watched out the rear window for signs of his whereabouts, but he was improving at the job. By the time we reached the guesthouse, he was nowhere to be found.

Chapter 37

The Arrest at Cat Tails

S arah drove past the Baldwin mansion and headed to the guesthouse where Tori had been hiding. There was no need to be discreet because everyone would know she was alive by the end of the day. It was finally time for Tori to come out and reveal the story to the people who knew and cared for her.

Sue waved to the server, who brought them breakfast as Sarah passed the mansion. The gardener knew Tori was alive, but no one knew how many people he had told. She may have been one of them. Maybe not—-as there had been a reward to anyone with information regarding Tori's where-abouts. He may have kept the secret to himself.

As Sarah drove through the woods to the remote guesthouse, no black sedan followed us this time. Sue mentioned it felt strange to miss a driver who was following us. "Who knows where he is?" she asked, shrugging.

"We couldn't miss seeing him in the woods," Sarah said.

"I haven't seen him since we left Nella's house," Sue replied. "He must have his agenda under control."

After Sarah had parked the SUV, Sue let me out of the back seat. As I raced up the stairs to the guest house, I was unleashed in front of them. I enjoyed the freedom to run in the drizzle, no matter how short. I mastered the stairs in leaps and bounds.

When we reached the cabin door, Tori's bodyguard let us in. "You must be Sue and Sarah," he told my two-legged friends. Tori has been expecting you."

"This is Daisy," Sue added while I sniffed his large frame and noted the smell of ketchup.

"I've heard about Daisy," he replied, patting my damp furry head. "I'm a dog-lover, too."

"What kind of dog do you have?" Sue asked, and the Big Man replied, "A Morkie—she's a Maltese crossed with a Yorkie."

"That's a fine mix," Sue said, describing my roots. "Daisy is half-Poodle, half Australian Shepherd."

The big man launched into a full-fledged conversation about his relatives and their Doodles. I knew the word Doodle, as did the name "Cute Dog," which applied to me. It was a long conversation that seemed to make them happy.

Tori entered the living room, dressed in cut-off blue jeans, a Cat Tails Pub T-shirt, and her favorite orthotic sandals. "I see you've met Steve," she said as we stood beside the bodyguard.

"Yes," Sarah replied as the man nodded favorably. "He likes dogs."

"That's a good sign," Sue said.

"I like your outfit," Sarah told Tori, and Sue agreed it was a good choice for her first public appearance in six months.

"I'm thrilled to be out of that cape forever!" Tori said. "It's hot!"

"I don't know how you stayed in this cabin in the woods for so long," Steve said. "I'd weigh a ton if I lived here. I eat when I'm bored."

No one mentioned they noticed. Sue said, "We have a friend who can help you. She's writing a cookbook for fitness."

"How is Jessie?" Tori asked. "She was trying to get me to add some CHEWS recipes to the pub, but Dave wasn't interested."

"Now that Dave will be gone, you might be able to work with her on that project," Sarah said, and Tori agreed.

"The locals will be happy to have Tori back at the pub," Sue told Steve. "She's a sensation in Sweetwater Springs."

"I don't know about that," Tori said humbly. "But Dave will be surprised to see me."

"You were too nice to him," the bodyguard said, and Tori explained she had her reasons.

We filed out the front door and down the guesthouse steps for the last time. Tori looked back over her shoulder and smiled at the bodyguard. "I hope you don't mind if I don't miss you," she chuckled.

"Not at all!" Steve replied, "I won't miss this place either."

I jumped into the back seat with Sue while Tori shared the front with her friend.

"Good luck!" he waved as Sarah drove away.

When we arrived at Cat Tails, Dave stood behind the al fresco bar wearing a black raincoat. The drizzle had flourished into a windy rain that sometimes flashed across the bar top. Tori noted that he was better than ever at mixing drinks, so much so that he almost looked like a bartender, and Sarah said he was probably doing large pours to make people like him.

"Do you recognize that black raincoat?" Sue asked, and Tori mentioned that it looked like the one she had given him as a birthday present a few years ago.

"It doesn't look new," Sarah said, and Tori agreed that it looked like it had been washed a few times.

"Did Dave have a black raincoat at the housewarming party?" Sue asked, but no one knew the answer.

"He wouldn't be dumb enough to keep it if he wore it to kill Phil, would he?" Sarah asked, and Tori said he wasn't a hired assassin and probably didn't know forensics could find traces of blood after washing.

"He's cheap," Tori said. "He wouldn't want to replace it."

Sue said. "If he wore that raincoat to kill Phil, it would have traces of blood on it."

Tori approached the bar as a threesome with a fluffy dog. Dave looked at me first. He wasn't a dog lover but had learned to accept that the locals loved their pets. Dogs were allowed in some areas if he wanted to compete with the other riverside pubs.

Dave's jaw dropped when he saw Tori in the Cat Tails T-shirt. "I thought you were dead!" he gasped.

"No, just missing," Tori replied.

"You faked your death!" Dave accused her while the locals around the bar watched.

"No, I just wanted to give you a chance to make some money at the pub so you could leave Sweetwater Springs," Tori said. "You never liked it here."

"You're right about that," Dave said, moving toward the half-swinging door for a quick getaway to his car.

"We know what you did," Tori said, following him. "We know you killed Phil."

"You framed Loretta for the murder," Sue said. "She's my daughter."

Dave's face turned pale, almost white. He looked like he would trip on his feet as he stumbled toward his car.

"You can't prove anything," Dave stammered as he stumbled toward the black sedan parked in the lot. A man stepped out of the sedan and flashed his credentials at Dave. "I'm a Private investigator, and we have the proof for the record."

Dave was trapped and desperate. He reached under his rain coat and pulled out a small handgun. He was shaking so much he nearly dropped it as Sheriff Stone wheeled into the parking lot. "Don't do it!" he said, jumping out of his car.

"You're in enough trouble already!" Deputy Livingston thundered. "Drop it!"

Dave dropped the gun onto the dirt parking lot. "Your parents would have killed me if they knew I left you for dead," he said to Tori, and she agreed. "I went back the next day to check on you, but you were gone!"

"You went back to check for the camera," Sarah said, "It was gone."

"Phil had already taken it!" Sue said.

I pulled on the leash to sniff Dave's raincoat. The faint smell of old blood filled my nostrils. I pawed at Sue to let her know something was there.

"Tori is lucky Mia and Sarah found her the next day," Sue told Dave.

"How could you just leave me there?" Tori asked. "I allowed you to make good on your mistake and leave Sweetwater Springs for a fresh new life. What do you do with it?"

"You Killed Phil!" the crowd chanted.

"I hope they put you away for a long time!" Sarah said. "You had a good wife. My best friend. You took advantage of her—and her parents!"

"That was stupid!" the crowd chanted.

"You're under arrest for the murder of Phil Coleman," Sheriff Livingston said, locking the handcuffs. He read his Miranda rights and was led to the backseat of the sheriff's vehicle, behind the bars that separated the criminals from the officers.

"It was a horrible thing you did to my friends and me!" Tori said, and Sarah and Sue agreed. "My life, Sarah's childhood, and Sue's daughter."

"Phil was bribing me $10,000 monthly in hush money," Dave said before the sheriff shut the door. "I couldn't pay him off. It was him or me."

"It was both of you!" the crowd chanted as the sheriff drove away. "Phil is dead, and you're going to prison."

It was the first murder in Sweetwater Springs in over twenty years, with only a few loose strings. The patrons of Cat Tails Pub were happy to see justice for a man they had never liked but tried to tolerate. Dave would be gone for a long time—hopefully forever.

It was time for justice to be served for the guilty so that the hardworking and innocent could prevail. Everyone was thrilled to have Tori back at the pub.

Chapter 38

Baldwin's Mansion

Thomas and Mia invited Sue, Luke, Sarah, and me to the Baldwin mansion for lunch the following day. Luke knocked on Sue's door late in the morning, making me bark. I usually knew when Luke arrived because I recognized his engine noise, but today, he arrived at the same time as the mailman. I looked back and forth between Sue and the front door to let her know he was there.

"It's Luke," Sue assured me, opening the door to let our friend inside.

Toby rushed from the loveseat to greet him, as he always did. Luke carried cat treats in his pocket and a beef stick in his hand for me. "Hi, Daisy," he said, passing me the beef stick while Toby jumped on the counter where he would give him the cat treats.

Sue smiled. "They're glad to see you," she said, and Luke replied it was the treats.

"They'd love you anyway," she said. "You're among the few people Toby trusts, and Daisy thinks you're the bomb."

"That's very special," Luke chuckled. "You look nice," he added.

"Thank you," Sue replied, wearing white slacks and a belted, striped shirt. "I hope it's not too bold of me to wear white," she added. "I can't eat without spilling." Luke agreed he was a messy eater, too. "Are you and Daisy ready to go?" he asked as Sue leashed me for the ride. "All set," she said.

The guard signaled the gates open when we arrived at the Baldwin mansion. Luke drove through the forest to the manicured lawn surrounding the home. "This place is lovely," he said. "I'm always impressed when I visit here."

"Your estate is lovely, too," Sue replied, and Luke smiled. "In a different way," he said. "I love the forest and the grounds here. It's wild and remote, yet sophisticated and elegant."

Sue agreed with his description. "I love the connection of your estate with the river. It keeps you in touch with day-to-day life."

"Baldwin's place is better for hiding from public life," Luke said. "Anyone could come here to relax and not be seen."

"Like Tori," Sue said as Luke opened the door for her to exit. "Or a celebrity," he replied, taking me by the leash to the front door.

The butler ushered us to the verandah, where Thomas, Mia, and Sarah awaited our arrival. For lunch, the outdoor air conditioning cooled the patio overlooking the main spring. After yesterday's drizzle, it was muggy, but the patio felt comfortable, seated on the floor between Sue and Luke in my short fur coat.

"It's good to see you," Thomas greeted us. "Thank you for coming," Mia agreed as she and Sarah rose for a hug. Everyone took turns rubbing my fur. "I'll bet Daisy would love to go for a swim," Sarah said, and Sue agreed that I'd love to dip my belly in the creek.

"I wish Loretta could be here," Mia said as their friends sat on the wicker chairs overlooking the crystal-clear spring gurgling underground beneath the lime rock.

"Me too," Sue said. Now that Dave has been arrested, Stanley expects her case to be dismissed, but until then, she's waiting for full release.

"Forensics has some work to do," Mia said. "The evidence is there: Dave's DNA is on the gun Phil was carrying. Dave's DNA is on Loretta's jacket after he ripped off her disposable raincoat. Dave's DNA is under Loretta's fingernails from when she tried to pry herself away from him when he held the gun in her hand and pulled the trigger to kill Phil. Phil's blood is on Dave's raincoat."

"Dave's DNA is on Nella's windowsill, where he tried to break into her house to steal the camera and the images of pushing Tori out of the kayak he was bribing him with," Sue said.

"When Dave goes to court, justice will be served," Mia said, and everyone agreed he'd go to prison.

The server brought lemonade and ice water and set them on the table. I was excited to hear the ice clinking against the pitcher's side, as it was my favorite crunch on a warm day. Sue poured water for Luke and herself and passed me an ice cube to chew on while they talked.

"I hope he goes to prison for a long time," Tori said, joining us on the verandah when Mia invited her to dine with us. Thank you to everyone for all you've done to help me get my life back on the right track," she said when the staff pulled up an extra chair.

"Dave didn't deserve your kindness," Thomas said, and Tori agreed he was right. "I kept holding out for the goodness in him, but he kept showing darker sides of himself."

"He felt trapped when he knew there was no way out," Sarah said. "It brought out the worst in him."

"You could have been killed when Dave pulled that gun in Cat Tail's parking lot," Luke said. "What were you thinking trying to shame a murderer into a confession by yourselves?"

"It became a dangerous mission," Thomas agreed. "I couldn't bear it if anything happened to you."

"I'm sorry if we scared you," Mia said. "I hope you're not mad at us."

"Of course not," Thomas replied. "I admire your courage and instincts to decipher the truth."

The server brought finger sandwiches of cream cheese, cucumber, and chicken salad with cranberry to the table between the guests. The chicken smelled delicious, and I hoped for a spill, but I wasn't a fan of cucumber.

"Don't be afraid to ask for help if you need it," Luke said, and Sue frowned. Where did you get that bodyguard?" she asked.

"All he wanted to do was eat hot dogs," Tori said, and I recalled the smell of ketchup the first time I met him.

Luke smiled. "He came as a package deal," he said.

Sue had an aha moment. "You mean with the man driving the black sedan," she said. "How else would you know we tried to shame Dave into a confession?"

"You hired a private investigator," Sarah said, joining Sue's epiphany. "He was about as good as Tori's bodyguard."

"They did the trick," Thomas said. "Do you think we'd let you pass through harm's way alone?"

"Were you in on it, too?" Mia asked Thomas.

"Not until recently when Luke told me what you were up to," Thomas said.

"I had no choice when you told me Tori was alive," Luke said. "I had to tell Thomas because he'd want to protect Mia when he discovered she was sheltering Tori on his estate."

Sue dropped a slice of cucumber under the table while she ate her sandwich. I wasn't impressed, but Luke's chicken salad was better. As I munched the goodness, I was glad they were both messy eaters.

"We didn't solve this case alone," Sue said, reaching for the cucumber, and Luke replied. "You solved it alone, but we had your back in case you got in trouble."

"That's what friends are for," Tori said. "Many people had my back throughout this ordeal, and I am thankful. I couldn't have survived without Mia and Sarah."

"We have that in common," Thomas replied, smiling at his wife.

"There's something I have to tell you," Mia said, looking at Thomas. "I hope no one preceded me in this confession."

Thomas looked baffled but was speechless, like everyone else.

"Sarah is my daughter," Mia said, and he smiled, relieved. "Is that it?"

"Almost," she added, "Phil was her father."

Everyone knew there was more to tell, but nothing else mattered today. Thomas would soon discover the secrets of Sarah's upbringing in good time. "Do you still love me?" Mia asked, and Thomas hugged her tight. "I love you, Dearly," he said. "I'm proud to be Sarah's stepfather."

Sarah had just received the best news of her complicated life. There was much to tell, and getting there took a long time. She smiled at Thomas while I rested on my belly in the shade under the table.

"I'm glad you're not a vindictive person," Tori told Sarah. "Of everyone, you had the most reason to be angry at Phil, yet you aren't bitter."

"Not at all," Sarah replied. "Because of Phil, I've met some of the most remarkable people in the world right here in Sweetwater Springs."

"You have a good attitude," Luke said. "That's one of the most important things in life."

"It will serve you well," Thomas said. "There's a lot of good to be done in Sweetwater Springs and elsewhere."

"Do you care that I'm a call girl?" Sarah asked, and Thomas replied that it was in the past. "Not now or ever," he said. "The future is a clean slate with better things to come."

The server brought petite cheesecakes and Tiramisu for dessert. She asked about coffee, but the guests declined the hot brew, which wasn't healthy for me. Luke tossed me another ice cube, but that was it for dog-friendly offerings.

"Do you think it's about time you told your parents the truth?" Thomas asked Tori.

"I'm excited to tell them," Tori replied. "They have been at your house. Did you tell them I've been living here?"

"No, I didn't tell them," Thomas said, and Mia and Sarah added that they didn't tell them either.

"I'd love to host the party of truth," Luke said.

"The whole town is talking about Dave getting arrested at Cat Tails," Sue said. "If you don't tell them soon, they'll already know."

"My parents are perpetual homebodies," Tori said. "Most of the people they talk to are family connections."

"They walk the dog," Sue countered, and Luke suggested breakfast at his place tomorrow. "I'll talk to my mother and let you know, but I'm certain she'll be happy to host everyone for breakfast."

"Sophie loves to cook," Sue said. "She can't wait to meet Val and Gio."

After lunch, I walked to the headspring of Mia's Run with Sue and her friends. This was my first time unleashed on the Baldwin property, but it wouldn't be the last. Over the coming years, Mia and Thomas would become good friends with Sue and Luke. There would be many reasons to get together.

The head spring had a lovely step for a belly soak. I lay in the cool water of the stairs, enjoying the sunshine while they talked about life, the river, and the town. Tomorrow was another day with news to spread. Everyone was delighted to meet up at Luke's house for breakfast, but Tori was happiest to share the truth she had been withholding from her parents.

Chapter 39

Tori's Story--Luke's Estate

S ue combed my fur the following morning, as always, before we started our day. I wouldn't say I liked this part of the daily routine, but I was getting used to it. She carefully combed my head first, making a puff of my kinky fur. Next, she combed my back, which was easy because my fur was short. And finally, my long fluffy tail—the worst part of the ritual—when I jumped on the back of the loveseat to escape with little success.

"We have to look presentable," Sue would softly say when I let her finish the job.

Sometimes, I felt jealous of dogs who didn't need their fur groomed, but honestly, combing or brushing was necessary with kinky fur like a Poodle's. You had to comb or cut it; it was worse to itch for three days after a haircut.

"I'll be careful," Sue said. "Be still, and we're almost done."

Toby watched my grooming with mild engagement. He had seen it often but was hesitant to get involved by watching from a distance. He was lucky to have soft, short cat fur. At times like this, I felt jealous of him, too.

Most other times, I'd rather be a dog than a cat. Toby slept most of his life away—with the rare exceptions of his infinite imagination. For heaven's sake, I'd seen him chase dust bunnies— while I was walking, playing, kayaking, or solving crimes between naps.

Today, Sue was taking me to Luke's house for breakfast. Artemis would be there, but Sue expected Gio to bring his furbaby, too. I was excited to meet a new playmate. Although I had seen Jelly Bean on walks, we had never played together.

When we walked into Luke's house, Artemis was waiting for me. Sue let us go outside while we awaited Jelly Bean's arrival. It was good to release some energy before our new, much smaller friend arrived.

"Hi, Sue," Luke said, hugging her. Sue smiled. "It's good to see you," she said.

"Where's Sophie?" Sue asked when we returned from two big races around the lawn.

"She's in the kitchen," Luke replied. "She's making the biggest breakfast spread ever."

"I'll bet she's excited to meet everyone," Sue replied.

"Yes, but she's pretending to take it in stride," Luke countered. "Cooking calms her nerves."

"I wish it calmed mine," Sue said, preferring easy recipes to lengthy old-fashioned ones. "Can I help her?" she asked.

"No, you'd be in her way," Luke said. "Let her make her peace before the guests arrive."

Thomas, Mia, and Sarah were next to arrive, followed by Tori. The guests met us in the glass sunroom, where breakfast would be served. It was a lovely morning, with the river in view. Artemis and I sat by the window, watching for river cowboys and dogs who liked to swim in the river, as I did.

"I'm so excited, I'm shaking," Tori said.

"You said your parents would understand," Mia reminded her, and Sue hoped it was true. All of us had been, in some way, large or small accomplices in Tori's disappearance.

"I haven't seen my parents in six months," Tori said. "It's the longest time ever."

"It's good to be close to your parents," Luke said as Sophie waltzed into the sunroom. "Nobody loves you like your mama does," Sophie added.

"A mother's love is forever," Mia agreed with a warm hug and introduced the others.

"I'm sorry I missed your housewarming party," she said. "Next time, I'll be there for your celebration."

"Thank you for cooking," Sarah said, and Sophie admitted nothing calmed her nerves like pounding dough. "I'll teach you to make bread if you'd like."

"I understand the movement," Sarah said, and Sue added that Jessie would love some bread recipes in her cookbook. She loves unprocessed food recipes for the CHEWS Fitness cookbook. "We're coming full circle," Sue said as Sarah promoted the farm-to-table lifestyle.

Gio and Val arrived at the estate and entered the sunroom last. Gio held Jelly Bean in his broad arms while Val carried two bottles of Prosecco and a plate of cookies. As the family reunited, I could feel a melding of shock, anger, and love.

Val set the goodies aside and rushed towards her daughter. "Sweetie," she said, hugging her long-lost daughter like she'd never let go. "You can't imagine how much we've missed you."

"I'm sorry, Mama," Tori replied, shifting towards her less welcoming father. "Don't you ever do this to us again," he said pulling her towards him. My heart couldn't bear it."

"It was hardly worth living without you," Val said. "We've been devastated."

"I'm truly sorry," Tori replied, feeling their pain. "I had to disappear—for your sake."

"For our sake?" Gio asked, frowning menacingly. "You broke our hearts for our sake?"

"Please, Daddy, let me explain," Tori said, backing away to tell her story. "Being your daughter wasn't easy, but I thought I could make a fresh start in Sweetwater Springs. I was thrilled when you bought us the pub as a wedding gift, but I knew you didn't trust Dave. You were right. He's been abusive for years. We fought all the time. But I believed I could make it on my own. I didn't want you to know how badly he treated me."

"You should have told us," Val said, but Tori replied that it wouldn't have mattered. Dave turned to mean, she said, describing the horrific evening he had left her for dead.

"Dave pushed me out of the kayak on Mia's Run and left me lying in the muck. Mia and Sarah found me the following morning, and Mia let me live in the guesthouse while I sorted out my life. Loretta and Sarah both had motives to kill Phil, but Loretta was framed at the housewarming party. Sue and Mia searched for evidence to prove their daughters' innocence."

"We did it for love," Mia said.

"Why didn't you tell us you were hiding?" Gio asked.

"I thought the same as Phil. If you knew Dave left me for dead by the creek, you would have killed him."

"Isn't that my business to decide?" Gio asked.

"I didn't want you going to prison," Tori said. "I thought it was better for Dave to leave Sweetwater Springs and start over."

"He's leaving Sweetwater Springs and starting over, all right," Val said. "In prison."

"I don't agree with you leaving us out of your secret," Gio said. "But I forgive you," he added, drawing his daughter close. "Promise me you'll never pull a stunt like this again," he said, and Tori agreed she'd never get married again, let alone fake her death for an unworthy man.

Sophie was mesmerized by the reunion when Gio approached her. "Cousin Sophie," Gio said while Jelly Bean sniffed Artemis and me. "It's nice to meet you."

Val walked over to greet Sophie. "Excuse our manners. It's been a revealing day," she said, kissing her wrinkled cheek.

"I won't break if you hug me," Sophie said, pulling her closer to whisper in her ear. "I'd be furious if Luke did something like this to me," she said.

"Were you in on Tori's secret?" Val asked.

"Only just recently," Sophie said. "I made Luke promise to hire a private investigator after he found the bodyguard for Tori."

"You did the right thing," Thomas said, "Although he wasn't much of a tail," Luke added.

"How long until Loretta is a free woman?" Gio asked, and Val agreed they'd love to meet her. "Hopefully, not much longer," Sue said. "The courts are slow, but we are pleased when there is justice."

Everyone went to the kitchen to serve themselves from Sophie's generous bounty. Luke did not have a serving staff since his mother was the chef at his house. Artemis and I followed the guests, friendly to all, unlike Jelly Bean, who preferred to stay close to Gio.

"This is delicious," Val said, sampling breakfast pie with Sophie's home-made crust. "I'm impressed."

The guests indulged in waffles topped with peach compote, whipped cream, biscuits and gravy, and thick slices of homemade bread. Gio returned for seconds, followed by Jelly Bean, who was closely attached. Luke returned for seconds and thirds since he wasn't likely to have such a feast on the road during his work travels.

They discussed Sarah's future and Thomas's dream of a luxury hotel in Sweetwater Springs. They talked about his dream of a theme park. They spoke of the river's pollution, most evident in Green Cove, where Phil and the mayor lived.

They drank Prosecco, chatted, and laughed while Tori and her parents reunited, and the rest of the guests got to know each other.

"There's one thing still bothering me," Tori said when the chatter diminished. "Does anyone know who scoured out my cabin just before the bodyguard came to live with me?"

I pricked up my ears while the guests focused on Tori's question. I recalled that I had barked between the windows in Tori's cabin because I saw someone hiding in the bushes who had discovered her whereabouts.

Gio replied, "I posted a reward for anyone who had information about your disappearance and could help us find you."

"How long ago?" Tori asked.

"Long enough," Gio replied vaguely, as he often answered.

"Who found me hiding in the guesthouse?" Tori asked, unwilling to settle.

"The gardener who put the camera in the tree that Phil stole and used to bribe Dave," Gio said.

"'Did he know it showed Dave pushing me out of the kayak?" Tori asked, but no one answered.

"How long have you known I was at the guesthouse?" Tori asked, and Gio said that was for him to know, and she would likely never find out.

"How much did you pay him?" Tori asked, and Gio said to forget about it. "You were worth every penny."

It was a revealing lunch with many questions, primarily answers, and delightful camaraderie among my two-legged friends. I wasn't sure how I felt about Jelly Bean, who seemed like a bit of a dog snob. But, so be it. Artemis and I could have plenty of fun and adventure without him.

Chapter 40

Cat Tails

When Loretta was released from custody, everyone was excited to see her. By now, the locals knew Loretta had been framed for Phil's murder. She was loved and trusted for her veterinary care in nearby Haywood, where many had traveled for years. Her clients were happy to share their support for her release with a gathering at Cat Tails Pub.

I was excited to see Cousin Luna, who Loretta had chosen as the dog to join her at the pub. Luna was my favorite playmate of Loretta's three dogs. I enjoyed running with Artemis in Luke's big yard, but my weekly romps with Loretta's dogs were the best days ever. I couldn't wait to see my four-legged friend from the farmhouse.

Sue invited friends, colleagues, and fellow detectives to Cat Tails Pub to celebrate Loretta's release. I proudly pranced beside her to join my four-legged friends at the dog-friendly establishment. Now that Dave was in custody, the friendliness returned to the pub Tori loved, but her husband loathed. Dave had used Tori's family money, and Phil had met his marks for various cons at the pub.

Phil had been a thorn in many people's sides, flashing his silver-plated gun to intimidate people. Some thought he was delusional about carrying Wild West paraphernalia, while others declared it part of the costume. I had sniffed him once and been uncertain of his intentions, but I suspected they weren't all good. His widow and daughter will join us today, along with many others.

"Hi, Nella," Sue said as her daughter reached down to pet me. "Is Beth coming?" she asked.

"She's over there," Sue said, waving, and Beth bounded to see her.

"We couldn't have solved this without our girls," Nella said, and Sue agreed they had been a big help to pull the case together.

Tori's parents, Val and Giovanni, joined us near the bar. I was happy Gio did not bring Jelly Bean, a one-man dog unsuitable for play. Today, I did not jump on Gio, who did not encourage it.

"Thanks," Sue said when Gio bent down to pet me from where I was seated. Gio smiled. "You're learning."

"Is Loretta here yet?" Val asked as Luke joined Sue and me.

"Two minutes," Sue replied when Thomas and Mia joined us with Sarah. "She's on her way."

"Should we hide?" Luke asked, although it was not a surprise party.

"Let's do it," Mia said. "It sounds like fun."

Everyone hid behind the bar, where Tori was serving cocktails. I sat beside Sue, squeezed into the crowd that watched Loretta's truck roll into the pub for the first time since her arrest. Her husband, Zeke, drove while her daughter, Lucy, sat in the back with Luna. When everyone piled out of the truck, Sue and her friends jumped from hiding and rejoiced in unison.

"Surprise!" they yelled, and Loretta smiled happily. "Thank you so much for coming!" she said, grinning ear to ear. "I wouldn't be here without your help," she said, hugging Sue and Mia first and then the others, who had done much to solve the caper.

Zeke took Lucy by the hand and led her into the crowd. "Thank you for bringing Mommie home," she said when he set her on the bar counter. The crowd clapped for her sweetness and bravery, which touched their hearts.

Jessie said, "You have a great mommy. We are lucky to have her back."
Lucy and Loretta smiled at their kindness.

"A round of drinks for all who helped us bring Tori back to the pub,"
Gio said as his daughter left the bar service to Peter to join the party.

"Cheers to Tori," the gardener said, and everyone chanted. "Here,
Here!"

Loretta joined her friends at a table near the river. Luna and I sniffed noses
in a long-awaited greeting while the growing table chatted about the past
and the future. Sitting still with so much energy was hard, so Loretta and
Sue took us for a swim before we settled under the table.

When everyone was seated, Loretta said, "Thank you for finding Phil's
killer. It means so much to my family and me." She looked at Tori. "I'm
sorry it had to be Dave," she said.

"It's for the best," Tori replied. "Dave hated it in Sweetwater Springs
and wouldn't let me forget it. He changed, but I didn't want to accept it."

"They fought all the time," Peter said as he served a plateful of chicken
wings and a massive dish of French fries. Anyone who works here could
vouch for that."

"I never trusted him," Gio said, and Val frowned. "You never trust
anyone, Dear," she said.

"You were right, Daddy," Tori said. "Dave was using me."

"He was using all of us," Val said. "And he was abusing you."

Beth and Nella's daughter jumped off the dock into the river while their
parents talked. Luna and I watched them with interest and jealousy because we couldn't swim, too. But Sue wasn't ready to let us swim without
the adults.

"The river is lovely here," Loretta said, admiring the clarity of turquoise
over the sandy bottom. Nella agreed but countered, "It's not crystal clear
at my house."

"It's been a long time since I've seen the Green Cove," Loretta said.

"It's still blossoming with algae," Nella said. "It won't clear up until Winter."

"Why is it clear in Winter?" Loretta asked, and Nella replied that there were many theories but little evidence. "There aren't many people on the river in Winter," she said.

"I want to pay a group of private scientists to study the reasons for the pollution," Thomas says. "I don't believe everything the experts say."

"Some people are afraid to step up and speak up," Gio said. "We want good hard truths, not job-securing coverups."

"It's easy to blame cows when no one can prove it, one way or the other," a man said, and Loretta recognized him as the cattleman from the housewarming party. "It's good to see you back," he told Loretta. "Your mom, the detective, keeps me out of trouble," he said. "I was on the list of suspects, too."

"Dave will go to prison for a long time," Sue declared.

"I'm sorry," the cattleman said to Nella, and she replied that Phil was a deceptive man. "I wanted to know the truth, too."

"Why did Phil want to buy the clinic?" Loretta asked, putting the question on the line that had given her the motive for the murder she did not commit. She looked at Gio. "I thought you wanted the clinic to launder money," she said.

"What?" he asked, shocked by the strange and unexpected accusation.

"I'm afraid I planted that seed," Chris said. "I am sorry."

Gio laughed. "It never ceases to amaze me the speculations people suggest regarding my family. I would never try to buy Loretta's clinic to launder money."

Thomas piped up. "I'm afraid it was my fault," he said. "I wanted to buy your clinic because it has a cave on the property."

"Why does that matter?" Sue asked.

"The cave leads to the aquifer," Thomas replied. "It's an easy place to directly monitor the purity of the water after it leaves the river."

"Interesting," Sue replied. "Anything else?"

"I can use it as a field trip to show guests of my theme park the inner workings of the aquifer. We can educate people about what the river looks like under the earth."

"I'd be proud to be part of that education," Loretta said. "Next time, just ask me."

"We will be more careful who we hire in the future," Thomas said. "Buyers like Phil give Baldwin Enterprises a black eye."

Luna beat me to a French fry Sarah had dropped, reminding me of my friend's penchant for food. Luna was the biggest chow hound of all Loretta's dogs. Sometimes, she didn't bother to be sneaky when she jumped on the counters at Loretta's house, dragging me into her mischief.

"What will you do now that you are giving up the nightlife?" Gio asked Sarah, who grabbed the falling fry without success.

"I want to help the At Risk girls," Sarah said, explaining that something had happened in their lives to turn them to criminal activities or risk of being trafficked.

"That's admirable," Val said. "What will you do?"

"I'd like to be a teacher," Sarah said. "Or a school counselor."

"I'd be honored to fund your education," Thomas said, and Mia smiled that her daughter could look forward to a better path to serve the community. "I hope you return to Sweetwater Springs," Mia said, and Sarah promised she would.

Jessie scooched a French fry under the table with her foot. She was too quick for Luna, who missed the opportunity to eat junk food.

"You must make healthier food at the pub," she told Tori, and she agreed to work on it.

"I'm afraid my customers don't have a taste for air-fried French fries and chicken wings," Tori said.

"The next generation will eat better," Jessie replied, and Sue agreed that Jessie's CHEWS for Fitness cookbook was making a difference. "Kids will refuse red dyes, lard, and preservatives one day."

"I'm waiting for the day kids refuse to eat fat and sugar," Jessie said. Sue declined to comment on the brownies and hot dogs Beth had eaten at Nella's house.

"I loved my tea house," Nella said. "I baked chocolate chip cookies, brownies, carrot cake, and limoncello bread pudding," she said. "I"m thinking of returning to work there since Phil is gone."

"If you can't stop eating sugar, at least eat it in moderation," Jessie said. They agreed that portion control mattered. "I'll work to make my recipes healthier," she said.

"Until then, my advice is to eat less," Sarah said, and Nella agreed it was the best advice for the transitional period.

"One more thing, Honey, I found your father's will," Nella told Sarah. "Phil left his silver-plated handgun to you."

"Thanks for the info, Mama Nella. You or Mama Mia should have it,'" Sarah said. "I love both of my Mamas, but don't want it."

"Let's open a museum in Sweetwater Springs," Mia said as she put her arm around Thomas. "It's the best place in town for a piece like Phil's."

"You can call it Mia's Museum," Thomas agreed. "Phil's gun can be the first exhibit."

It was the first time Sarah called Sue and Mia Mama, but it wouldn't be the last. Love and friendship grew with every caper. Phil's murder was our story and the first of its kind for the amateur sleuths. Cat Tails Pub was the best place in town for people to talk—and dogs like me to spread the stories of crime and justice in Sweetwater Springs.

Chapter 41

About the Author

Dr. Stacey is a veterinarian and author of animal fiction, a memoir of the Cross-Florida Greenway, and a children's book.

After nearly thirty years of veterinary practice and teaching, Stacey retired to write books about her passion, the human-animal bond. As a veterinarian, she was inspired by how pets uplifted people. She was encouraged by stories of people who served the community better with pets, such as school counselors, librarians, teachers, and veterans. Pets gave people purpose, loyalty, trust, and unconditional love.

Stacey takes her Doodle on weekend adventures with her family and friends. Penny is the ambassador for meet-and-greets. You may find them on the trails, kayaking the river, or walking the neighborhood. Penny is a magnet for connection with dog lovers everywhere.

Stacey lives in Dunnellon, Florida, where she enjoys spending time with friends, family, Penny, and her cat, Andy— rescued during a summer storm. When she's not loafing with her pets, she writes books, reads cookbooks, practices yard work, or rides her horse on the greenway. Her secret dream is to reimagine recipes that are easy, bold, and delicious with healthy fats and little sugar.

Her cozy mysteries are narrated by a canine companion for a lighter look at crime-solving in Sweetwater Springs. Daisy, the Doodle, is perceptive, insightful, and eager to lend a sniff to the subject. Her crime-solving skills bring justice to the residents of the scenic small town. The perpetrators face accountability for their crimes through the results of her canine cognitions.

If you enjoyed her book, Stacey asks you to leave a review on Amazon. If you borrowed her book from a friend or a Little Free Library, where she donates free copies, please mention it in your review. You don't have to buy the book to review it.

Stacey writes books as Stacey Bonner Gerhart and her maiden name, Stacey Bonner.

Chapter 42

Other Books by Stacey Bonner, DVM

*P*ippin and the River of Wonders: *A Voice for Wildlife* for Children 9-12, by Stacey Bonner Gerhart, DVM

Paws to Walk in the Woods: Dogs, Horses and Kindred Spirits on the Trails of the Cross-Florida Greenway, A Memoir By Stacey Bonner, DVM

Pets and the Miracles of Love: A Veterinary Novel to Enrich the Head and the Heart— from Dr. Penny's Notebook, by Stacey Bonner Gerhart, DVM

Alley Cats, Alligators, and All Spice: The Dog Walkers Discover Stray Cats, Food, and Friendship in Everyone's Favorite Riverside Town—From Doc and the Dog Walkers by Stacey Bonner, DVM

Stacey writes books under her maiden name, Stacey Bonner, DVM, and as Stacey (Bonner) Gerhart, DVM.